Praise for Jessica Clare and her novels

"Blazing hot." —*USA Today*

"Ms. Clare had me at billionaire. . . . A fast, sexy read."
—Fiction Vixen

"Great storytelling . . . delightful reading. . . . It's fun and oh-so-hot." —*Kirkus Reviews*

"Just thinking about it puts a smile on my face."
—Heroes and Heartbreakers

"Buckle up and take the ride—you'll enjoy every peak, valley, twist, and turn." —Cocktails and Books

"Sexy and fun." —Smexy Books

The Cowboy and His *Baby*

JESSICA CLARE

JOVE
New York

A JOVE BOOK
Published by Berkley
An imprint of Penguin Random House LLC
1745 Broadway, New York, NY 10019

Copyright © 2019 by Jessica Clare
Excerpt from *A Cowboy Under the Mistletoe* copyright © 2019 by Jessica Clare
Penguin Random House supports copyright. Copyright fuels creativity, encourages
diverse voices, promotes free speech, and creates a vibrant culture. Thank you for buying
an authorized edition of this book and for complying with copyright laws by not
reproducing, scanning, or distributing any part of it in any form without permission.
You are supporting writers and allowing Penguin Random House to continue to
publish books for every reader.

A JOVE BOOK, BERKLEY, and the BERKLEY & B colophon
are registered trademarks of Penguin Random House LLC.

ISBN: 9781984803986

First Edition: May 2019

Printed in the United States of America
1 3 5 7 9 10 8 6 4 2

Cover art: *Cowboy* by Nicholas Russell/Getty Images;
Dogs by Bildagentur Zoonar GmbH/Shutterstock;
Landscape by Carlton Ward/Getty Images;
Windmill by Ray Tango/Getty Images
Cover design by Sarah Oberrender
Book design by George Towne

For Cindy and Kristine—
an author couldn't ask for a better team.

CHAPTER ONE

Annie Grissom had been in the movie business for six years now, and she'd been asked to train animals to do a lot of things. She'd taught dogs to walk on their hind legs, bark a phrase that almost sounded like talking, play follow-the-leader, and any number of tricks that would look incredible with a bit of movie magic. Tricks that made audiences sit up in their chairs a little straighter and say to each other, "How did they do that?"

But she'd never, ever been asked to teach a dog to race through a grass fire.

"I'm sorry, Mr. Sloane," she said for what felt like the hundredth time that day. She was always apologizing on this particular movie, especially to the director. Annie paged through the script again. "I'm not sure I see where the whole 'grass fire' scene is in the movie."

"It's something I brainstormed last night. Since we're doing a ranching movie, I thought it'd be perfect. Now, can you make Petey do this or do I need to find a new star for my picture?" He glared at her as if her reluctance was a huge annoyance.

"Spidey," she murmured, trying to think as she pretended to flip through the script again.

"What?" Mr. Sloane yelled at her. Such a yeller. The yellers were always the worst to work for. Ironic because they usually got the job through nepotism or a family friend, not by their own merits, so they tended to scream quite a bit to ensure things were done the way they wanted. She'd signed on to this movie knowing Mr. Sloane wasn't a well-known director, but she hadn't thought he'd be this bad.

"My dog is Spidey," Annie said, doing her best to keep the smile on her face. "And I don't mean to be a jerk, but he gets nervous when people yell."

"What?" Mr. Sloane blasted in her face, his nose purpling.

"That's one of the rules in the animal care contract," she continued. "No yelling on set, no touching the animal except by the trainer, and no outside food provided to the animal. All of these things can interfere with my work."

His eyes narrowed at her. "Are you trying to tell me how to do my job, Miss . . ."

"Grissom," she reminded him smoothly. "And I never would, no. I'm just the dog trainer. But I do know my dog, sir, and he gets very nervous around strong voices."

Mr. Sloane grunted, crossing his arms over his chest and tucking the well-paged (and mostly ignored) script against his shirt. "So you're telling me that if I lower my voice, you'll get him to do the scene?"

She bit her lip. That was also part of the problem. "Complicated stunts can take a while. I need time to run him through the scene, get him comfortable with what's happening around him. Even if I manage that, I'm not sure how he's going to react to fire."

"So you need more time," he said flatly. "As usual. Why

am I not surprised?" He pinched the bridge of his nose. "This is a movie production, Miss Grissom. You know that time is money."

"I know." Annie also knew that these sorts of things were supposed to be given to her in advance so she could work on them with Spidey. Throwing them at her—and the dog—last moment wouldn't be beneficial for anyone. "And I truly do appreciate that time is money. I just don't think that he's going to react well to a cold run of a grass fire."

"You're telling me you can't get him to do it." Mr. Sloane scowled at her, shifting on his feet as if he could make himself look more imposing. "I hired a dog trainer. If you're not going to train the damn dog then what do we have you here for?"

Annie ignored his nasty attitude. He was stuck, and she knew it. They'd already filmed most of the scenes and he couldn't switch dogs out. He'd insisted on having a nearly white Boston terrier with one black ear, and it had taken her forever to find one with the right coloration that was also a rescue. Spidey actually had no black ear at all, but makeup fixed that. Even now, he was sitting on the grass nearby, his head between his paws, watching her intently.

Such a good boy. He deserved better than this movie and this particular director. She changed her tone to soothing to try and deal with Mr. Sloane. "I know animals can be very difficult and stressful to work with on a film, Mr. Sloane. You're doing a great job understanding how animals can be tricky." Didn't hurt to throw in a compliment or two even if they were lies. "But if we're changing the scenes, I need to be notified in advance so I can get Spidey ready. This is a big deal."

The director frowned at her and gave a little shake of his head. "This will be the scene that makes the movie. I need it to happen. If you can't get it to work, you're fired."

Annie bit her lip. She knew what he was saying was hot

air—this far into the production he couldn't replace her or her dog. But it still made her anxious, because the more he yelled, the harder it was going to make it for every future scene. Spidey was already sensitive to raised voices and if he associated fear with Sloane and his set, she wouldn't be able to get anything out of him, no matter how many treats she encouraged him with.

"Is there a problem?" A woman moved up next to them, her clipboard in hand, a polite smile on her face.

Annie nearly breathed a sigh of relief. The representative for the American Humane Association was on set today to ensure that the animals were being treated fairly, and she'd stepped in just in time. Of course, Annie couldn't tattle on the director—that was a sure way to get fired from this picture and every movie in the future forever and ever—but she could emphasize her point.

"Mr. Sloane and I were just discussing an upcoming stunt." Annie pretended to page through the script, though she already had it memorized. "I have Spidey's training scheduled down to the hour, Mr. Sloane." Gosh, she was just full of lies this morning. "So if we're putting in a wild-fire scene, I need to know what stunts we're removing so I can juggle things appropriately."

The representative's eyebrows went up. "Wildfire scene?" At Sloane's terse nod, she gestured at the rest of the set. "With this many horses on set? Do you really think that's wise? And the weather's been so dry lately."

"It's all going to be very safe," Sloane barked at her, and then suddenly there was a new focus for his ire.

Annie murmured something about going to work with Spidey and slipped away from the group, heading over to the covered umbrella set up on set. Wyoming was nothing but rolling plains and endless sunlight. Great for shooting, terrible for short-haired white dogs that sunburned at the drop of a hat.

Like poor Spidey.

Even now, her little buddy was waiting patiently under the umbrella in the shade. He loved basking in the sun but he also turned bright red underneath his white fur, so she'd trained him that he needed to wait for her under the umbrella. She just adored that little guy. Of all the dogs she'd worked with in the past, she had a soft spot for a few, and Spidey was at the top. He was smart, funny, eager to please . . . and had the weirdest personality. Spidey loved people and horses and being on the movie set. However, he was terrified when people raised their voices, and certain objects set him off into a barking frenzy. Like . . . a ball. If she showed him a ball, he'd lose his mind, barking and snarling, until it was out of sight. It was the strangest thing.

At least her little guy liked cheese.

She sat down on the grass next to him and petted one soft, un-dyed ear. "Who's my best boy?"

His tail had been cropped off by his previous owners, so he had nothing to wag, but his hindquarters shook with excitement and he panted happily, his stubby snout turned up toward her with adoration.

Annie loved and snuggled the dog in the shade, trying to undo any anxiety that he might be experiencing due to Sloane's yelling. Then, she pulled out the doggy sunblock and slathered him with a fresh round of it, trying to figure out how she was going to get Spidey to race through a burning plain when animals instinctively hated fire.

She sighed. It was something that could be done, with weeks of prep work . . . weeks that she didn't have.

Maybe the director would change his mind again. After all, he had several times already. Hopefully she just needed to wait him out.

In the meantime, she stroked Spidey's short, wiry fur and told him over and over what a good boy he was.

*   *   *

A lot of time on the set of a movie was spent waiting around. There were scenes to be set up, lighting that needed to hit just right, animals to be prepared for their spot on set, and actors, who could be more stubborn than any dog or horse. The lead actor for *The Goodest Boy* was a nice guy named Chad Weathers. Chad had a string of superhero movies that did well in the late 90s and then everything flopped after that. He'd been forced to take on roles like this one, where he played a cowboy with a talking dog who tries to help him find love. The script was saccharine, and the dog trainer in Annie couldn't understand why a rough-and-tumble cowboy in the Old West would have a Boston terrier for a dog instead of something hardy, but hey, she wasn't paid to think.

The director was in a rotten mood after his conversation with her, and Chad objected to some of the new scenes in his script, which meant everyone was walking around on tiptoes this afternoon. Annie did her best to stay out of all of it, working with Spidey on a few conversation commands. One scene in the movie involved the dog picking up a box with a wedding ring and setting it down carefully at Chad Weathers's feet, so she'd been teaching Spidey that particular "fetch" trick and showered him with treats every time he did it right.

There was a quick scene with Spidey at Chad's side as they walked through the Old West set, and then Chad yelled at the director and stormed off to his trailer. Sloane did the same, and that was pretty much the end of filming for the day.

Annie sighed, working another coat of sunblock over her charge. "No wonder we're over budget," she muttered to herself. "It's not your fault, Spidey."

"Definitely not," said another voice, and Annie looked

up to see Katherine approaching. The other woman waved, sitting cross-legged in the grass across from Annie and carefully away from Annie's dog. "These two chuckleheads are making us all run over schedule. It ain't the animals' fault, that's for damn sure."

Katherine was the closest thing Annie had to a friend on the set. She tended to be a bit of a loner. After years of being dragged from movie set to movie set, most Hollywood kids either grew theatrical or grew introverted. Annie was the latter. But Katherine was from Boston, had the accent to boot, and had never met a stranger. She was an assistant to the horse trainers, which meant she spent most of her time picking up droppings or running errands, but she kept a cheery attitude and she loved animals. More than that, she respected the set rules and never tried to pet or feed Spidey, which Annie was grateful for. The big actors always thought the rules didn't apply to them, and it was hard to argue with an Oscar winner who was paid millions that he couldn't pet her cute dog on the head.

Katherine was just as tired of the shenanigans on set as Annie was. She pulled off her heavy gloves and set them in her lap, taking a break under the shade of the umbrella.

"Are they still talking about the wildfire scene?" Annie wanted to know.

Katherine shook her head. "That certification lady talked him out of it. Said it was too dangerous for the horses."

Annie said nothing, but her mouth twisted a little and she caressed Spidey's round head again. Dogs never got as much respect on set as horses did.

"Now he's talking about doing one long running shot of a cattle-roping scene," Katherine said. "He wants a big pay-off for the climax. Lots of horses. Lots of racing over the hills and scenery."

Annie blanched. "Is Spidey supposed to be in that scene?" At Katherine's nod, Annie sighed. "He's brachycephalic. He can't race for long distances without getting overheated. He's not made for that sort of thing." Just like she'd told them and told them a hundred times when they'd insisted on having a Boston terrier instead of a cattle dog, and now, well, here they were.

Katherine shrugged. "Maybe they can get a stunt dog for it if it's a high overhead shot."

"Maybe." It'd be tricky to get the director to understand the need behind it, though.

"At any rate, Sloane's cooped up with the writers and with Chad for the rest of the day. We're free to go back to town." She beamed at Annie. "A few of us are meeting up at the bar for some drinks. You should come. Celebrate the fact that we're almost done with this picture and then we can work on a real movie. I hear one of the big studios wants to make a tentpole Western for summer release and they'll be casting soon. Maybe they'll need dogs."

She smiled at Katherine, because it was sweet of her to think of Annie. It reminded her that not every set was full of bad people, and just because the director was difficult didn't mean this wasn't a good experience. "I'm not sure if I should go out tonight," Annie said, hesitating. "I'm not much of a drinker, and Spidey can probably use some attention—"

"We won't be out long," Katherine said. "And Chad's assistant is going. You could always put a bug in his ear about how a long, extended shot from a distance wouldn't make Chad look nearly as heroic as some close-up cuts."

"You know just what to say to get a girl to cave in, don't you?"

"That I do," Katherine said proudly. "Let's get on the bus, go home and change, and see what kind of nightlife this tiny town has to offer."

Annie bit back a sigh and studied Spidey's little face, tracing a finger along the curve of his skull. His eyes were closed and he did look tired. He wouldn't mind a few hours alone in his crate. "I guess I can pick him up some cheese while we're in town."

"After we get our drink on," Katherine said firmly.

"After," Annie agreed.

CHAPTER TWO

"I see movie people," Jordy joked, lifting his beer to his lips. "They're everywhere. And they don't even know they're obnoxious."

Dustin just snorted and shook his head. He played with the label on his own bottle of beer, using Jordy's comment as an excuse to look around the tiny Painted Barrel Saloon. For a town of about two hundred folks, the bar got a surprising amount of activity, and with the outsiders swarming in to have a drink tonight, it was packed. Unlike Eli, who was hiding out back at the ranch with his pretty wife, Dustin enjoyed seeing new faces around town. Painted Barrel felt small enough most days, and new people brought fresh conversation. New women? Well, he was never averse to seeing a few new faces.

"You should find yourself a nice city girl to flirt with," Old Clyde told Jordy. "One that's not smart enough to realize you're full of crap."

Jordy just snickered, unoffended. "Wouldn't mind meeting a girl," he said, watching the female faces in the bar avidly. "Been a long time since I've been on a date. Not a lot of women in town."

"You had a date?" Old Clyde joked.

This time Dustin grinned. "Prettiest little thing on four hooves."

"Ha ha," Jordy told them and nodded at Dustin. "You're the ladies' man around town. You wanna give me a few pointers on how you manage to always win them and I just strike out?"

"I can," Dustin said, finishing off his beer and then setting the bottle on the table. He gave it a nudge toward Jordy. "But this round's on you if I do."

The younger cowboy immediately got to his feet and worked his way through the crowd, holding on to his hat as he headed toward the bar for refills. At Dustin's side, Old Clyde snorted. "Don't know what advice you could give him other than 'stop being such a damned idiot.'"

Dustin just shook his head. "He's just eager. He'll work out of being an idiot at some point." Hopefully. "Kid's just young. Everything's new to him."

"Ain't that new," Old Clyde said. "He's what, all of five years younger than you?"

Huh. Dustin guessed he was, though Jordy acted much younger. "Sheltered," he suggested. He'd been on his own since the age of sixteen, so he hadn't had the family to protect him from the harshness of life. In a way, he kind of envied Jordy. It wasn't that Dustin's life was hard—it was just that he knew all the things he didn't want. Jordy was still wide-eyed and eager and almost innocent, and that made him seem a lot younger.

And then he snorted to himself, because Jordy was about as innocent as any other young man with women on his mind. Even now, he was talking to a gorgeous, tall woman with brown skin and a long black braid who clearly wanted nothing to do with the young cowboy.

"He needs to figure out that women don't want you to slobber all over them," Dustin commented, peeling the last of the label off his beer. "Surefire way to scare them off."

"Wouldn't know. I'm too old for women and their crap," Old Clyde said. "Just want to relax with my dogs."

"Spoken like a true bachelor."

Old Clyde shrugged. "Was married once. We're both happier pretending the other doesn't exist. When are you going to settle down?" He nudged Dustin. "You're about hitting that age that a man starts thinking about family."

Twenty-nine? Was that the age that everything changed, then? "Never settling down," he told his friend.

"No one ranches forever. Well, except me, but then I get stuck with idiots like Jordy." Clyde snorted. "Poor kid's a fool."

Dustin glanced over at the bar. Sure enough, Jordy had a consternated look on his face as the beauty very carefully steered away from him, rolling her eyes. *Ouch.* Suitably crushed, Jordy headed back to them, three beer bottles in hand. "Not gonna ranch forever," Dustin told Clyde idly. "I have plans."

"Lots of hot women here tonight," Jordy said as he thumped down at the small table across from Dustin and Clyde. He handed out the beers. "And they don't seem to be into cowboys."

"Now, that isn't true," Dustin told him. "Every woman alive's into a cowboy. It's all in how you play it."

"Oh, whatever." Jordy took a swig of his beer and flopped back in his chair, utterly defeated.

Was Dustin ever so young? He felt old even at sixteen, he was pretty sure. With a smile, he took his new beer and began to play with the label. "If you don't want my advice, just say so."

Jordy made an impatient sound. "Everyone knows you get any girl you want. So yes, I want your advice."

He might have gotten every girl he wanted, but maybe that was also why he felt so very bored with everything, too. Nothing held his interest around here any longer, and that was a sure sign that it was about time for him to pack up and leave soon. Find another ranch, find another town, a new adventure. Maybe this time he'd finally cash out his savings and get that boat. He wasn't sure yet. "All right. First step is figuring out what you want from a girl, Jord, my friend. Are you looking for a long-term relationship or just some fun? You have to choose accordingly." He gestured at the bar. "You can't just home in on any pretty face and fling yourself at her."

Now Jordy just looked confused. "What the hell do you mean?"

"I mean, if all you want is a good time, you find yourself a Good Time Girl. You can't fling yourself at a keeper and expect her to just want a quick flirt. And that girl you were hitting on at the bar? She's a keeper and she knows it. That's why she doesn't have time for you."

Like a puppy, Jordy cocked his head. "How can you tell?"

Dustin shrugged. "I can just tell. I can always tell." Maybe he recognized Good Time Girls because he was a Good Time Guy—never ready to settle down, not looking for more than a night of easy flirting. Anything other than a Good Time Girl was a keeper and thus off-limits, because he wasn't that kind of guy.

"Okay, then what about the blonde next to her?" Jordy nudged his chin forward, indicating the women crowding the bar itself.

Dustin glanced over. "Good Time Girl."

"How's that?"

Dustin shrugged. "It's the way she carries herself. I can just tell." Even as Dustin spoke, the girl reached over and planted a kiss on the man standing next to her, who looked just as surprised as anyone to be the recipient.

"All right, so I need you to scan every potential woman for me and find me a date. What about Nina?" Jordy immediately asked.

"Nina that works at the grocery?" When he nodded, Dustin answered. "Good Time Girl. She likes to go out and have fun." He'd dated her once. They'd fooled around with some kissing, but never took it any further than that, much to Nina's dismay. Dustin was more a fan of the thrill of the chase. He loved spending time with girls, loved flirting, but the moment they wanted something more than just flirtation, he backed off. He didn't want to give the wrong impression. Unfortunately, because he dated a lot, he already had the reputation of being a bit of a ladies' man, but at least he wasn't leaving a string of kids (and broken hearts) through the Rocky Mountains. Wasn't right to lead a girl on if he wasn't interested in giving her more.

And Dustin already had plans for his future.

Jordy looked a little frustrated. "I'm more interested in finding a keeper, I think."

"The first girl was a keeper," Old Clyde pointed out.

"But she wasn't interested in keeping me," Jordy admitted with a sheepish grin. "I want a girl that'll like me for who I am. Someone I can settle in with. Someone that lets me hold their hand through church service."

Yeah, Dustin was pretty sure he was never as young as Jordy. "I see. Well, you might not find the right girl in a bar. Doubt she's gonna be one of the movie people, too." He was seeing a lot of Good Time Girls in the crowd.

"What about the redhead in the corner?" Jordy said. "The small one."

Dustin glanced around and didn't see a redhead. Of course, the place was hopping with people. On a good day, Painted Barrel Saloon had five, six tables and they were almost always full. Tonight, the place was standing room only, and the bartender was racing back and forth trying to keep up with demand. "What redhead?"

"There's one at the bar, in the corner. Lots of freckles." Jordy grinned. "Kind of cute but she's not much of a smiler."

"Didn't see her. I'd have to watch her for a few to be able to tell." It was never in a girl's appearance or what she wore. He'd learned long ago that girls wore clothing to impress other girls, not him. It was in how a girl acted, how she laughed. It was her outlook on life.

"She's at the bar, like I said." Jordy pulled out his wallet, slapped a ten down on the surface, and shoved it toward Dustin. "Go talk to her and find out if she's my type."

He groaned inwardly. Wanted to tell Jordy that this was all stupid talk that came over beers, that if he wanted a keeper, he needed to go talk to her himself. That Dustin knew how to spot them only because he'd flirted with and dated so many that he could recognize a restless soul, but he was terrible about keeping them and couldn't offer any advice on that matter.

Old Clyde kicked Dustin's leg under the table. *Damn it.* With a glare at Clyde's weathered face, Dustin got to his feet, snagged the ten, and then moved his way through the crowd toward the bar. It was packed, so he took his cowboy hat off so the brim wouldn't smack any unsuspecting patrons in the face, and held it against his chest protectively. As he did, he scanned the crowd. Fair amount of both men and women, all sorts of ages. Most of the faces he didn't recognize, which meant that they were the out-of-towners, the movie people. Some were clearly married and only out drinking because there wasn't much else to do in Painted Barrel. They sat at one of the tables and looked bored, checking their phones. Others were clearly here to party, evidenced by the crowd around the bar and the way they sandwiched in close together, laughing and talking over one another. People always piled up like sardines near the alcohol, as if they weren't gonna get the same drink sitting down at a table somewhere. Ah well. He looked around at the women, trying to find one that would be Jordy's type. He was a good kid. Well, okay, not exactly a kid. A few years younger than Dustin, but with a far more innocent heart. Sure. A young, innocent thing would be perfect for a guy as idealistic as Jordy.

And she had to like ranching, Dustin supposed, since Jordy wasn't good for much else. Heck, for his first year on the ranch, he wasn't much good at ranching, either. He scanned the people crowded at the bar, looking for red hair and a shorter stature. Sure enough, there was a woman hiding at the very far end of the bar, practically pressed against the wall in order to avoid the wildly gesturing man next to her who was absorbed in talking with another woman, his back to the redhead. All right, then. He supposed he could rescue her from her current situation and suss her out for Jordy at the same time.

He took a few steps forward and then managed to wedge himself in at the bar next to her, setting his hat on the counter. "Ma'am."

She gave him a polite little smile and then broke eye contact, scanning the bar as if looking for a familiar face to come rescue her.

"Not here to harass you. Just thought I'd say hello and let you know that my friend wanted to buy you a beer." It didn't hurt to talk Jordy up while he was here, he supposed. He liked the look of her, though. Like the other cowboy had mentioned, she was rather wholesome-looking for this crew. The movie people were a melting pot of cultures and races, which was a breath of fresh air in this town, but most of them also tended toward a wilder lifestyle. He was pretty sure the woman on the other side of him was wearing leather in inappropriate places. There was a lot of cleavage in the bar tonight, a lot of short skirts and tight pants—both male and female. Wasn't anything wrong with that, but it just made this woman stand out all the more.

For one, she was wearing a sweater so ugly that his granny would have turned her nose up at it. Orange and brown with a checkerboard pattern on the sleeves and a chevron across the shoulders, it looked like something someone would wear if they lost a bet. "I, ah, like your sweater."

She gave him a withering look.

Now that made Dustin grin. For such a wholesome-looking thing, she could cut with a glance. She was incredibly innocent-looking, just as Jordy had suggested. Her carrot-orange hair was parted down the middle and hung below her shoulders in thick, unruly waves. Her eyebrows were just as orange, her lashes pale, and every inch of her skin seemed to be covered in freckles. She was fascinating-looking, and with only a hint of lip gloss on her pink mouth, it was clear she wasn't dolling up to impress anyone.

He liked that.

She also seemed pretty uninterested in him, which meant she was definitely a keeper. He attracted the party girls; they were drawn to his hat, his rugged good looks, his easy smile. A challenge wasn't something he came across often, and even though he was supposed to be talking Jordy up to her, he couldn't resist a little flirtation, just to see how she handled it. "Name's Dustin. You're not from around here, are you?"

"Nope." She looked over at the bartender desperately, but he was at the far end of the bar, talking to a pretty blonde.

"You got a name, sweater girl?"

"Yep."

Dustin laughed, because she was so clearly making it difficult for him. And when her mouth curled in the barest of reluctant smiles at his amusement, he had to keep trying. He leaned in and caught a whiff of a sharp, odd smell that he didn't recognize. What on earth was she drinking? Didn't matter, he decided to turn on the charm. He knew how to flirt with the best of them, and women usually responded to a ready smile and a guy that could make them laugh. "If I guess it, you gonna give me more than one-word answers?"

"Unlikely." And her mouth twitched, as if she was trying to hold back her own laughter.

"*Mmm.* Guess I'll take that risk." He tilted his head, studying her. "I could go for a corny line and say your name is Angel, because you are one that came down to Earth, but then I think you'd shove my hat down my throat. You don't seem the fussy type, so I'm guessing it's not something ridiculous like Chandelier."

She only narrowed her eyes at him.

He put his hands up. "I can sense defeat. I only wanted to come over and say hello and tell you that my friend was admiring you from afar."

"Your friend," she repeated. "Which friend?" When he gestured at Jordy, she gave him a pointed look. "He was hitting on my friend Michele when he came to the bar last time. Then he hit on Katherine. And Mandy. Now he's decided I'm his next target?" She caught the eye of the bartender and put her money down on the table, closing out her tab. "No thank you."

As she left, the sweater stretched tight over her chest and he saw the outline of something square and blocky and got another whiff of that strange sharp scent. He felt a little guilty for chasing her off. He'd have liked to talk to her without the bar scene. She seemed like a sharp, wry wit and that appealed to him. Ah well. Dustin gestured at the waiting bartender. "Three more longnecks."

The redhead's seat hadn't been empty for longer than a flash when a new person slid into it. A woman, this one with short brown hair and a killer smile. She cast him a flirty look. "Hello there, stranger."

Dustin grinned back, because it was the polite thing to do. Normally he'd pick up what she was throwing down. She wanted to have fun tonight, another Good Time Girl looking to spend her evening with someone else who wanted to party. This was a dance he knew well. They'd talk for a bit. He'd buy her a drink or two. The flirting would get hot and heavy. They'd move to the dance floor and things would go up a notch. They'd drive around town until dawn, having a good time and end up somewhere they could watch the sun rise over the mountains. Maybe she'd want to go back to his place—he always said no. Maybe she'd drag it out a date or two more. Never more than that. Then she'd show she wanted more than just a good time and he . . . well, all he wanted was the thrill of pursuit.

It suddenly made him tired, how predictable all of it was. The redhead had been interesting in her complete and utter distaste for his flirty ways. That was new, at least.

"Can I buy you a drink, cowboy?" the beautiful woman at the bar asked, arching an eyebrow at him.

When had having a good time suddenly gotten . . . dull?

CHAPTER THREE

Dustin managed to extricate himself from the beauty at the bar without hurting her feelings. It took a lot of smooth talking and a purchased drink, but when he left she was smiling, and he was relieved. Normally he'd take her up on what her smile was promising, but tonight it just reminded him that he'd lived out everything that there was to experience in this town already. He felt trapped and ready to move on.

He felt even more trapped when a familiar blonde stopped in front of him.

"Well, well," Theresa said, flicking an imaginary hint of dust off his collar. "Look who we have here. You've been avoiding me."

"Have I?" Dustin kept his tone friendly even though he wanted to groan with frustration. "Can't imagine why."

"Be careful or you're going to hurt my feelings." She mock-pouted at him, her bright red lips full and attention-grabbing. Theresa was dressed to kill in a slinky black number that looked completely out of place in Painted Barrel, not that it had ever stopped her before. She was hot, of course, and he'd dated her a few times before he'd realized what a train wreck she was. Now he spent a lot of time deliberately avoiding her.

"I'm a mite busy at the moment," was all he said to her, though he kept his smile polite as he tried to sidestep.

"You always seem to be too busy for me lately." Her lower lip thrust out even as she sidled closer to him. "I thought we were dating."

"I'm not sure why you'd think that," he told her politely, removing the hand she put on his chest. "We went on two dates last year. That's it."

"But you haven't seen anyone since."

Now how did she know that? "Does it matter?"

"Does to me," Theresa said with a sly look. "If you're waiting for me, I'm right here."

"I'm not waiting." And before she could give him another pout, he stepped away. Theresa, and her overbearing craziness, was another reason why he was feeling a bit trapped around town lately. It made him a little sad to realize he'd be moving on. He liked working at the Price Ranch. He liked Old Clyde and Jordy, and Eli and Cass, who weren't here tonight because Cass was feeling under the weather. It was like a little family, and maybe that was why Dustin was feeling the itch to start somewhere fresh. He wasn't good with family.

He dropped off the beers to Jordy and Old Clyde, and made his excuses. Told them he wasn't much in the mood to celebrate and he'd find his own ride back to the ranch. How exactly he was going to do that, he wasn't quite sure, but the night was young enough, and one of the firefighters had started doing Uber or Lyft or one of those car services in his spare time. Maybe Dustin would call him. Didn't seem right to ruin Clyde and Jordy's fun. They'd all had a long spring, with calving season just now settling down. This was their first night to relax in a while and he wouldn't spoil it just because he was in a mood. So he clapped the two cowboys on the shoulders and headed out the door for some fresh air and peace and quiet.

Outside, the fresh air was bracing. The moment he stepped out of the crowded bar, he immediately felt better. That was one of the things he liked best about the ranch life—the surroundings, quiet and serene. It felt like the entire town of Painted Barrel was squeezed inside the bar itself. The music was muted, and the air was brisk and had a snap to it despite the warm days, thanks to the mountains. Overhead, the stars were brilliant and for a moment, it felt like he'd left civilization behind.

A dog whined.

"Good boy," murmured a sweet voice.

Dustin glanced down the wooden front of the bar itself. The building was old, and since it was a "saloon" the owners had done their best to give an Old West feel to the place. It had a narrow covered porch made of wood and a couple of rocking chairs set outside, and near the cluster of cars, there was a hitching post, since one or two old farts still took their horses into town in defiance of modern life. Old Clyde and Dustin had driven into town in Jordy's Jeep, and Dustin had nearly forgotten that Clyde took his dogs with him. He took them everywhere, and the leashed duo were sitting on the end of the porch, just where Clyde had left them.

Seated on the ground next to the dogs was his feisty redhead.

Well, now.

He crossed his arms and leaned against the building, watching her for a moment. She hadn't noticed his presence yet, and while the dogs were wagging their tails at the sight of him, they thumped even harder when the woman pulled out something from her sweater and held it up.

"Let's see if your owner's trained you right," she told them in a low voice. "Who wants to give me their paw?"

Immediately both dogs offered a paw to her, and she laughed, the sound sweet and full of delight. Hell, upon hearing that laugh, Dustin wanted to offer her a paw, too.

She gave them another bit of something, the dogs chewing, and he heard the crinkle of plastic.

"Such good boys," she told them again, stroking their heads. "I'd take you both home with me if I could."

"I think their owner might object," Dustin drawled, moving forward with deliberately heavy footsteps to get her attention.

He expected her to gasp and jump up, a guilty expression on her face at being caught, but she only grinned and turned to look at him over her shoulder. "I like your dogs more than I like you."

Dustin couldn't help but chuckle at such honesty. He moved forward, sitting on the railing across from her as she rubbed one dog's ears and then the other's. Inside the bar, she'd been interesting, a low-key, oddly solitary figure amid a gang of party-minded people. Here, with the dogs shedding all over her and licking her face? She was radiant.

He was transfixed. Her hair blew about her face and as he watched, the bigger dog, Gable, climbed into her lap and nearly bowled her over, eliciting a fresh peal of laughter. She looked like a completely different person, and it charmed him. Nothing was more appealing than a woman full of joy at petting an animal.

If every night in Painted Barrel was filled with a girl like this, he wouldn't be so damn bored of it all, he realized. When she looked up at him expectantly, Gable still licking her freckles, he crossed his boots and leaned against the rail-post. "I hate to transfer your lack of affection to someone else, but those aren't my dogs."

"Oh." She looked surprised. "They clearly know you, though."

"Yeah. They belong to my friend."

She made a face. "The one buying a drink for every single woman he saw in the hopes of getting laid?"

So cutting, that comment. He loved it, because she wasn't wrong. "Nah. My other friend, the eighty-year-old sitting back and laughing at the one buying a drink for every single woman he saw."

The woman smiled wider. "Well, if it's not you, and it's not your friend, I guess that's all right, then." She rubbed one dog ear expertly. "It looks like he takes good care of you, doesn't it, buddy?"

"You like dogs?" Damn, what was wrong with him? Next he'd be asking her stupid stuff like "Do you like air?" or "Isn't the weather nice?" Normally he was smooth around women, but it was because they knew how to play the game the same way he did. It was like this one had no idea there was a game, and that intrigued him as much as it left him at a loss of how to make small talk. He could compliment her on her appearance, or her clothing, say something flirty—a dozen things sprang to mind and he quickly discarded them. He wanted this laughing, real person to stay. He didn't want her to shut down and glare at him.

"If I didn't like dogs, I might have a hard time with my line of work," she said, her tone tart, and when the smaller dog, Leigh, stuck her face into the front of the woman's sweater, she didn't get upset or squeal with outrage. She chuckled and carefully removed her, rubbing the thick white fur. "Your dad needs to work on training you better. I think she'd tear me apart to get to my cheese."

He frowned, not entirely sure he heard that right. "I . . . uh, beg pardon?"

She looked up at him again, as if he was an afterthought to the fine evening she was having petting someone else's dogs. "My cheese. It's in my sweater." She reached in to the front of her sweater and pulled out an enormous, square block of cheddar that she'd apparently had stuffed in her bra. "I stopped by the store before I got dragged to the bar and my purse is back at the hotel, so I put it in my shirt."

"Well, that's . . . new." He rubbed his jaw, fascinated. "Don't think I've ever heard that one before."

She just chuckled.

What did a fella say to something like that? "You a big cheese fan?" Smooth, Dustin, real smooth.

The woman sputtered with laughter. She laughed so much and so freely that he felt doubly bad for making her uncomfortable inside the bar. It was clear that the terse, tight-jawed woman inside wasn't the one she normally was . . . and he preferred this laughing woman. "Yeah, I guess that sounded stupid, didn't it?"

"It definitely sounded odd." She tilted her head at him and then broke another tiny tidbit off of her cheese block. Immediately, both dogs went to attention. "The cheese is for my pup at home. It's part of his training." She gave the bit to the dogs, making sure both got a taste, and then glanced over at him. "I'm a dog trainer on the movie."

"Ah. Well, I figured it was either that or you were a lactose vigilante of some kind." At her smile, he wanted to sit down right next to her and just bask in her happiness, but he didn't dare. Not when she was laughing and happy and all he wanted in the world was more of that. "I'm sorry about earlier. Ruining your night and running you out of there. Wasn't my goal."

"I see. Is that why you followed me out here?"

"Nah." Dustin shrugged, glancing around the quiet streets. "Kinda wanted to get away myself. Too crowded, too loud." Too much of the same old thing.

"I understand. I'm not much of a party person myself. I'd rather be with my dogs. The only reason I came out was for more cheese."

"That's as good a reason as any, I suppose." He couldn't help but grin down at her. Despite the ugly sweater and the way she shoved her hair out of her face as if it were a bother, she was one of the most fascinating women he'd met in a long, long time. He wasn't entirely sure why. Perhaps it had something to do with her quick and immediate refusal of him—a put-down that his overinflated ego needed, he suspected. Dustin was one of a handful of single men in the area, and probably the best-looking one. That meant if he had his sights set on a woman, he usually got her. It had to be the thrill of the chase, he told himself.

Or her freckles. He did have a thing for freckles. As she rubbed Gable's ears, he decided to prompt her again. "So . . . you're a dog trainer. Do you have a lot of dogs, then?"

She grimaced, and even that was pretty. "I wish. Right now I just have the one dog, Spidey. He's for the movie. Because of travel and the job, sometimes it's easier to focus on one dog and one dog alone—that way there's no jealousy or competition between animals. If it was up to me, I'd have a dozen like this big boy here, though." And she fondled Gable's multicolored ears. "Tell me about them?"

"Well, that one's Gable and I'm guessing he likes long walks on the beach. The other's Leigh, and judging from her personality, she's a bit more of a Scorpio."

Her laughter pealed into the night, and he felt warm down to his boots. "No, silly. What breed are they?"

"Oh, riiiight," he said, drawling the words out as he teased her. "They're from the same litter, actually. Leigh's the little one, the runt. The mother's a Great Pyrenees and the father's an Australian cattle dog."

"So mutts, then." She smiled. "Mutts are the smartest."

"Well, these two are pretty damn smart and they're good

at chasing cattle. More than anything, though, they love Old Clyde, and that's all that matters. He got them as pups after his last pair of dogs died within a few weeks of each other."

Her face softened. "Oh, poor man."

"Yup. Eli—that's another cowboy on the ranch I work at—his dog got pregnant from one of the other cattle dogs and him and his girlfriend kept a couple of the pups for Old Clyde so he'd have company. Kept one for themselves, too. Of course, Cass doesn't really much understand the concept of 'working' dog so she spoils all of 'em. I swear when mealtime rolls around, we suddenly have a kitchen full of dogs begging for bacon."

"They need a firm hand," she murmured, stroking one demanding nose. "Treats are nice, but they should be a reward. It'll make them work harder to please you when they know they're going to get something great out of it."

"That's what your cheese is for then, I take it."

She nodded and then looked sad and distracted. "My poor little Spidey's giving everything he's got on set but the director still isn't happy."

Her crestfallen expression made him want to deck whoever was giving her—and her dog—a hard time. "Sounds like your director isn't much of a dog lover."

"No," she said flatly. "He's really not."

"You want me to go over there and read him the riot act? Get all John Wayne in his face?"

The woman looked up at him, her eyes shining with mischief. "As much as I'd love to see that, we've still got a week of shooting before the movie wraps, and I'd just like to be done."

"Well, all right. You just let me know. It's the least I can do since I ran you away from your beer."

She got to her feet, dusting off her pants, and dog hair

went flying everywhere. "I'm not sorry. The company out here was much better than in there."

He toyed with the brim of his hat. "I'd be flattered except I'm pretty sure you mean the dogs and not me."

"I absolutely mean the dogs," she told him, laughing. "They're such good boys."

"One's a girl."

"All dogs are good boys," she declared, and was that flirtiness in her tone? He was fascinated.

"So they are. I stand corrected."

She smiled up at him, tucking the block of cheese back into her sweater, and then gestured across the street. "I'm going to head back to my hotel. It was nice to meet you . . ."

"Dustin. And I wouldn't be much of a gentleman if I let a lady walk herself back to her hotel at night." He tipped his hat at her. "So consider me your official unofficial escort." He was trying not to lay the charm on thick, lest he scare her away. When she hesitated, he continued. "No creepiness or ulterior motives. Here." He took out his wallet and handed her his driver's license. "You can hold on to that if it makes you feel more comfortable."

She took the license, then hesitated for a moment, glancing down the wide street. "Is it not safe to walk alone?"

"Oh, Painted Barrel is safe, but I'm a bit old-fashioned, and it gives me an excuse to walk off some of this beer."

Her smile grew shyer. "All right." She pulled out a phone with a cracked screen and took a photo of his license. "Let me send this to Katherine in case I show up headless on the news in the morning."

"You wound me. I'm more of an ass man."

She blinked, then laughed, handing back his license as she finished the text. "I'm going to ignore that."

"All right," Dustin said agreeably. She wasn't chasing him off despite some cautious flirting, so it was progress. He thought about offering her his arm, but he didn't want to make her even more uncomfortable. She was a mite skittish as they stepped down from the saloon's porch, so he undid their leashes, then whistled and the dogs jumped up to follow him. When her face lit up, he knew that was the right call. And because she got quiet, he decided to be the one to talk for a bit. He told her about Gable and Leigh, how Old Clyde named them after actors in *Gone with the Wind*, his favorite old movie. How the ranch had six working dogs, all with different personalities, and they all helped out with cattle roundups. How you could never have too many dogs on a ranch, really. She wanted to know all of their names and ages and their breeds, and it occurred to Dustin that he still hadn't gotten her name.

Of course, asking now might scare her off, he realized as they stepped up to the front of the hotel. He held the door open for her and she paused, looking at him.

They were both quiet for a long moment, a small smile on her mouth.

"I guess this is good night," he murmured.

"I guess so," she said, tucking one orange lock of hair behind her ear—which was also freckled, he noticed. He liked that. She opened her mouth to speak, and then her phone buzzed with a text. She pulled out her phone, and then quickly put it away again, her expression changing.

"Bad news?" he asked.

"Katherine says I should ask you out on a date." She averted her eyes, gazing around everywhere except at him.

"Well . . . I do like the way Katherine thinks," he admitted, grinning. "But I won't push. How about I give you my number and if you need to pick up more cheese sometime, you give me a call. I know all the best cheese places in the state."

Her laughter was like music to his ears, and she pulled up her phone and typed in the number he recited to her. She bit her lip, then gave him another shy glance. "You know I'm probably not going to call you."

"I won't expect it. But I'll still be sad if you don't."

"If I do, I expect some wine with my cheese."

Dustin laughed. "I think I can manage that."

She smiled at him and gestured inside. "I'm going to go now. It was nice to meet you, Dustin."

"Nice to meet you too . . . Jennifer? Betsy? Frances?" he guessed, taking wild shots.

"Annie. No relation to the redhead in the movie. Or the comics. Just bad luck." She smiled again. "Good night."

He nodded, and when the door shut behind her, he watched through the glass until she disappeared up the stairs of the quaint, old-fashioned hotel. Well. That was unexpected. He suspected he'd be thinking about Annie for a long time after tonight, and hoped she'd call.

Of course, now he was going to have to do a web search and see who the redheads in the movie and in the comics were.

CHAPTER FOUR

Later that night, Annie lay in bed and stared at the ceiling as she petted Spidey's round little head. The dog snored—all dogs with short muzzles did—but she didn't mind it. It wasn't like she could sleep anyhow. She kept thinking about the cowboy.

Dustin.

There was a certain kind of guy that Annie tended to attract. Most of the time they were slim and intellectual. She'd dated scholars and engineers, writers, actors, and even the occasional barista. None of those relationships ever worked out, because men tended to expect the wrong thing from her. If they were from LA, they thought she was either a crunchy hard-core vegan type (she wasn't) or they assumed she'd gotten her job at the studio because she slept around (she didn't). Either way, dating in LA was hell, and she was usually too sweaty and smelling of dog to really attract anyone on set. Not that she minded—dating while working on a movie was a bad call, because you couldn't avoid each other if things went south. And they always, always did.

Dustin didn't look like the type of guy that'd be interested in her, though. At first when he'd come to talk to her at the bar, she'd been shocked . . . and then worried it was a prank. He was gorgeous, tall and muscular and so tanned she could practically smell the outdoors on him. He'd had a stunning smile, a face that could have been on the posters for the movie she was working on, and such an overwhelmingly masculine presence that she'd practically swallowed her own tongue. There he was, moving his way across the bar toward her like Prince Charming heading for Cinderella.

Of course, then he'd tried to schmooze her, and that little fantasy'd burst like a soap bubble. If there was one thing Annie hated, it was guys that were fake. She got enough of that in Los Angeles. To make matters worse, he'd then pointed out he was only talking to her because his buddy wanted to get to know her. That had been enough "fun" at the bar for one night. Katherine and the rest of the crew had been having a blast, but Annie'd just wanted to go home. So she'd paid out her tab and made her excuses, then squeezed out the door and into the brisk night air.

Then, she'd discovered the dogs waiting outside, and she'd never been one to resist a friendly canine. She'd been captured by their doggy charm and their happily wagging tails . . . and then the cowboy had returned. At first she'd thought he'd followed her, but he'd seemed as surprised to see her as she'd been to see him.

And when he hadn't been trying to impress her, he was . . . cute. Flirty, but not overly so. Self-deprecating and funny. She'd wanted to see more of that guy. So when he'd offered to walk her to her hotel, she hadn't protested. When he'd given her his phone number, she hadn't protested that, either. It felt good to see him smile at her, to hear his low, rumbling laugh. Maybe, just maybe, she'd been wrong about him.

She wouldn't call him, though. Even though she thought he was devastatingly handsome and appealing, her schedule didn't allow for a boyfriend, especially one who lived in the middle of nowhere in Wyoming. Painted Barrel was a small town and the moment the production of *The Goodest Boy* wrapped up, she had no doubt that she'd never end up here again. Her next movie was a mountain picture that would be shooting in New Zealand. She needed a mountain-type dog—like a St. Bernard—for that particular movie, so once this one was in the can, she'd find a home for Spidey, look for a dog to rescue and begin training, and then head out to New Zealand for initial shooting. As long as the stunts weren't too crazy, it'd be a tight timeline but she could make it work. A boyfriend didn't fit in the picture.

Heck, even poor, sweet little Spidey didn't fit in the picture. She stroked the dome of his head, her fingers moving over the short white hair. He gave a little groan of pleasure, not opening his eyes. The movie had been stressful for him. Spidey was a bit high-strung as some terriers were, and he'd rather race around and play than wait around in the shade to do one or two tricks. Also, the director was a screamer despite the fact that no yelling was specified in the contracts. It was one of those things where if she called her agent and complained, it'd end up making more problems than it was worth, especially given that Sloane's wife was one of the producers. Not too much longer, at least. Then she could find a good home for Spidey, even if the thought of leaving him behind made her heart ache.

The hardest part was leaving them behind, especially when she didn't want to.

That was precisely why she couldn't get involved with Dustin.

Funny how her brain kept circling back to the cowboy. She pulled her phone off the nightstand without disturbing the sleeping dog and glanced at his license photo. Dustin

Worthington. She did a search for him online (because apparently she was that person) and nothing came up, so she went to Facebook and searched him there. Sure enough, he had an account, though it didn't look as if it were used regularly. Most of the posts were other people tagging him in pictures. There was Dustin with three other cowboys, arms on one another's shoulders, hat brims almost touching. Dustin near a horse, grinning at the camera. Dustin with a girl in a photo from two years ago.

Dustin with another girl.

And another girl.

Annie frowned to herself, scrolling through the pictures. They were all different states, different years, different women. He wasn't kissing any of them in any of the photos, but there was the occasional loose embrace that told that they were close. Nothing from the current year, though, so she supposed she should be happy with that.

Still . . . it was clear that Dustin was a player. He was exactly the kind of guy she didn't want. Frustrated, she clicked her phone off and tossed it aside on the bed.

The next day dawned with a cold and rainy downpour. Annie dressed Spidey in his little raincoat and took him for a quick walk, then checked her email. Sure enough, the shoot was delayed until tomorrow due to the weather conditions. She hated that she felt relieved. It meant they'd be on location for yet another day, but it also meant that she wouldn't have to deal with Mr. Sloane, which was a win. She sent an email asking for script changes and any updates to stunts she needed to train Spidey on, and then idly paged through the rest of her inbox while Spidey ate breakfast with happy little grunts.

One email was from the LA office that she was agented out of. You said you needed a mountain dog for your next

movie? Is the city Casper close to you? Bernese Mountain
Dog in a shelter there. Not a St. Bernard but might fit the bill.
A picture was attached, and her heart broke at the sight of
the sad dog. His—or her—head was down, the body lan-
guage that of utter defeat as it stared out the bars of the cage.
Some dogs didn't do well in shelters, and this sad face
looked on the verge of despair. There was a full food dish
next to him and he looked small for his breed, which told
her he wasn't eating.

And his eyes were so, so melancholy.

She did a quick check of the map—a two-hour drive.
The timing was all wrong, of course. She was still on set
with this current movie and needed to give all of her attention to Spidey. She couldn't afford to have him distracted,
and another dog would definitely be a distraction. She
didn't have a car that could take her out there. It was just a
bad call all around.

Even so . . .

Annie didn't know if she could leave him. She worked
with animals because she loved them. Part of her job was
training dogs and finding them loving families once she was
done with them. Sometimes they went home with the movie
crew to a kid who was thrilled to get a dog and a parent who
knew their dog would be well trained and happy. Sometimes
she had to search a little harder. But . . . just because the
timing wasn't right for this dog didn't mean she should
abandon him.

Life didn't wait for perfect timing.

She looked at the shelter profile again. He—it was a
boy—had been there three weeks. It was a no-kill shelter . . .
but still. Her heart broke for those sad eyes all the same.
Annie gazed at the picture for another minute, deciding,
then flipped over to her contact list.

She could call Dustin.

Despite telling herself (repeatedly) that he was bad news

and she shouldn't call him or see him again, she was still thinking about him. He really was cute. Would he be that cute in daylight or was she just building him up in her mind after their meeting?

But . . . he did have a car.

And she could get over this silly, distracting obsession with him. She could stop checking his Facebook page every ten minutes like a stalker. She was bored, that was all. She was bored and he was charming and sexy and it had been a long time since she'd dated anyone.

Like, a *really* long time.

Annie told herself she was doing this for the dog. If she got there and he was what she needed, she could save his life. Bring some hope back to those defeated eyes. It really didn't have anything to do with a handsome, charming cowboy.

Nothing at all, no siree.

She stared down at his number, hesitating. Then, before she could lose her courage, she flicked to the text message screen and wrote him. Hi there—this is Annie from last night. She wondered if she should send something flirty and light to impress him. Her mind went blank, though, so she added: The dog lady.

There was no immediate answer, so she felt stupid. Of course last night was just him talking to a woman in the hopes of getting in her bed. The thoughtful walk back to her hotel? Him looking to score. She should have known better. With a roll of her eyes at her own stupid hopes, she got into the shower and decided she'd forget all about good-looking cowboys and their breathtaking smiles. Maybe she'd just enjoy the rain and let Spidey unwind with a day of no one asking him to perform. That might help his doggy anxiety a little. She didn't think he was the anxious sort but the longer they were on set, the more agitated he got. He needed a break. They all did.

By the time she'd toweled off and dressed, though, her phone had a text waiting.

DUSTIN: I remember you. Thought you weren't going to contact me. :)

He sent her a smiley face. A cowboy that sent smiley faces. She didn't know what to make of that. Feeling flustered, Annie fired off another quick reply. I wasn't, but something came up. What's your day look like?

DUSTIN: Well, I just had my hands in a cow's uterus five minutes ago, so as days go, it hasn't been uneventful.

She had no idea how to respond to that. Uh, pardon? Breech calf came the response. Had to help it into the world.

ANNIE: Oh. I hope you washed your hands before using your phone.

DUSTIN: I'm dying here. Did you text me just to check my hygiene?

She bit her lip. Should she? Oh, who the hell cared what the rules on this sort of thing were? I need a favor. There's a shelter in Casper that has a very sad-looking dog who looks like he needs a rescue and he might work for my next movie. You mentioned if I needed anything to give you a call. Want to drive me into the big city so I can see him?

Annie held her breath, waiting for his response.

I absolutely can, came the eventual reply, and she exhaled deeply. How late are they open? I have some babies to bottle-feed and a few cattle to doctor and a barn to clean before I can head out. Can you give me until three in the afternoon?

For some reason, she liked that he wasn't dropping everything to come and spend time with her. Responsibility was . . . nice. A welcome change. Of course. I'll call the shelter and see if that's a problem. And I'll give you gas money, too.

My treat, he sent back. I have to go now—hungry calf butting my leg. Text me if you need anything else, otherwise see you in front of hotel at three.

See you then, she sent back, and then flopped back on her bed with a sigh.

It was a date. Kind of. Not really.

So why was her heart fluttering like wild?

The rest of the day was relatively quiet. Annie gave Spidey tons of attention and lavished love on him. She took him for three walks despite the pouring rain. She took a nap. She went over the script and tried to think of places where impromptu tricks or director demands might be added. She went through her emails.

She went through her wardrobe twice, looking for something appropriate to wear to a shelter but still flattering. Most of her clothing was made with comfort in mind and the ability to hide dog hair, so she had a lot of patterns and pull-on-type clothes. Jeans and T-shirts. Jeans and sweaters. Jeans and . . . well, more jeans. Eventually she picked out her least torn-up jeans and a plain gray sweater. Her hair went into a ponytail since it was raining, and she washed her face and wondered if she should borrow makeup from Katherine. The most she had was lip gloss and tinted sunblock.

Then again, if he didn't like the way she looked, she shouldn't care. With a scowl at her reflection for even daring to get flustered at a guy's attention, Annie went back into her room and dug out Spidey's leash and his lined raincoat.

"Want to go on a car ride, buddy?" she asked, checking the time. Almost three.

Spidey whined with joy and did a crazy little hop, his ears sticking straight up with excitement. He did love the car. Annie hoped that Dustin wouldn't mind a tagalong, but if he did, that was too bad. She was a package deal. She put her arms out and Spidey jumped into them like a cannonball and started licking her face. Laughing, she pulled him back even as she locked her room behind her and went down the stairs.

Katherine was down in the small sitting area that doubled as a "parlor" and common area for the long-term hotel guests. Her legs were sprawled across the lap of one of the gaffers, and she leaned against Jan from makeup as they all watched TV. Katherine glanced over at Annie. "You want to come watch *The Great British Bake Off* with us? We can make room."

Feeling her cheeks heat, Annie shook her head and hugged a squirming Spidey a little closer. The dog was a chunk—easily eighteen pounds—but if she put him down right now, he'd get dirty from the mud tracked all over the pretty hardwood floors. "I have to run an errand out in Casper. A friend's driving me."

She sat up slowly, her eyes going wide. "Who's your friend with the car?"

"Just a local." Her tone sounded defensive and she inwardly winced. "You don't know him."

"I bet I do," Katherine said with glee, her dark eyes lighting up. "Does he wear a cowboy hat and impossibly tight jeans?"

"We're just going to a shelter—"

"That's not a no!"

Gosh, now they were all staring at her. Her face felt like it was on fire. Gossip on a movie set was rampant. They were away from family and friends, so lots of people tended to hook up—and those that didn't gossiped about those that did. Everyone would be giving her smirking looks by the time they got back on set unless she nipped this in the bud. "We're just going to a shelter!" Annie exclaimed again. "It's no big deal!"

"Do you need to borrow some condoms? I have extras."

"No," she choked out, strangled. "He's just a friend."

"You can have hot friends," the gaffer said. "But we're going to give you hell about 'em."

The others laughed.

"It's not the hot cowboy," Annie protested again. "It's . . . just a friend."

"Just a friend," Katherine echoed, a wide grin on her face. "But not that guy."

"Not that guy," she agreed.

"Well then, this is a mighty coincidence." Katherine's expression was downright gleeful. "Because guess who's coming up the steps?"

Oh lord, there went her cover story. Clutching Spidey to her chest, Annie stared as Dustin ran into the building, rain pouring from his hat. He paused in the entryway, gave himself a little shake to fling water off, and then stepped inside, holding the door open for her. "Miss Annie, you ready to go?"

Had she forgotten how rich and buttery his voice was? How handsome he was? Because her heart hadn't forgotten. Even now, it fluttered traitorously as he said her name.

The others just snickered.

She'd hear it later. She knew she would. Suddenly, though, she didn't care. Dustin was grinning at her, Spidey was licking her chin, and she didn't have to deal with awful Mr. Sloane today. She was going to enjoy herself, darn it.

CHAPTER FIVE

The rain was still pouring down, icy from the mountains despite the fact that it was late spring. Annie shivered a little, wishing that she'd thought to bundle herself up half as well as she had her dog. But it wasn't a long sprint out to Dustin's bright red truck. Before she could head down the street to it, he took Spidey from her arms and grinned. "Wait here."

And then he was gone with her dog, pulling his jacket over Spidey's face so the dog wouldn't get wet. She couldn't even protest that he wasn't supposed to touch her dog—no one was while she was training him— but it seemed a silly thing to point out now. As she watched, he opened the door to the truck and carefully set Spidey in the back seat, as gently as he would a child.

Her heart might have melted a little at that.

Annie was no shrinking flower and she'd had worse than a bit of rain, so she jogged after them, ignoring the fat, cold drops that pelted her head. Dustin looked surprised to see her when he turned around, but he held the truck door for her and made sure she was inside before heading over to the driver's seat and sliding in. His hat sluiced water onto the dashboard and he flicked it away, grinning at her. "Hope you don't mind a little water."

"If I did, it's too late now."

He laughed. "So it is. You ready to do this?"

She wasn't entirely sure. Her heart was fluttering a mile a minute, as if she were running a race instead of sitting in a truck with a cute cowboy. No, she decided. "Cute" wasn't the right word for Dustin. Spidey was cute, with his smooshed-in snout and big eyes and stout little body. He made you want to squeeze him and hug him close.

Dustin was . . . not the same.

Dustin was dangerous. His smile made her feel nervous and excited at the same time. His eyes were the most gorgeous shade of blue that seemed to turn green at certain angles, with sexy little crinkles at the edges as if he found the world just a little bit more amusing than everyone else. His face was strong-jawed and open, and if his eyebrows were a little heavy and his nose a bit bigger than it should have been, he made up for it with that killer smile. His features were each a little "too much" but on him, they were perfect—as bold and appealing as the man himself. She couldn't see much of his hair under the hat, but she remembered it was dark and cropped short against his skull.

Really, she was spending far too much time paying attention to how he looked. This was just friendly, that was all. She wasn't looking to hook up.

"I appreciate you taking us," Annie told him, her tone brisk and efficient. "And I'm sure if we rescue the dog, he will thank you, too."

"I don't mind. Told the others I'd be back to finish up my chores after dark." He shrugged, turning on the car and then slowly easing out of the parking space along the main street of Painted Barrel.

"I can pay for the gas."

"You can, but I won't let you." He glanced over at her again. "My treat."

"This isn't a date."

"No ma'am."

"I just need a friend with a car."

"Of course." His tone remained even and easy, as if he were amused at her protests.

"And after this, I'll probably never call you again."

"Unless there's another dog to rescue," Dustin agreed smoothly.

"Right." She sighed. "Wow, I sound like an ass even to myself."

He chuckled, gazing at the road as the wipers worked merrily across the windshield. "I wasn't going to say it. Figured you were just filling the air with words until you got comfortable."

A smile tugged at her mouth. Maybe she was. "Either way, it's very nice of you to take me, and I sincerely appreciate it."

"I like the company."

"You barely know the company."

His grin widened. "That's partly why I like it so much. This is a small town and more of the same gets tiresome. I like new people. Reminds me that the world's bigger than this little place and I should get out and see it."

There were a million questions she wanted to ask about that, but she wasn't sure if it'd be prying. Spidey snorted in the back seat, and she glanced over her shoulder at him. The truck was an extended cab, and across the bench in the back, fluffy towels had been laid out, along with a rope toy and a sock monkey stuffy.

"Figured if we got him, he might be nervous," Dustin said when he noticed her looking. "I brought some dog treats, too. And a ball, somewhere. Cass was showering me with crap the moment she heard what we were going to be doing."

She laughed. "Cass is your friend's wife?"

"Eli. Yup. She's nesting. Pregnant and all. We're all being smothered by her need to take care of everyone," he teased, even as thunder rumbled overhead.

"It's very thoughtful of her."

"I even brought us snacks," he said, gesturing at the satchel near her feet. "Couple of bottles of soda, some fresh-baked cookies, and two bags of chips. Again, Cass." He shook his head. "Guess she thought we'd starve to death before we hit Casper."

Annie looked anxiously at the skies as the thunder rumbled again. "You think we're okay to drive in this weather?"

"It'll be fine. We'll just go slow on any steep roads between here and there." He glanced over at her. "What time do they close?"

"I called and they said they'd stay open another hour if we were coming by, just for us." When all he did was nod, it got quiet again. Annie peeked over at him from under her lashes, doing her best not to stare and well, kind of failing. She felt that awkward need to fill the silence, say something to make herself seem witty and fun and again, nothing sprang to mind. "So . . . ah, you work with cows?"

Ugh, she was an idiot. The moment the words left her mouth, she wanted to take them back.

Dustin's lips twitched. "Several hundred of them."

At least he wasn't laughing at her. "Do you own the ranch?"

"No. I've been working there for about two, two and a half years now. Before that, I worked at a ranch in Idaho. Before that, Montana."

"So you roam around a lot?"

"A fair amount. Once one place gets to be too much of

the same, I start looking for new opportunities. Kinda hate being in one place for too long. Makes me feel trapped."

"I guess I'm the opposite. I've been moving around with work so much that sometimes I just want a nice long stretch where I don't have to go anywhere. My home's in Los Angeles but I think I've been back there for all of three weeks in the last six months."

He chuckled, gaze on the road. "Maybe we should trade places."

"I don't think I want to stick my hands in a cow's uterus."

His laughter grew. "That's the all-too-common and unglamorous side of being a cowboy, I'm afraid. When it's calving season, there's no time to be squeamish. You just have to hold your breath, reach in, and hope for the best."

She wrinkled her nose at the thought. "Do you deliver a lot of the babies like that?"

"The calves? Not too many. Usually we just step in if something looks like it's not going right or if the mother's struggling. Most of the time they just drop 'em in the pasture and we find them when we check the herd and do a head count."

Annie tried to picture it, but cattle were very different than dogs and she was a city girl. She couldn't picture ten cows together, much less hundreds. "And this is what you wanted to do for a living?"

"You sound so skeptical."

"I guess I am."

Amusement colored his tone. "It wasn't that I dreamed of being a cowboy, though as far as jobs go, I like it. It was more like I knew what I didn't want to end up as."

"And what was that?"

There was a long pause. "My father."

She bit her lip, worried she'd pulled the conversation into unpleasant territory. "Should I not have asked? I'm sorry."

"No, it's all right. I don't mind."

The rain slackened up a little, just enough for her to hear the gentle snoring of Spidey in the back. He loved a car ride and didn't mind storms—this long drive might be perfect for the little guy's nerves. If nothing else, he'd enjoy the trip.

"My dad," Dustin continued, thoughtful as he drove, one big hand carefully guiding the steering wheel. "My dad was a great guy, actually. Still is, though I haven't talked to him in a long time. We didn't see eye to eye when I was a kid, though. He was born in a small town in Iowa. Grew up there, married his high school sweetheart and the only girl he ever dated. I think he would have liked to go away to college or join the military, but he got my mom pregnant and that was the end of that. Took over the family business when his father died and expected me to take the reins after him. Lived in the same house all his life, surrounded by the same people, and he'll die there." He shook his head. "That's not me."

"You have grander plans?" She understood that. How many times had people looked at her and seen her mother's daughter instead of someone who was her own person?

"I don't know about 'grander.'" He gazed out the window, pausing for a long moment. "I just remember how defeated he was all the time, and how I didn't want to be like that. How small his world was. He always talked about traveling, but never did. Had to run the business and all."

"What was the business, if you don't mind me asking?"

"Tailoring and dry cleaning." Dustin smiled when she chuckled. "It's not glamorous, but my father was very dedicated to his customers."

"Nothing wrong with that if it pays the bills."

He nodded, stealing a little glance over at her that made her skin prickle with awareness.

"How did you start as a cowboy, then?" Annie asked, feeling a little flustered at his attention. "It's a bit of a change from dry cleaning." She clasped her hands in her lap so she wouldn't fuss with her clothing out of nervousness, and fought the urge to grab Spidey from the back seat so she could pet him.

"I ran away from home when I was sixteen," he told her, his easy expression telling her that the memory wasn't a bad one despite the gravity of the situation. "At that point I'd realized that I wasn't good enough at baseball to play pro, wasn't good enough at school to get a scholarship, and my dad was making noises about me helping out at the cleaners on weekends. I thought that was the first step to turning into him, so I picked a fight. A nasty one. Told him he was a waste of space and a nobody, and I didn't want that to happen to me. I made a big scene, made my mother cry. It wasn't pretty, and my dad was furious at me for upsetting my mother. I was so angry I packed a bag, wrote a note, and left. Thought it'd be real easy to get a job doing whatever I wanted, because I was good-looking and charming." He looked over at her and cast one of those winning grins. "I also failed to realize that a lot of doors aren't open to a sixteen-year-old dropout."

"What did you do?"

"Held up signs on street corners, hitched across country, whatever I could do to scramble a few bucks here and there." He looked over at her again.

She noticed he was looking at her a lot, and she squeezed her fingers in her lap, determined not to fuss with her hair. "And then?"

"And then I met a guy who wanted me to come and muck out his stalls for twenty bucks and a burger. I was so hungry at that point I'd have said yes if he wanted me to muck out a hundred stalls. He gave me a ride to his ranch, gave me a pitchfork, and told me to get to it." His teeth flashed white with a smile. "I had no idea what I was doing, but I gave it a shot anyhow. Worked my ass off that day and when the guy came back out to pay me, he took one look at my efforts, laughed his head off, and then told me I was an idiot, but a hardworking one. He gave me a job for the winter—room and board in exchange for hard work. I took it; it didn't pay but it was food and a roof over my head. After winter was over, he offered to have me stay on for another year, this time with pay. I did, and by that time, his kid was old enough to help him around the ranch so he didn't need me. He had a buddy that needed help in Montana, though, so I headed there, and have bounced around from ranch to ranch ever since."

"Hands in cow uteruses across the west," she agreed, then felt herself flushing at the stupid joke.

Dustin threw his head back and laughed. "Yeah, I guess so. Wasn't born into ranching, though, or even thought about it. I keep saying to myself that maybe I'll do something else with my life, but then the next day dawns crisp over the mountains and I get to spend my day on horseback in the sunshine, and I figure there are worse things."

"You make it sound nice."

"Oh, sometimes it's awful. Sometimes the cows get sick and I end up having to give a hundred shots in a day. Sometimes the calves die and you feel like it's your fault. Sometimes you end up covered in so much mud that you feel like you'll never get clean again. Every job has a downside."

Annie nodded at that. "They do."

"So why are you in movies? You like the fame?" He looked over at her, his expression intent. "Become a big star?"

"No. Not at all, really. The thought of being on camera makes me break out into a cold sweat." She gave a little shudder, rubbing her arms. "I don't like being the center of attention. I think I do movies just because that's what people in my family do. My uncle is a sound editor. My mother's an extra. My cousin's a key grip—that's someone who handles the camera equipment. Everyone I know is involved with movies or television in some way or another. I always loved animals, so when a friend of my mother's had an opening to assist on a dog movie, I took it. It was my first real picture experience and my job was to run around and collect dog poop and clean cages. The entire movie was about a pack of show dogs that were crossing one end of California to another to get to a competition. I didn't like the movie itself, but I loved those dogs." She smiled wistfully. "One of the trainers thought I was good with the animals and worked with me. I took some classes, got certified, and got an agent and went to work. Here I am, years later." She spread her hands. "Like you, it's just something I happened into but I like it. Well, I like most of it. I love the animals. I'm not sure about all the people. Do you have dogs?"

He shook his head. "Never seem to stay in one place long enough, unfortunately. I love the ranch dogs but I haven't committed to one of my own just yet." Dustin looked over at her. "Does this ruin my chances with you?"

"That's cute. You thought you had a chance?"

They both burst into laughter.

CHAPTER SIX

It was the loveliest afternoon she'd had in a long, long time. The rain continued to hammer at the truck all the way into Casper, and it made the interior of the cab seem cozy and private. Despite the initial awkwardness, they managed to chat and laugh the entire two hours into the city. Dustin was smart and self-deprecating, and he made her giggle at his astute observations. He told her stories about crazy happenings at the ranch, interesting things that occurred in town, and the time one of the dogs ran off with his boot and he'd ended up hopping after it across an entire field.

Annie shared stories of her own, but they never seemed as exciting or funny as Dustin's. But he seemed to like hearing them, so she kept talking, and before she knew it, they were in Casper and driving through the city to get to the shelter.

The moment they pulled up she felt a nervous hitch in her belly.

"You okay?" Dustin reached over and touched her hand. "We don't have to go inside if you don't want to."

She offered him a weak smile. "This is the hardest part of the job. I have to find a dog I can train, a dog that will be all right around groups of people, a dog that can perform on camera. And he has to have a certain look. A lot of people get their dogs from breeders because they can at least take the 'look' part out of the equation, but I try to rescue. Even so, if he doesn't fit what I need for the movie . . . I have to leave him behind. And that's difficult. I feel like I'm betraying them every time I do." She didn't add the part where she usually spent the evening crying because all of the wistful, hopeful faces in the shelter with the wagging tails made her so sad. It was part of the job, and she told herself that over and over again. Someday she might actually even get used to it.

"Nothing wrong with having a soft heart," Dustin told her. He squeezed her fingers. "I'm here to provide moral support if you need it."

Strangely enough, that made her feel a little better. "I'll settle for you watching Spidey while I sit with the new dog."

"I can do that, too," he said easily. "I'm a man of many talents."

She blushed at that.

The rain let up a moment later and Annie managed to get Spidey harnessed without getting soaked. She set him down on the pavement despite the puddles, because he'd want to walk and stretch his legs, and she was grateful when Dustin immediately took the leash, leaving her hands free. "Why don't I let him sniff around a little before we join you inside?"

"Great idea. Thank you." Annie beamed at him for being so thoughtful, then headed in, steeling herself.

Shelters always made her emotional. As an animal lover, it tore at her heart to see so many little lives in need of saving when she was unable to do it. She both loved and hated the sad eyes and the wagging tails, because she was bound to disappoint them, just like how they'd been disappointed by the people that put them in this place. She knew she couldn't save them all . . . but it didn't mean she didn't want to try.

The interior of the shelter was neat and clean and the woman at the front desk was snuggling a kitten. Annie smiled at her. "Hi. I called about the Bernese mountain dog? Has he been adopted?" Perhaps in the hours that it had taken her to get here, some family had wandered in and found the perfect playmate for their little boy and everyone would go home happy.

The woman beamed at her. "Hi, I'm Cara. You're looking for Moose. And he hasn't been adopted yet, no. Do you want to sit with him for a few?"

Annie's heart gave another little squeeze. "I do. Thank you."

"Right this way." She put the kitten into a plush bed shaped like a strawberry, then gestured for Annie to follow her. Cara opened the door to the kennel area and immediately, dogs began to bark and howl at the tops of their lungs, desperate for attention. Her heart squeezed again every time they passed a cage with a tail-wagging pup and had to keep on walking past. Annie wanted to apologize to each and every one of the dogs for not picking them, for needing a specific kind of dog for the next movie. She even avoided eye contact, as if that would make things better somehow. Then, they were at the back of the long room and at the last cage.

And there was her dog. Moose.

He was enormous. There was no denying that. The thick, shaggy coat made him look bigger than he actually was but even so, he overflowed the square brown dog bed he was lying on. She noticed his food bowl was full—never a good sign with big dogs who had big appetites—and he didn't raise his head as they approached. The big, liquid brown eyes were sad and his tail didn't wag as he looked at them.

Obviously, he was depressed. Annie's heart ached for him even as she worried that he might not be the right dog for her. Dogs that did well on set tended to be adaptable. They loved new people and new situations. A dog that struggled in strange atmospheres wouldn't perform when she needed him to. With the right affection and patience, she was sure that he'd be a wonderful dog, but she didn't have the time or the situation. But because she couldn't leave without trying, she waited while Cara went into the kennel, coaxed him up, and then guided him to the visitor's room. "I'll leave you two here for a bit and you can see what you think." Her eyes were full of sympathy. "Some dogs don't do well in shelters and that doesn't mean he's not the right boy for you."

"Thank you," Annie said softly, sitting down in the only plastic chair in the sparse room. No dog toys, no treats, just her and a small, antiseptic room. There was nothing she could use to distract or entice the sad, defeated Moose in the hopes of seeing a spark of his personality. *Hmm.* She clapped her hands on her knees, trying to call him over, and when that didn't elicit a response, she sank down on the floor next to him and petted his big, fuzzy head. His hair was matted and underneath all that fur he felt thin and bony. Poor thing probably wasn't eating. With time, she could fix him. She knew it.

But that was the one thing she seemed to be running short on lately.

He was a beautiful dog, though, and purebred, unless she missed her guess. Hopefully he'd been loved by someone. She wondered if he knew a few tricks. "Can you give me your paw, Moose?"

No response.

"Sit? Stand? Heel? Roll over?"

Annie went through basic commands, and he didn't act as if he'd heard any of them, even when she pulled out treats. So she petted Moose's head and she fretted. She couldn't take a chance on him, not if he wouldn't be right for the movie. She wouldn't be doing either one of them any favors if he couldn't learn what she needed, and he'd be miserable on a busy movie set if he needed quiet.

But how could she leave him here when it was clearly killing his spirit?

There was a gentle knock at the door, and she looked up to see Dustin there, a muddy Spidey in his arms. She gestured for him to come inside, her heart heavy.

"How's it going?" Dustin asked, closing the door behind him.

She wanted to tell him that it was going terrible, that this poor dog was depressed, but his tail started to wag. He stared up at Dustin and some of the hope returned to his expressive eyes.

"I'm not getting anything from him," Annie admitted. "This is the first sign of life he's shown."

"Maybe he needs a friend. Is it okay if I put this meatball down?" He gestured at Spidey. When she nodded, he gently set the Boston down on the ground.

To her surprise, Moose kept staring up at Dustin and wagging his tail slowly, hopefully.

"I think he likes you," she told him, surprised. "Maybe he responds to men instead of women."

"Is that true?" Dustin knelt and spread his hands, trying to draw the dog to him. Immediately, Moose got up and went over to Dustin, who began to rub the fuzzy head. "Huh. Maybe so." He looked up at Annie. "You going to get him for your movie?"

"I don't think I can. The moment we wrap this one, I

would need to start him on a training regimen. Even if I did take him, I don't know how he'd react with crowds or if he can learn tricks. I think I could eventually get him to trust me, but he'd be better off with a guy, clearly." As she watched, his tail slowly wagged and he looked up at Dustin adoringly. "But I hate the thought of walking away. He's a beautiful dog but it's obvious he's depressed. I feel like if I leave him, it's a death sentence."

"This is a no-kill shelter," Dustin pointed out. "But I know what you mean. He probably needs to run around and be out in the open, don't you, buddy?" He rubbed the dog's big head. "A movie'd probably be all wrong for you."

"I really can't take him with me," Annie said, and it hurt to say it aloud. "I want to, but mostly because I think it'd be cruel to leave him here." She hesitated, torn.

"I'll take him, then."

She blinked at Dustin in shock. "You what?"

He pulled the dog against him, manhandling him in an affectionate way. Moose let him—in fact, he seemed to love it, eyes closing in delight as Dustin roughly rubbed him. "We've got a half dozen ranch dogs already. He'll fit right in with the crew. Even if he doesn't work out for you, he'd be a good buddy for me as long as he doesn't try to eat the cattle."

"I don't think his breed is aggressive," she said faintly, still shocked at his generous heart. "A-are you sure? A dog's a big commitment."

"I like him. I like you." He glanced over at her. "He'd be great on a ranch. It makes all of us happy. I don't see the problem here. I didn't show up today to get a dog, but I like this fella." Dustin patted Moose's hip and the dog looked as if he'd fall over in bliss.

"He does seem to like you." Heck, she was almost jealous. Then again, could she blame Moose? Dustin was beyond charming—of course he was half in love with the cowboy. She was, too. "Dustin, I don't know what to say."

"Well, you could tell me your last name and let me treat you to dinner."

She could feel herself blushing. Again. Seemed like all she did around him was blush. "You're not doing this for me, I hope? It's too big a commitment—"

"I'm doing this for him. I can't let this sad little guy stay here, either." He gave the dog a head rub that told her that no matter what, he'd be good with Moose.

Annie was so relieved and happy she wanted to cry. Or fling her arms around him. She wasn't entirely sure which one yet. "Grissom. And I could cheerfully kiss you right about now."

"Annie Grissom. That's a pretty name. And I might take you up on that kiss later."

Even though her cheeks were hot with embarrassment, she was smiling.

CHAPTER SEVEN

Turned out that Annie wouldn't let him take her to dinner, but she was happy to have burgers with him while sitting in the truck at a fast food drive-in. They had milkshakes and fries with their burgers, and she fed tiny bits of burger to Moose, who was content to eat as long as Dustin kept touching him.

"Attachment issues," was all Annie would say.

He felt bad for the little guy, and when Moose put his chin on Dustin's knee, constantly nudging forward, he figured it was the right call. He could use a buddy at the ranch, after all. And maybe when it was time to pack up, he'd see if Moose was a sailing dog, too. He suspected Moose would be okay with anything as long as he got to stay at his side.

Even though the dinner was just in his truck, it was nice. Annie didn't want much, it seemed. She was happy and full of life and didn't care about anything except the dogs and his company. She wasn't out to impress the town with the fact that she'd gotten a date with him. She wasn't looking to "land" him. She just wanted to rescue a dog. She liked simplicity, and he liked that, too. Most of the women he flirted with—he hesitated to use "dating" since he never stuck around—wanted something from him. They wanted a trophy boyfriend, or a dirty hookup, or to prove something. He ended up disappointing all of 'em.

But Annie was different, and he didn't want to disappoint her. He wanted to make her smile. He wanted to hear her laugh.

If he was a teenage boy, he'd say he had a crush. Did grown men get crushes? Because every time she flashed a smile or he caught a glimpse of a new freckle, his heart pounded. He liked her bright red hair and her pale lashes and her small stature. He liked the way she looked in her plain sweater and didn't mind the dog hair covering her or sitting in his truck instead of going to a real restaurant.

"I enjoyed today," he told her, fishing a fry out of his bag. Moose gazed up at him with such sad, woeful eyes that he offered it to the dog, instead. To think that he'd been annoyed at Cass for constantly giving the ranch dogs treats, and here he was, stuffing his meal down a dog's throat himself. Pot, kettle and all that.

She beamed at him. "Me too. I think he likes you, by the way."

Dustin just chuckled, offering another fry to the dog, who took it with delicate care. "He just likes fast food."

"Who doesn't? It's been forever since I've had junk. Painted Barrel's low on drive-thrus. And this boy's eating for what's probably the first time in days." Her smile was radiant, and it took his breath away. "I'm having a wonderful afternoon and I can't thank you enough for taking the time out of your day to humor me."

"You can thank me by going out on another date with me," he told her, and when she looked surprised, he wondered if he'd pushed it too far, if she was going to get skittish on him. He had to try, though. He hadn't been this fascinated with a woman in what felt like forever.

"Was this a date?" Her tone was light and teasing, but she glanced down at her lap before looking over at him, and he realized she was shy.

"Parts of it count."

"Which parts?"

"The parts where I want to lean over and kiss you."

"Oh," Annie said softly. Her lips parted and she grew silent, then said, "Are there a lot of those parts?"

"Happens about once every two minutes," he admitted with a smile. "Hope you don't think less of me for being a little single-minded."

"Not at all. I appreciate honesty." There was a hint of color rising under those freckles. "Do you think we should kiss?"

Dustin kept his expression carefully neutral, because reaching across the cab of the truck and pulling her against him would probably be frowned on. Probably. "I'd reckon that's your call."

She thought for a moment, her gaze flicking to his mouth as if considering her options. "If we kiss, I don't want you to think I want a boyfriend."

He laughed. "If it helps, I don't think I'm boyfriend material."

"But you still want to kiss me." It was a statement, not a question.

"You look pretty kissable to me. And I like kissing. And I like you, so I figure I'll like kissing you."

"Can't argue with that logic." Annie licked her lips. "All right. Fine. Let's do it."

Such enthusiasm. He bit back a laugh. "As long as we're sure it doesn't mean anything to either of us," he said gravely.

"Oh, just shut up and kiss me so I can quit wondering about it."

Was she wondering about it? He liked that he wasn't the only one. "Lean in, then."

Obediently, Annie leaned forward, and as she did, he noticed she was breathing rapidly, her hands fluttering slightly in her lap. Nerves? That seemed ridiculous, given that she was so damn appealing. He loved the freckles on her eyelids, the pale lashes, the curve of her cheek, the way she responded with sarcasm. He loved her big heart and the fact that she stoutly told him she did not want a boyfriend.

Annie Grissom had him fascinated, all right.

So he touched her chin and met her halfway.

Her mouth parted under his, soft and sweet. She tasted like strawberry milkshake and Dustin had to bite back a groan when she pulled his hat off and tossed it aside, as if she made out with cowboys every day. They shared a light, teasing caress, more of a flirtation of lips than anything else, and he was content to keep it light. Gentle. Playful.

But then she made this lovely, deep noise of pleasure in her throat, and he was lost.

Screw playful.

Dustin's hand went to the back of her neck and he cupped it even as he slicked his tongue against the seam of her mouth. She moaned, opening up to allow him in. With a plunge of his tongue, he claimed her mouth with a hard, possessive stroke, loving how she responded. Her tongue played against his, her hands sliding to his shirt to hold him in place—as if he'd leave—and the kiss grew deeper, more urgent. He was lost in the moment, lost to everything but the feel of her mouth against his.

It was a fantastic kiss. He wanted to keep going forever, to pull her into his lap and strip that sweater off of her and discover if she was freckled everywhere. As his tongue slicked against hers again, Annie gave another sultry little moan.

One of the dogs howled in response.

They broke apart, and Annie giggled, looking over at the back seat. "Naughty Spidey!"

Dustin just laughed. Thwarted by a dog. It figured. But . . . it was probably a good time to stop, because if he touched her for much longer, he was going to forget all about stopping.

By the time they got back to Painted Barrel, the rain had disappeared and Annie was exhausted. She could only imagine how tired Dustin was, but he didn't show it. He pulled up to her hotel, hopped out of the truck to get her door, and they leashed both dogs to give them a walk. Moose clearly had some training, as he didn't pull on the leash, utterly content to be at Dustin's side. The dog was half in love with him.

She didn't blame him.

"Will Moose and I get to see you again?" he asked after a few minutes of quiet.

"I like how you threw the dog in there."

"Well, sure. I need to make sure you say yes."

Even though she didn't want to laugh, she did. He was such a flirt. Why was it so much fun? She should be irritated at his constant teasing but all she did was blush and giggle and enjoy it. "I'm not sure it's such a good idea. I'm not in town for much longer."

Dustin shrugged, as if the idea didn't bother him at all. "We'll make the best of the time you are here, then, if you want to get together. If not, just tell me to buzz off. You won't hurt my feelings none. Moose, however . . ." He gave a gusty sigh and shook his head, indicating the leashed dog with the sad eyes. "He's sensitive."

She snorted.

"Come on, look at those sad eyes."

"Yours or his?" she teased.

"Both." He pulled his hat off and held it to his chest.

"Miss Grissom, we'd love to have the honor of taking you out for burgers again. Or just watching Netflix."

Annie could feel the smile tugging at her mouth. Even though it was a bad idea, she couldn't refuse. What was a little flirty fun for one week, after all? It wasn't as if it'd change her life. A brief fling with no strings attached would be utterly harmless. "You can call me tomorrow and see if our schedules match."

He just grinned as if he'd won the lottery.

They stayed outside talking for a while longer, standing close together while the dogs sniffed the nearby greenery and then each other. When fat droplets started to sprinkle down once more, she shielded her face with her hand and glanced over at him. "I think I should go inside now."

Dustin held his hat over her head, leaned in, and gave her a quick, gentle kiss on the mouth. "That's so you won't change your mind on me."

And what did she do? She giggled like an idiot, babbled something about seeing him tomorrow, and then wandered onto the tiny hotel porch just as the rain began to pour down once more. She watched as he and Moose raced back to his truck, the dog already devoted and following at his heels. If nothing else, she was so, so happy that they'd rescued him and given him a new start. He deserved that. Everyone did.

"Come on, Spidey," she murmured to her round little butterball of a dog as they went inside. She was so busy yawning that she didn't see Katherine until the other woman put her magazine down and got off of the ugly floral couch in the foyer of the old-fashioned hotel.

"Well, well," Katherine called out. "Look who the cat dragged in." She wiggled her eyebrows at Annie to take the sting out of her words. "You have a fun day? I saw you sucking face with that cowboy."

Annie picked Spidey up before he could eat a chunk of mud on the floor, a sure sign that he was hungry. He tended to hoover up anything in reach if he missed a meal. "We were just checking on a rescue dog in Casper. He wasn't for me, though."

"So you kissed the cowboy until the pain in your heart went away?" Katherine teased. "You sly dog. Here you told me you never hook up on set."

"I don't," Annie protested. "Really, I don't. This was . . . just a little harmless fun. That's all. It doesn't mean anything."

"Girl, I know it doesn't. If it was me sucking face with a cowboy, we both know it would mean nothing." She had on-set hookups all the time, and they both knew it. "But this is you we're talking about. You're like a sister to me. I don't want you getting your heart broken by some guy in a pair of tight Wranglers."

"We both know we're not going to be in town long enough for that," Annie told her, holding a wriggling, muddy Spidey against her chest. "It's just a little fun with a cute guy, that's all."

"You know Steve and I went to dinner tonight and heard plenty about your cute guy," Katherine said, a knowing look on her face. "This town's small enough that everyone knows everyone. They also apparently know everything about each other, because your boyfriend? Dustin? He's the town player. He flirts with all the girls and his dance card's always full. If it seems like it's good to be true, it probably is." She reached out and squeezed Annie's shoulder. "I know you don't want to hear it, but I also don't want you ending up as just another notch on some guy's bedpost."

"I'll be careful," she promised Katherine. And she would.

It was just a harmless flirtation. That was all. He was fun to talk to and fun to make out with.

It didn't have to be more than that.

* * *

The next day, with Katherine's warning ringing in her mind, she vowed to herself that she wouldn't call or text him. The shoot that day was long and difficult, and Sloane was in an exceptionally bad mood. To make things worse, the fields were muddy and so any shot with Spidey in it had to be paused so he could be scrubbed free of dirt so each frame would match the last one. The horses were cranky. The dog was cranky. The actors were extremely cranky, and by the time they wrapped for the day, she just wanted to forget all about *The Goodest Boy* and everyone involved in it.

When she got a text from Dustin, it seemed like a sign.

Moose says hello, he sent, along with a video filmed from horseback of the dog trotting alongside. Moose looked so happy that she had to respond.

Her quick rejoinder turned into a dinner invitation, and when she told him she was too tired to go out somewhere, he offered to come by with sandwiches. And Moose, too.

How could a girl refuse that?

So one night turned into the next, and the next. The days were spent arguing with Sloane on the set as he came up with more and more ridiculous new ideas to try and film the climax of the movie. Luckily, the actors seemed about as done as she was and all the ideas were shot down, though not without furious arguing on all sides. Annie had never worked on such a disaster of a movie and told Dustin so. Strangely enough, though, she wasn't looking forward to it ending, because that meant she'd be leaving.

And she was having far too much fun with Dustin.

Their dates weren't really "dates." She never went to the ranch. She'd offered a few times to meet him there, but he'd said it was too crowded, or they wouldn't have privacy. She understood that. Most of the time they headed up to her room to relax and watch TV or to cuddle with the dogs. They'd grab the leashes and take the pair out for a walk up and down the main street of Painted Barrel and drop in at the local convenience store to pick up snacks. One night he brought food over to her place and tried his best to make her macaroni in the room's coffeepot.

It was all low-key, silly, and fun.

She loved it.

She loved his sense of humor, and how he never seemed to take life seriously. No matter how bad of a day he had on the ranch, he would always show up to meet her with a smile and a joke, and it was as if nothing could bring him down. Annie admired that. She worried too much, she knew, but when she was around him, she worried a little less about the things she couldn't control.

Heck, she just loved being around Dustin. She didn't feel like she had to impress him, to be some LA glamour girl. She could just be Annie, a stay-at-home, dog-crazy sort of girl that liked long walks in the countryside and quiet evenings under the stars. She looked forward to her phone pinging with text messages from him throughout the day. He sent her all kinds of pictures from horseback, sometimes of a sea of cattle, sometimes of wide-open landscapes. Because she was quickly becoming besotted, she changed her wallpaper on her phone to a selfie he'd sent her when he was bottle-feeding one of the calves. Darn thing melted her heart every time she looked at it. She'd offered to come over and help with the calves, but he'd declined and showed up at her hotel, instead.

Really, Dustin was amazing. And she wasn't looking for a relationship, but the time she spent with him just made her so happy. So content.

The only thing she didn't like? She wasn't exactly feeling the love from the locals. Not that she needed approval from anyone to see him, but things were a little . . . weird when they went out together. A few times they'd run errands around town, using it as an excuse to walk the dogs and stretch their legs. If they ran into an elderly woman, the stranger would give Annie a small shake of her head, as if disappointed in her. If they ran into a younger woman, she shot daggers at Annie with her eyes.

All the men smirked at Dustin.

And Katherine? Katherine just gave her pitying looks, as if Annie was so hypnotized by a handsome man paying attention to her that she didn't know how to think logically.

So it was . . . weird. It was as if they all knew something she didn't, and she thought of what Katherine had told her, that Dustin was notorious around town for being a player and dating a lot of women. Well, he was gorgeous, so she could understand why the local women weren't warm to her, but the whole "player" thing didn't match the Dustin she knew. He was playful, yes. Flirty? Absolutely. Out to use her? It didn't feel like it—he never did more than kiss her and tease her sweetly. He held her hand. He let her snuggle up against him on the small sofa in her hotel room. He never slept over. He never asked to.

They kept things light and fun.

They kissed. A lot.

Oh, how they kissed.

She'd done a fair amount of dating in the past, but no one had ever kissed her quite like Dustin did. He touched her like he had no goal except to please her. As if he had all the time in the world to do nothing but leisurely make love to her mouth with lips and tongue and need and lord have mercy, it was amazing. Toe-curling amazing. They could sit on the sofa for what felt like hours, touching and nibbling and tasting until her lips were swollen and she was dizzy with arousal, and she still never got enough.

Katherine kept telling her to be careful.

Of course, this all was temporary. None of it would matter in a handful of days, because she'd be heading back to Los Angeles, the movie wrapped. Dustin would more than likely be out of her life. It wouldn't matter that he was a player.

For now, she was just going to enjoy being with him.

CHAPTER EIGHT

Her last day on the set was a nightmare.

"I feel like we need to do the wildfire scene," Sloane said again, gesturing at the script. "We still don't have the punch we need to make this movie memorable." And he looked pointedly at Annie.

Not this again. "I know what my dog is capable of, and a wildfire scene isn't it," she told him, pulling Spidey into her lap. They sat under the big shade umbrella, and she was on the ground so to be at Spidey's level. The dog was getting more nervous by the day, to the point that he was acting up even when simple tricks were required. It only made Mr. Sloane more agitated, which made Spidey even less likely to perform.

In short, it was turning into a disaster.

She couldn't blame the dog, though. Heck, she didn't want to be here, either. He was really giving her everything he had. He'd done the horse roundup scene perfectly, but when it came time to simple interactions with the actors (in a scene where he was supposed to be "listening" to what they were saying) he spent more time watching her than paying attention to his cues.

He was done, poor little guy. And he wasn't the only one. Because the last few days on the set were so stressful, everyone was cranky and on edge. They were all glaring at her like she was the holdup and the problem. No one wanted to be finished more than Annie, though. But she also knew her dog, and she wasn't going to risk him.

"Just a small wildfire," Sloane told her, as if he was being reasonable. "We can manipulate the film after the fact to make it look bigger."

She shook her head. "He's not prepared—"

"You've had a whole week to prepare him! We talked about this the other day!" He threw down the script in front of her, and she felt Spidey cringe in her lap. "I specifically brought it up a week ago—"

"And I told you a week ago that it wasn't doable. I didn't have the time and the dog doesn't have the nerves. We just can't do it. If you want to CGI it in, I'm more than happy to bring him to the studio and train him to do whatever you need for the motion capture."

"Do you think this picture is made of money, Miss Grissom? We're already over budget as it is."

People were starting to stare and the looks she was getting were distinctly unfriendly. Normally everyone on the set supported each other and worked well together, but things were running long and tempers were frayed. If she caused the picture to be delayed more than it already was, she'd be making enemies. She was already going to have a black mark against her reputation once word got out about how much she and the director clashed, and in a small business like movie making? Reputation counted for a lot. It was what got you hired.

All of this made her stomach hurt, nerves starting to

affect her, too. She knew how Spidey felt—right now Annie wanted nothing more than to run away from the set herself.

So she tried a different tactic, stroking a hand down Spidey's short fur to calm his quivering. "There's another problem we haven't considered—he's a white dog and all that fire is going to leave him covered in soot. That's going to be worse than the mud." When Sloane frowned, obviously considering her words, she decided to push a little further. "It's not the same as having, say, Chad Weathers do an epic wildfire scene."

Sloane's eyes narrowed. He turned to his assistant. "Get Weathers out of his trailer. We can have him film this. He's always talking about doing his own stunts—here's his chance."

Saved. For now . . . though she was going to be in deep if Chad Weathers found out she'd hinted that he could do the scene, instead. She just hugged Spidey against her chest and waited for the day to be over.

Dustin's phone had been quiet that day. Normally they texted back and forth during slow periods. Annie would send selfies of herself or photos of Spidey, glimpses of the set, or just anything that crossed her mind. He wasn't much for texting normally, but he found it fun to send her notes throughout the day. He even sent pictures of himself, though he felt a bit like a tool for doing so. She liked it, though.

Today, however, she was silent. At first he thought she might be mad about something and wracked his brain as to what would have annoyed her, but then somewhere after repairing his fifth fence post, he remembered that today was the last day on set for her.

It meant she'd be going home soon.

He wasn't all that sure how he felt about that. Normally by the time he and a girl split ways, it was a mutual thing.

She'd have made it clear what she was looking for, and he'd have made it equally clear that he wasn't it. They'd drift apart and he'd be glad of it.

But he wasn't quite ready to drift from Annie, not yet. Not when he was still utterly fascinated by her. Not when he thought about her endlessly all day and looked forward to each and every text, no matter how trivial. Not when he couldn't stop thinking about kissing her, or how soft her hair was, or how pink her mouth when they made out. No, he definitely wasn't ready to stop seeing Annie. Maybe it was because he was very aware of how temporary it was between them that he'd settled in so easily. They'd seen each other every day, determined not to waste time.

The afternoon filled up with a couple of calves that wandered into thick mud around the watering hole and had to be carefully retrieved so they didn't break a fragile leg. After that, he and Eli and Clyde discussed moving the cattle to a different pasture in the morning that'd be less muddy. This particular pasture was still green with thick grasses, but the stock ponds here were also boggy and the animals had a hard time getting down to drink, especially the calves. It was a little early to switch fields, but if the calves were going to be putting themselves in danger, they needed to take action. So they rode out to the new pasture, checked the fences and the mud situation, and decided they'd move them there in the morning. For now, it was getting late and they were ready to head in for dinner. Eli kept glancing in the direction of the house, his horse nearly as antsy as he was, and it was clear he was ready to get back to his new wife.

Dustin pulled out his phone and checked it. No messages from Annie.

"We keeping you from your woman?" Old Clyde asked, and Dustin glanced up, expecting to see the weathered cowboy shooting a smirk at Eli. Instead, they were all staring at him.

"What woman?" Jordy asked. "You got another girl-friend?" He made a sound of disgust. "Is there a woman in this town you haven't dated?"

"Plenty," Dustin said defensively. He didn't say who he was seeing, though. He didn't want to hurt Jordy's feelings.

"The redhead?" Old Clyde guessed. "The one with the dog. I saw you with her on Main Street the other day."

So much for not hurting Jordy's feelings. "We're just having a good time," he said evasively. "She's not staying long-term."

"The redhead from the bar?" Jordy asked, tugging on the reins of his dancing, high-strung horse. "With the freckles?"

"Yeah. You mad?" He felt a surge of guilt. Annie was fantastic, and Jordy had been interested in her. It didn't feel right to steal her from him.

"Me? Nah. She didn't like me at all. No violation of bro-code here, buddy." Jordy gave him an easy smile. "But if she's got a hot friend, you could hook me up."

Dustin chuckled, shaking his head. "Most of her friends are four legged and have tails."

"That why we got a new dog?" Old Clyde asked.

"Not the only reason," Dustin admitted, scanning the landscape for Moose. The dog was at the edge of the herd, parked in the grass, watching happily. He'd taken to ranch life as if it was utterly familiar, and he suspected it was. The dog had settled in right away, a gentle giant among the other ranch dogs and an adoring shadow to Dustin. He liked the big guy and had no regrets about adopting him. He needed to be wild and free, that was all. Dustin knew what that was like.

"Well, if you've got a lady to impress, we should head in." Eli pulled off his hat and wiped at his brow. "And I want to check on my wife. She was sick all night."

"You could text her," Dustin suggested.

Eli just stared at him with narrowed eyes. "Why?"

"Because that's what modern people do?" Jordy countered. "This ain't the 1870s, bud."

Eli snorted. "I don't need a phone. I can go talk to her."

Dustin shook his head, amused. Of all of them, Eli was the one most resistant to the constant connection to others. He was pretty sure the guy would be perfectly happy completely isolated from the rest of the world as long as he had his wife at his side. Once, Dustin might have thought that was insane—he liked people, liked their stories, liked getting to know strangers. But now, well . . .

Maybe he could see it, if it was just him and Annie.

Of course, he might be mooning over a woman that wasn't interested in him any longer, and wouldn't that just be ironic. He did his best not to frown as the other cowboys teased him and they all headed in out of the pastures and back toward the ranch, the dogs chasing around the horses with excitement. He'd give Annie a call—a real call, not this texting crap—when he got out of the shower. Texting was far too easy to avoid. If he could talk to her, he could find out what was going on.

You realize you're screwing your career, here," Katherine told her as they got off the crew bus and went inside the hotel. "You think Sloane's going to stay quiet about how big of a pain in the ass this movie was? That all will be forgiven the moment he gets back home? He's married to the freaking producer."

"I know," Annie said, her stomach churning with nerves. They'd gotten steadily worse throughout the day and right now she felt like throwing up. Everything Katherine said was true. "But . . . he wasn't being reasonable."

"He doesn't have to be reasonable! He's the director!"

She hugged Spidey in her arms, ignoring the dog's

squirming. "And I'm the dog trainer. If I don't think the dog can do it, it's my responsibility to say so."

"No," Katherine snapped, shoving the door open and then holding it for Annie, as if she couldn't decide whether or not to be angry enough to be impolite. "Your job is to make the dog do tricks. It's the Humane Society's certification expert's job to determine whether or not it's unsafe. I think you're just being an ass because you don't like Sloane."

"That's not true," Annie protested, but the moment the words left her lips, she wondered if Katherine was right. Was she deliberately being difficult? She'd certainly worked with a lot of bad directors before . . . and she probably would again. The thought was depressing. Why was she doing this job when she despised all the people she worked for? "At least I'm pretty sure it's not true."

"You've been distracted all week," Katherine lectured. "You know what I think it is? I think you're too busy giggling with your cowboy to focus on the movie and because the movie stars your dog, we all have to suffer."

That stung. "What, I'm not allowed to date someone? That must be a new rule on set, because no one else is paying attention to it."

Katherine paused at the foot of the stairs. "All I'm saying is I hope he was worth it, because you know that it's going to get around that you were difficult to work with on this movie. I'm your friend and I'm trying to give you advice because this industry sucks, and there's no need to make it harder on yourself."

She didn't know if she was touched by Katherine's words, or irritated. The bad day was polluting her thoughts and all she wanted to do was forget anything and everything related to the stupid movie.

"Except you, buddy," she murmured to Spidey, rubbing his head as she headed up the stairs.

Once inside her room, she unharnessed Spidey and put down a bowl of fresh water, then flopped down on the bed and stared up at the ceiling. Now that the movie was done, there were still a million things to do. Head to the laundromat. Pack her clothes. Decide if she was going to rent a car or fly home with Spidey.

Prep Spidey for adoption.

Locate another dog for her upcoming movie and start training him.

Contact her agent and let her know how much of a disaster the film was so she could spin it. Or heck, contact her agent and tell her Annie needed a break. Just the thought of another movie made her tired right now. Plus, the thought of giving up Spidey made her heart hurt. She wasn't ready to do that, not yet. She had a hard time letting go of any of her charges, but every now and then, one snagged her heart and didn't let go. Spidey with his big, sad eyes and his little grunts of happiness had definitely captured hers.

And then, of course, there was Dustin.

And Moose, naturally.

But mostly Dustin.

She fumbled for her phone in the pocket of her oversize sweater. She'd turned the thing to silent when the incoming texts were distracting her and she was too busy arguing with the director. Then, she'd forgotten all about it and now the entire day had practically gone past without talking to Dustin. He'd be wondering what happened.

At least, she hoped he would be.

Before she could send him a text, though, her phone rang. *Dustin.* She picked it up, surprised and pleased. "Hello?"

"So you're not avoiding me after all." His voice came through, rich and smooth and slightly teasing.

She found herself smiling. "No, just had a hell of a day and couldn't scrape together five minutes to look at my phone. I'm glad you called me, though."

"Wanted to see if you were interested in getting together tonight. Dinner?"

"I'm not much for going out on the town tonight," Annie admitted, thinking of all the blaming eyes that would be focused in her direction. "Maybe your place?"

"How about I come to you?" he suggested, instead. "I'll bring food."

She smiled. "Sounds good."

"Be there in an hour." He ended the call, and she smiled idly to herself.

Of course, then she started thinking about Katherine's words. How Dustin was just using her. How they always ended up in Annie's hotel room instead of going to the ranch. Of course, he'd said before that they had no room over at the ranch. That it was even less private than her hotel. But still.

She hated that the seed of doubt had been planted.

Annie slicked lip gloss over her lips and fluffed her awful looking hair, just because she needed a night of kissing and making out to remind her of the good that had come out of this particular movie set. She had Spidey, after all, and he was the sweetest dog. He'd make someone a great companion . . . and that made her heart ache. She didn't want to give him up, but at the same time, she had another movie coming up in about two months, and she didn't have the time to devote to both him and a newcomer. Plus, her mother would have a heart attack at the thought of keeping a dog while Annie was on location. It wouldn't work, and that made her sad.

At least Moose had a happy home.

Thinking of Moose made her think of Dustin, and her body flushed with heat in response. She studied her clothing. Tonight was the last night she'd be here, more or less. She could schedule a flight a few more days out, but her hotel room was paid for by the movie production through tomorrow and that was it. Anything after that would be on her dime. Still, she could spend a few days with Dustin, she figured. Enjoy a little personal time before she had to go back to LA.

Squeeze in another makeout session. Maybe more.

Of course, she wasn't exactly wearing her sexiest gear. Not that she had sexy gear. She wrinkled her nose at her bulky tan turtleneck sweater—because the spring in the mountains was cold—and decided to change. The slinkiest thing she had was another sweater, this one black and soft as a baby rabbit's fur. It clung to her body and made her curves look fantastic while still being modest enough to wear out in public. Her jeans were all right, but her bra and panties were boring, boring beige.

Why did her bra and panties matter, though? They were just playing around . . . weren't they?

But if she only had a day or two left with Dustin, she wanted to go further. They'd been hot and heavy for a week now, and every touch made her think of more. Made her think of the way his mouth would feel on her breasts, on her skin, the way his hands would feel as he caressed her thighs . . . yeah, she was having a lot of dirty dreams about Dustin. She wanted to see him naked. She wanted him to see her naked.

But maybe, maybe not in this bra and panties. Annie picked through her lingerie drawer and couldn't find anything that matched or looked sexy together. Eventually, she decided on a pair of basic black bikini panties and to skip the bra entirely. So she stripped down and got dressed again from the skin out, and by this time, her sweater was full of static and clung to her body rather inappropriately . . . but it did look fantastic. She admired herself in the mirror once more, and jumped when there was a knock at the door.

Spidey gave a low bark then looked at her for approval.

"Good boy," she told him, patting his head before moving to the door to answer it.

Dustin stood in the doorway with a bottle of wine and what looked like a long, wrapped baguette of some kind. His hat today was black, his shirt a checkered blue and black that stretched taut over his shoulders, and he looked good enough to eat. The gaze he gave her was equally admiring. "You look nice."

Annie's nipples pricked at his intense gaze. "Thank you," she murmured, pulling him inside. Then, because she couldn't wait any longer, she took the wine and bread out of his arms, set them on the nearest counter, and then grabbed him by the front of his shirt and plastered her mouth to his.

He groaned, his arms immediately going around her. His mouth was sweet and tasted faintly of peppermint, and his tongue slicked against hers in a practiced, expert way that made her toes curl against the carpet. She gave a happy little sigh as the kiss grew deeper, their mouths meeting over and over again with hungry need. Kissing Dustin made her forget the world around her. It made her forget her bad day, or the fact that she was leaving—it made her forget everything but the way his mouth felt on hers, the way his lips were soft but firm, the way his tongue managed to tease hers in a way that was completely sexy and made her tingle all through her body.

Dustin nipped at her lower lip before breaking the kiss, and then pressed a small one to the tip of her nose. "That was a nice greeting."

"*Mmm.*" She slid her arms around his waist and tucked her head against his shoulder. "I had a bad day."

"I see that." One hand rubbed her back idly. "You want to talk about it?"

"Not really. I'll just get mad all over again."

"You want to eat, then? I have enough sandwiches for you, me, and that little butterball you call a dog."

She chuckled. "You made sandwiches?"

"Nah, Cass did. She shoved one in my arms the moment

she heard I was going out. She's good like that." He rubbed her shoulder. "Eli's a lucky man."

For some reason, she felt a little stab of jealousy to hear that. Cass lived with them, didn't she? "I hope I get to meet her before I leave."

He just rubbed her shoulder. "I hope so, too. You'd like her. Not a mean bone in her body."

And that was a good answer. Mollified, she pulled out of his arms and moved toward the tiny table in the corner of the room. "Shall we eat, then?"

They split up the sandwich, with Dustin getting the majority of it and Annie pulling out bits of meat from hers and giving it to Spidey. He was well trained enough that he wouldn't touch it without looking at her first. She knew giving him scraps was destroying the training she'd carefully built up, but the movie was done and it didn't really matter anymore, did it?

The wine was delicious, and she took healthy sips of it while gazing at Dustin. He told her about his day, how he hoped the weather would hold because the last thing they needed was more rain and mud, and normally she'd be interested in it, because she liked to hear him talk about life on the ranch. Tonight, though, Annie kept thinking about his lips.

She thought about kissing, and more. So much more. It occurred to her that she was more attracted to Dustin than she had been to anyone else in a long, long time. Cowboys hadn't really been her thing before meeting him, and now that she had? Well, he was giving cowboys a good name, that was for sure. He breathed sexiness and charm, and she only had a day or two left here.

It'd be a shame to go home and not hook up with him.

Even as the thought crossed her mind, Annie was both shocked and excited by it. She wasn't a virgin. She'd dated a few guys off and on, and one boyfriend back and forth for a few years before they'd finally called it off. She knew how sex worked, and while it wasn't always great, it could be downright enjoyable even if she didn't climax. She bet Dustin would make sure that she climaxed, though.

The thought made her toes curl against the carpet again, and she drank more wine.

He tilted his head at her. "You all right?"

"More or less," she admitted. "I'm just distracted tonight."

"Anything I can help with?" He set his wineglass down, and she noticed his gaze flicked to her loose breasts, prominent under the sweater. Desire shot through her again, and she wanted to forget all about work, or travel, or anything else. Tonight she just wanted Dustin.

"Actually, yes," she murmured, and got to her feet. He watched her with interest as she moved to his side and gently tugged the hat off his head, then tossed it onto the bed. His eyes gleamed and a smile curved his mouth as she stood over him. He was the perfect height to touch her breasts like this, with him seated in the chair and her standing, but all he did was put his hands on her waist and look up at her, waiting. Waiting to see what she wanted from him.

Because even though Dustin was a flirt, he was also a gentleman. And she liked that, so so much.

"I was wondering if you had condoms," Annie told him, and she hated how shy she sounded. She wanted to be sexy and bold. She wanted him to think she was delicious and daring and exciting, not a shy miss afraid of her own body.

He looked surprised.

CHAPTER NINE

When Dustin didn't answer right away, she started to get nervous. "We don't have to do anything—"

"Now, I didn't say that," Dustin murmured, his hands sliding over her hips. He dropped his gaze this time, looking thoughtfully at her body. "I do have condoms. I just want to make sure we both want this. It's a big step."

"I want this," she told him. "I want you."

Dustin looked up at her face, studying her. "I want this, but only if when you leave, it isn't goodbye."

Her breath caught in her throat. "What do you mean?"

"I mean I like you, Annie. I like you more than I've liked any woman, maybe ever. And I don't want this to be casual between us. I know you have to leave, but I'm hoping we can keep making this work." His thumb rubbed against her sweater, and she wanted to strip it off so he could touch her skin. "You deserve more than a casual fling."

"Then we won't keep it casual," Annie promised him, her heart beating faster. "We'll figure this out, you and I."

He grinned at her, that lazy, pleased grin that made her entire body flutter with desire. Goodness, she had it bad for him. When his hands flexed on her waist, she wanted to shuck her pants like a wild woman and get naked just so he could touch her everywhere.

Really, how on earth had they lasted a week with just kissing? Now that the boundaries had been removed, she was going crazy with the need to touch him. She moved in and cupped his neck and the back of his head, her fingers moving over the short stubble of his close-cropped dark hair. She bent down and kissed him, and despite the urgency burning inside her, the kiss was light and sweet and playful, and it made her ache with the potential of it. His tongue skated over the seam of her lips, encouraging her to open up to him, and she did, loving the possessive stroke of him as he claimed her mouth. She moaned.

From the bed, a half grunt, half groan rose, and they broke apart. Annie looked over, and there was Spidey, his little white head cocked, as if he were trying to figure out what they were doing. He grunted again, the sound turning into a whine, and then offered his paw.

"He doesn't get a turn," Dustin teased, his arm locked around her waist.

She giggled at the ridiculousness of it. "He doesn't understand what we're doing. Let me go shut him in the bathroom with his blanket." With one more quick kiss to her cowboy, she detangled herself from his grasp and picked up Spidey's favorite chew toys and his blanket. "You ready to take a nap, boy?"

Excited because he knew the goodies meant he got alone time, Spidey hopped off the bed and danced his way to the small bathroom, and Annie was glad she'd trained him to enjoy having his own "space." Dogs liked to have a den of their own, and because it was a pain to drag his cage back and forth out of the bathroom, she'd learned early on that training the dog to sit quietly in the bathroom worked much the same. She gave him his chews, stroked his head and told him what a good boy he was, and then shut the door quietly behind her.

Dustin was standing next to the bed, unbuttoning his shirt and looking so breathtaking it took the air out of her lungs. My goodness. Even the way he stood—the slight cock of his hips, the casual, wide-legged stance—was masculine and made her ovaries twitch. "He's good now," she murmured, unable to take her eyes off of him as she grabbed some sanitizer and cleaned her hands. And because she could feel the nervousness growing in her belly, she kept the topic safe. "How's Moose doing?"

"Followed me like a shadow for the first few days," Dustin told her, pulling his shirt free from his jeans. She noticed he had a big shiny belt buckle with some weird logo on it, and she forgot to ask what the logo was because then he was half naked and she got a good look at his chest. It was like he was sculpted from stone, this gorgeous, delicious man. His shoulders were wide, brawny perfection, and he was tanned as far as the eye could see. There was a scattering of dark hair between perfect pectorals, and then a happy trail that disappeared into his jeans. She wanted to touch him and find out where that trail went.

My goodness, she was distractible. Dustin was saying something, but she wasn't paying much attention. Something about Moose. It was all white noise in her ears, though, because she was moving forward and touching him, her fingers skimming down that hard chest, from collarbone to pectorals to six-pack to rock-hard obliques that made her breathless.

"You're beautiful," she told him, fascinated.

"I guess we're done talking about dogs." Dustin sounded

amused. His hand went to her waist and he hooked a finger in her belt loop and pulled her against him. "You're rather easy to distract, sweetheart."

"It's not my fault. You're so . . . you." Annie gestured at his chest. "I mean, just . . . wow."

He grinned. "You're doing wonders for my already inflated ego." He slid his other arm around her back, pulling her against him until her breasts brushed against his chest. "Now come here and kiss me."

With pleasure. Annie opened her mouth under his, loving the sweep of his tongue into her mouth. Kissing him was so good, so perfect. It was as distracting as his chest. Of course, now that he was shirtless, she got to feel all that hot skin under her hands, and the tips of her breasts were rubbing up against him as their mouths locked together, and she was getting all aroused just from the graze of them against his chest.

A little moan escaped her and when Dustin pulled back, breaking the kiss, the playfulness was gone from his eyes. "I like you, Annie Grissom," he murmured. "I think I like you far too much."

"No such thing," she told him, and her fingers went to that happy trail, stroking it until she got to the waist of his jeans. "No such thing at all."

"I'm taking this sweater off you now," he rasped, the look in his eyes intense.

Annie shivered, loving the way he gazed at her. Instead of answering, she just lifted her arms over her head and waited.

He pulled it over her head in a flash, so quickly that her hair floated around her face in a staticky cloud. But then she was nothing but bare skin to her waist, too, and when he pulled her against him for another deep, soul-shattering kiss, she could feel his skin against hers and it changed everything. Dustin was warm and hard everywhere, and she wanted to rub all over him. Another little moan rose in her throat, and his hands moved over her back, stroking her.

"Damn, but you're pretty. Freckled everywhere, too." He pressed hot kisses to her mouth, then moved to her jaw as she twined her arms around his neck. Her breasts teased against his chest again, the tips so hard and aching that she felt as if she'd shatter when he finally touched them.

But then his mouth was on her neck, hot and urgent, and she'd forgotten all about how good necking could be. Annie gasped when his tongue slid along her throat, because she could feel it deep between her thighs, leaving her hot and aching there. "Dustin," she whispered. "Please."

"I'm going to," he murmured, his mouth moving to her collarbone. "I'm gonna please you everywhere, sweetheart. That I promise."

She clung to him, and when he pulled her toward the bed, she eagerly let him tug her along. She wanted more of this. She wanted more touching, more caresses, more exploring. She wanted to take her jeans off—and she wanted to see him without his. Good lord, she was practically panting at the thought of seeing him naked.

With one last, sweeping kiss, Dustin laid her down on the bed on her back, and then rose up over her, just gazing down. He watched her for so long and without saying a thing that she had to fight not to squirm, worried he was going to find her lacking. She had enough up top, she'd always thought, though maybe a few more freckles than she wanted. But she wasn't Hollywood pretty, and she knew Dustin had dated a lot of women. Maybe she didn't measure up. Hesitant, she lifted a hand to cover her breasts.

He immediately pulled it away again. "Don't you dare," Dustin told her. "I haven't gotten my fill of looking at you yet."

Her nipples tightened at hearing that, and she could feel her body growing hotter and wetter between her thighs. It took everything she had to remain still, waiting for him to do something, to move, to touch her.

Something. Anything.

"Damn," was all he said. He rubbed a hand over his mouth and shook his head. "Just . . . damn."

"Bad damn?" She had to ask.

"No such thing," Dustin told her, and traced a fingertip over one nipple. "I wanted to kiss every freckle but there's so many of them that I think I'd lose control first. You're too beautiful. And these breasts . . . perfect."

Annie arched her back as he touched her, lost in sensation. Her breath was coming out in jagged pants. "Touch me," she begged him. "Please. I want your hands on me."

He groaned and shook his head as if to clear it, then cupped one breast. She gasped at how hot his hand felt against her skin, how urgent, how perfect. "Look at you," he murmured. "So beautiful." His thumb skated over her nipple again. "Can't get over how pretty you are."

"That's . . . nice," she managed. "Thank you."

He laughed, shaking his head. "Never thought I'd hear a girl tell me thank you when I'm praising her breasts. Then again, they are mighty fine breasts." He leaned over her and his mouth closed over one nipple, drawing lightly.

Annie moaned again, her hands moving to his hair. It was so short she couldn't hold on to it, but that didn't matter. She clung to him and writhed while he tongued her breast, caressing the other with his hand. By the time he lifted his head, she was panting again, as if there wasn't enough air in the room.

There was never enough air in the room when she was with Dustin, it seemed. She was always bowled over by him, always struck dumb at his handsomeness, at how sexy he was, and how he made her smile and laugh when no one else did.

I love you—the words bubbled up in her throat and she

bit them back, because it was too soon. But she wanted to say them anyhow.

He kissed her stomach, his tongue teasing over her navel, and then his hands were at her waist and he undid the buttons of her jeans, sliding them down her legs. Then she was clad in nothing but her panties, and she sat up on the bed to help him get undressed, too. She put her hands on his belt, unbuckling it and then pulling his jeans down, and then his boxers were revealed to her. Plaid. For some reason, that gave her the giggles.

"What, you don't like my britches?"

That made Annie giggle harder. "Britches? Are you serious?"

Dustin just grinned. "I'd have worn something more suave if I'd have thought I was going to get laid tonight."

And that made her sigh. Because he was coming to spend time with her without any expectation of getting sex, and wasn't that just perfect of him? How on earth had he been single this long? She really was the luckiest woman. She waited for him to kick off the rest of his jeans, his belt rattling, and then he slid his boxers down his legs.

Dustin was naked.

She'd wondered what he'd look like naked. In a few of their intense kissing sessions, she'd brushed up against the hard bulge in his pants and known he was well-built, but she wasn't sure how well-built. This, well, this took her a bit by surprise. Because my goodness, but the man was packing some serious heat. His shaft was long and thick, probably the largest cock she'd ever seen. No wonder the man was so cocky . . . ha. He knew he was well-built and he knew he was sexy.

Really, it was unfair for one person to be so gifted in every dang department.

"I'll get condoms," he told her, then leaned in and pressed a sweet kiss to her forehead that reminded her that she was maybe the lucky one this time around. He moved back across the room, showcasing buns that were pale enough that they looked luminescent in the room's dim lighting. Clearly he didn't tan all of himself, and it should have been amusing, but for some reason, it just made him seem human, and that made her ache for him all the more. He picked up his wallet, pulled out a pair of condoms, and then squinted at one package.

"What are you doing?" she asked.

"Checking the expiration date."

That made her laugh. "Oh, come on."

He just grinned at her and then opened the wrapper of one with his teeth. "You never know."

She watched as he rolled the condom onto his thick length, her breath catching at the sight of him. His cock seemed impossibly large as it jutted out from his body, and she clenched her thighs tightly together, trying to ease the hollow ache low in her belly. When he was done, he moved back to the bed and she lay flat, trying not to get nervous. But then he was in the bed with her, his big body covering hers, and there was nothing but Dustin—warm, wonderful skin and a mouth that kissed her so sweetly that she forgot who she was, sometimes. She loved the feel of him, and when he gently pushed her thighs apart, she clasped her legs around him and drew him closer.

He claimed her mouth with another hot kiss, and then nuzzled at her breasts, the heat of him resting between their bodies in a silent tease. When he kissed her again, she arched up against him, trying to hint that yes, she really would like him inside her. "Impatient minx," he murmured against her mouth, and then she was smiling as she rocked up against him and dug one heel into his backside.

"No one said I had to be patient," she told him.

"Fair enough." This time, the kiss was possessive and

fierce, and when he reached between them, Annie felt the head of him press against her core.

He sank into her in one hard stroke and she gasped, startled at how large he felt and how intense everything was.

"You okay?" Dustin went still over her. When she nodded, her fingers clenching on his shoulders, he grinned. "Need a moment?"

"No." She gave a little sigh, her body adjusting to his size. "No, I think I'm good now." And when he stroked again, this time it was all pleasure. He was hard and invasive, yes, but in a way that excited her and made her want to push back against him, to increase the friction between their bodies until something between them gave. She wanted to claw at his shoulders and bite at his gorgeous skin. With a little growl, she leaned in and did just that—gave him a fierce nip.

This time, it was Dustin that sucked in a breath. "Did I say minx?" he growled. "Clearly you're a wildcat." He grabbed her hand in his and as she gave a delighted laugh, he hauled their joined hands overhead, until her knuckles were resting against the headboard. His face inches from hers, he gazed into Annie's eyes.

And thrust.

She whimpered, all playfulness disappearing in that intense moment. The way he looked at her was so good, so deeply intense. It made her feel like the only woman in the world.

He kissed her, and this wasn't a sweet kiss but a claiming, exquisite one that seemed to pierce her soul. He continued moving atop her, working her body with an expertise she'd never had before. It was like he knew just how to pace himself to make her wild, just how to stroke deep, leaving her hungry for more. A slow burn started in her belly, a precursor to an orgasm, and she encouraged it, meeting his thrusts with her hips, clawing at his back until the tease of a climax became a reality. Then it was on her, and she was sobbing Dustin's name even as she was filled with wonder at how quickly—and how intensely—she'd come. That was a surprise—as was the tender way that Dustin held on to her, his forehead pressed to hers as he came, too.

When their joined breathing slowed, he gave Annie another kiss, as if reluctant for things to end, and then eased off of her. The moment he did, he cursed aloud.

"What is it?" She sat up on her elbows.

"Condom broke. It's nothing. Let me get you a towel."

Annie bit her lip, waiting as Dustin cleaned up in the bathroom and then returned with a warm, wet towel for her. She scrubbed herself—too shy to take up his offer to do it for her—and then they settled back in together, his arms going around her and pulling her against his chest. He tucked Annie against his shoulder, stroking her hair.

"Should we be concerned?" she murmured.

"I don't think it was a bad break, but I don't know. You on the pill?"

"Not exactly. But there's a pharmacy in town, right? I'll get a morning-after pill."

"Okay." He was quiet.

Worry gnawed in her belly and she couldn't help but think about his parents. The story he'd told her about how his father had gotten his mother pregnant, and between that and the family business, he hadn't been able to leave town. How that had eaten Dustin alive and to make sure it wouldn't happen to him, he'd left home at sixteen. Gosh, she hoped he wasn't thinking about that. She poked a finger in his ribs. "You're quiet."

"I'm just wondering how soon is too soon to be in love," he mused.

A warm glow shot through her. She leaned in, kissed his nipple. "A week?" she teased. "Isn't that about how long it takes celebrities? I'm sure it's equally speedy for us plebeians, too."

The slow, easy grin spread across his face once more. "Ain't nothin' plebeian about your body, Annie Grissom."

"Why thank you, cowboy," she teased back, one finger dancing down his flat stomach. "You had two condoms, huh?" At his nod, she circled his navel lightly. "How long do you think it'll take for you to be ready for round two, then?"

"Not long, sweetheart." He wrapped his arms around her and rolled over, taking them both along until she was on her back once more and he was over her. Dustin's smile was heartbreakingly gorgeous as he gazed down at her. "Not long at all."

S ometime before dawn, Annie awoke––sort of––to a kiss on her shoulder. "Stay in bed," Dustin murmured. "It's early and I have to go to head to the ranch."

"Mmmokay," she mumbled, clutching her pillow against her face. She was not a morning person and they'd stayed up pretty late doing filthy things to each other.

He just chuckled and kissed her forehead. "I'll take Spidey for a walk and then bring him back up. You sleep and text me when you wake up." He smoothed her hair back from her brow. "Don't leave town without seeing me again, okay?"

She nodded and went back to sleep.

A few hours later, she woke up to Spidey's incessant licking of her arm. Lick. Lick. Lick. Lick. Lick. Lick. Right. He was hungry, and the licking was his subtle way to remind her that he was alive. She rolled over in bed, groaning at the sunlight streaming in. Her hair was a rat's nest around her head, snarled and messy, and she was naked. She never slept naked. Why—

Oh.

A hot flush crept over Annie's face as she remembered last night. Sex with Dustin had been . . . well, just wow. She'd had good sex before. She'd had great sex once. Sex with Dustin was off the charts, though, and she'd been sad that they'd only had two condoms because they'd definitely wanted to go more than that and—

Shoot.

Annie leapt out of bed, racing to the bathroom. She'd forgotten about the broken condom. She needed to get to the pharmacy and get a morning-after pill, just in case. She grabbed her shirt as she ran, flinging it over her head. She could just splash water on her face, then—

Oh dear. The reflection in the mirror was a woman who'd spent all night destroying her bed with her man. Her hair was indeed a wild nest, she had hickeys all over her neck, and her lower face was pink from the abrasion of Dustin's beard stubble. On a hunch, she pulled her shirt against her and sniffed. Even through the clothing, she smelled like sex.

Shower first, then a frantic race to the pharmacy. No problem.

"Five minutes, Spidey," she told the whining dog, and then jumped into the shower.

Ten minutes later, she twisted her wet hair into a clip, grabbed his harness leash, and they went out the door. The hotel itself was crowded, and everywhere she looked, she could see her coworkers—production assistants, gaffers, grips, sound techs, people she'd worked with for the last three months. They all had suitcases out, readying to leave. The maid service cart was in front of the room across the hall and she could hear vacuuming.

The urge to go back to her room was strong, but the need for a morning-after pill was even stronger.

As if she did the morning walk of shame every day, Annie headed down the hall, avoiding eye contact and doing her best to look inconspicuous. A few people smiled and waved, but no one stopped her, thank goodness.

The pharmacy was just a short jog down Main Street, but then again, everything in Painted Barrel was off Main Street. She let Spidey do his business and then they headed inside. The moment the doorbell clanged, though, the employee behind the counter was staring at her. It was a woman, and a really pretty one. She had bright blonde hair and even brighter red lips, and she frowned at the sight of Annie.

"You can't bring dogs in here," she practically snarled.

"I'm sorry. I'll just be a moment," Annie promised, picking Spidey up so he wouldn't walk on the floor.

"This is a pharmacy," the woman hissed at her. "I don't care if he's a service dog or not, but people have allergies!"

Oooh, right. Wincing to herself, Annie went back outside and tied Spidey to a nearby mail drop. She didn't like leaving him alone, but it was quiet and there was no chance of him getting in the street at least. Five minutes, she silently promised him, and then trotted back inside, heading for the feminine hygiene aisle. The store wasn't very big—no more than four dingy rows of shoulder high shelving, but surely they'd have the morning-after pill.

They did. Naturally, everything was locked.

She squinted at boxes and peered at things, but there was no sign of a morning-after pill. She'd have to ask the pharmacist. Figured. Bracing herself, Annie went back to the front cash register, where the blonde was glaring at her. "Hi. I'm looking for the morning-after pill?"

"We keep that behind the counter, skank." The blonde looked furious.

Annie blinked at her in shock. "I . . . I'm sorry? What did you say?"

"I can't believe you slept with him," the blonde hissed. She glared daggers at Annie. "That's my man."

"I . . . what . . . who?" This felt surreal, like something in a bad dream. Her stomach started to hurt. "I think you have the wrong person."

"Are you sleeping with Dustin Worthington? Tall, dark-haired cowboy? Good-looking? Because that's my man." The blonde gave her another scathing look and then added, "Bitch."

Annie's jaw dropped. She couldn't breathe. "I . . ." She stared at the woman's name tag, trying to make out if there was a last name. Just a first name—Theresa. Surely Dustin wasn't married, was he? There was no way. He lived out on a ranch—

Wait. She'd asked to go over there a few times and he'd said it wasn't private. What if it was because this woman was living there? Annie stared at the blonde in horror. "I think there's been a mistake," she whispered. There had to be.

The blonde just gave her another ugly look. "Please. He sticks his dick in everything that comes into this town. The only mistake was you thinking you could come in here and brag to me."

"I wasn't . . . I didn't . . ." She swallowed hard—or tried to, but the gigantic knot in her throat wouldn't go down. For a moment longer, she stared at the blonde, and then turned and left the store, racing out to where Spidey was tied. She fumbled with the dog's leash, desperately pulling at the knots with trembling fingers, and when he was finally free, she scooped him up and ran back to the hotel.

Thankfully, she made it up to her room before she started sobbing.

It wasn't true. It wasn't.

But it made so much sense. She'd wondered why someone as handsome and charming as Dustin was interested in her. She knew, now. He had a girlfriend—or a wife, she'd forgotten to look at the woman's finger. He didn't ever bring her home because he had someone there. Katherine had tried to warn her.

And Annie had been such an idiot. The stunt with the condoms? Checking the dates? That had seemed so stupidly sincere, but would he need condoms if he had a steady girlfriend/wife? Of course not. The whole "is it too soon to fall in love" schtick? She'd fallen for it like an idiot.

Sobbing, she collapsed on the floor and hugged Spidey close, letting him lick her face. Dustin had played her. He'd played her and she'd fallen for it like an idiot. He'd carefully kept them apart from the rest of the town and she hadn't thought anything of it because she didn't want her coworkers to know.

She was so stupid.

CHAPTER TEN

Dustin's phone buzzed with texts all morning long, but unfortunately, all of them were from Theresa. He ignored the first few, like he always did, and then when they didn't stop, he blocked her without bothering to read any of them. He wasn't interested in hearing what she had to say.

It was probably time to get a new phone number, he reckoned.

There wasn't a single text from Annie, though, and that struck him as strange. Last night had been . . . well, he'd broken one of his own rules about dating. Treat 'em like a Good Time Girl. Have fun but never get serious, and never take it past kissing.

Yeah, he'd broken all those rules last night. He'd slept with Annie and lost his heart in the process. Then again, he suspected his heart hadn't really been his since the moment she'd looked up at him, eyes shining as her arms went around one of Old Clyde's dogs. There was just something pure and sweet and good about her that called to him. She wasn't fake or pretentious. She was the type of girl he'd never get tired of, never wonder what she was thinking or if she was lying. She was real and honest and he loved that. When he was with her, he didn't feel that nagging restlessness. He just felt calm and peaceful. Happy.

Maybe she was just sleeping in. He'd probably tired her out. Biting back his proud smirk, he focused on the cattle ahead of him as they herded them toward a nearby pasture. He wasn't going to think about sex while working. He wasn't. He had to focus, because if he let the cattle drift away, Jordy'd never let him hear the end of it.

He still thought about Annie, though. Annie with her soft red hair spread over the sheets. The freckles that he'd kissed. The way she'd sighed when he'd touched her breasts—

A horse rode up next to him and a cowboy hat smacked him in the arm. "Where's your fool head, idiot?" Old Clyde bellowed at him. "You're letting the damned cattle wander everywhere."

Dustin glanced around. One or two had split off from the group, but the dogs were rounding them up. "It's fine, Clyde. They're rejoining the herd."

"It's fine for Jordy, maybe. It's not fine for you." He scowled at Dustin from atop his horse, the pinto as calm and unruffled as ever. That was Clyde for you—all scowls and barking conversation, but the best damned trained animals of any ranch he'd ever been on. "Where's your head?" the old man demanded again.

"Hey, I heard that," Jordy called from across the way. He was on the other side of the cluster of cattle, making sure no one wandered on his end.

"Of course you heard it. I wasn't being quiet!" Clyde bellowed, and then smacked Dustin with his hat again.

"Pay attention, boy. If you're just gonna sit around and day-dream, you can go back to the ranch."

"I'm fine," he promised, grinning. He was more than fine. He was great, really.

By lunchtime, though, he was less great.

No texts from Annie. He'd have settled for a damned smiley face, but she hadn't even sent that. Frustrated and tired of waiting, he texted her, instead. You up?

No response.

The afternoon passed with excruciating slowness. Dustin flipped between worry—was she okay? Was something wrong?—and anger. Was she blowing him off now? Had he come on too strong and she'd decided it was too much for her? He sent another text, and another.

When he got out of the shower, she still hadn't responded, so he tried a different tactic.

DUSTIN: If you're there, respond to this please, or I'm calling you.

I'm here, came the immediate reply. I just don't want to talk to you. Leave me alone.

He frowned to himself, sitting on the edge of the bed and absently patting Moose's big head as he texted. What's wrong?

ANNIE: You should know.

He should? I'm not a mind reader, sweetheart. Tell me what's bothering you.

ANNIE: I think the thing that's bothering me the most is that I don't understand people as well as I understand animals. I just don't understand why you'd think this is okay.

DUSTIN: What do you mean?

ANNIE: You know what I mean. Now leave me
alone. I don't want to talk to you ever again.

He texted her again. No response. Cursing aloud, Dustin
called her this time.

His number had been blocked.

He didn't get it. What had changed since he'd left her this
morning? Irritated, he got dressed, shoving his feet into his
boots before throwing on a T-shirt. "Come on, Moose. We're
going into town."

A half hour later, he pulled into town. The Painted Barrel
Hotel was lit up as usual, but when he went up to Annie's
room, there was no answer. Frustrated, he headed down to
the front desk. Constance, a nice older lady who knew Clyde
from back in the day, was behind the desk. "Hello young
man," she told him sweetly. "Who are you looking for?"

"Hi, Constance. I'm looking for Annie Grissom. She's
not answering her door."

She typed on the computer with one finger, peering at
the screen. "Oh, she checked out earlier today. She was
with all those movie people. They're done now, you know."

"I know," he managed politely, and gave her a winning
smile even though he felt like snarling. He made polite conversation with her for a few minutes more, then excused
himself and went back to his truck.

Dustin drummed his fingers on the steering wheel,
thinking.

His number had been blocked. She didn't leave an address. She really, really didn't want to talk to him. He didn't
understand what he'd done wrong. Normally he was the one
chasing a woman, but it seemed every time he got close to
Annie Grissom, she pushed back.

Was last night a lie, then?

He'd lain in her bed with her in his arms, and he'd felt . . . happy. Whole. Complete. For the first time in his life, he saw decades rolling past, with Annie in his arms. They'd train dogs or whatever she wanted to do. He'd move out to Los Angeles if she really wanted that, or maybe he could convince her to go on his boat once he bought it. They'd get a house together. Start a family. It didn't matter that they'd been moving fast.

When things were right, you knew. You just *knew*.

He'd known Annie was right for him.

That's why none of this made any sense. It felt like betrayal. It left him hollow inside and wondering if he'd read everything wrong.

Dustin tried her number again, desperate. Still blocked. Swearing, he wanted to fling the phone against the dashboard, but he didn't. He buried his hands in Moose's thick ruff and thought hard.

Facebook. Of course.

He looked up Annie Grissom. There were dozens of Anne, Ann, and Annie Grissoms on Facebook, but none were his Annie. He found one with a dog picture and when he saw a California city, he took a chance and sent a friend request. And waited impatiently.

Finally, he just sent her a message.

Annie, I don't know what I did wrong, but I want to talk to you. Did I hurt you? Scare you? That wasn't my intent. Last night was special to me, and I thought it was to you, too. Please unblock me so we can talk. I'll be waiting—Dustin.

He refused to believe that she'd just completely block him out. She wasn't that heartless.

* * *

Annie rented a car at the airport so she wouldn't have to deal with the airline's dog policies—there were too many scary stories in the news for that sort of thing—and she drove back to Los Angeles.

It was a long, horrible drive and she pretty much cried the entire time. She stopped once at a chain pharmacy to get a morning-after pill, cried some more, and ignored the withering looks the old cashier gave her. Right now, she was feeling a bit like the whore of Babylon, and who was to say she didn't deserve it?

She'd been messing around with another woman's boyfriend, after all. And that made her cry even more, because she'd liked him so much that she'd wanted him to be the real thing. Now, though, she just felt used.

She took the pill and tried not to feel like the world's worst seductress. It wasn't her fault, she reminded herself. Dustin was the big fat liar in this situation. He'd really had her snowed, too. He'd seemed so nice and fun and genuine.

She was terrible at reading people, apparently.

The bitchy blonde at the store had been so pretty, too. She'd looked perfect, with artfully curled hair, expert makeup, and big boobs. Her skin had been tanned and flawless, without a single freckle. It was enough to make a pasty redhead vomit in envy.

She didn't, though. She just kept driving. Of course Dustin had a gorgeous, perfect local girlfriend. No wonder he hadn't wanted to go out in public with Annie. She hadn't pushed it, either, because she just loved staying in, and wasn't she an idiot?

"I hate men, Spidey," Annie told her dog, glancing in the rearview mirror at him. "Except you. You're all right."

He just panted and gave her a happy look, clipped into his seatbelt harness in the back seat. Spidey was happy to be done with the movie at least. She was attuned to his moods, and he'd been calmer ever since they'd left the presence of the others. She'd found a small bare spot on the inside of one of his front legs and realized that he'd been stress-licking it and she'd been too wrapped up in Dustin to realize it.

So now she was a bad pet parent on top of being a bad judge of people. It just got worse and worse. By the time she hit the East LA Interchange, she hated Dustin and hated herself. She vowed she wouldn't speak of this to anyone ever again. Not Katherine. Not her mother.

No one.

Wyoming was done. Finito. That part of her life was over. She never had to see Sloane or anyone from the set of *The Goodest Boy* ever again.

She certainly never had to see Painted Barrel or Dustin Worthington ever, ever, ever again.

After two days of driving and lots of breaks, she pulled up into the driveway of the tiny house in Culver City. Her mother's car was there, and she suppressed a tiny sigh of frustration at the sight. Well, there was nothing to be done about that, either. Annie glanced over at Spidey. "We're home, boy."

For better or for worse.

Every day, Dustin watched his phone like a hawk. She'd call, he knew. She was angry over something, but at some point she'd tell him what she was so pissed about and then they could talk it through. She'd let him back into her life. She'd tell him where she'd gone. She'd answer the message he'd sent her on Facebook.

Something.

Anything.

But a week passed. Then two. Then three. Even though

Dustin still had feelings for her, something hardened in his chest. He didn't like that he felt like a fool. That she'd used him and ditched him. Maybe she had regrets over their night together, but it wasn't his damn fault. She'd wanted sex as much as he had.

If she wanted to cut him out of her life, though, that was fine. He didn't need a sweet redhead with freckles and a happy smile. He was probably better off alone anyhow—no one to tie him down.

Sometimes things worked out for the best, even if they didn't feel like it.

CHAPTER ELEVEN

Weeks Later

Y ou're going to give your mother an ulcer," Kitty Grissom said, slurping down her third mimosa of her
Mother's Day brunch.

"Are you sure it won't be the drinks that do that?" Annie
teased her mom, but she wasn't drinking her own plain orange juice. Something about the taste was making her
stomach upset, so she sipped water, instead.

"Very funny," was all Kitty said.

"Darling, at least your daughter takes you out for
brunch," Kitty's friend Vivian declared, her (fourth) martini sloshing as she waved her arm around. "My sons won't
even call me. It's dreadful. Positively dreadful. I mean, I
got them their first jobs in this business. You would think
that they'd be grateful! Instead, they act like I'm a pariah of
some kind."

"My daughter is wonderful," said Honoria, who was
nursing an enormous glass of wine. "Except she had those
babies and got fat as a blimp. Now she'll never get a role.

What's the point in living in Hollywood if you don't want to work in the industry?"

All three women murmured agreement as Annie stared at the menu.

"She has a great point, sweetie pie," Kitty said to Annie. "When does your next movie start?"

"I told you, Mom. It got shelved. There's already a St. Bernard movie shooting that they feel it's too close to and they don't want to compete. Something else will come up."

Kitty reached over and smacked Annie's arm, her heavily made-up eyes widening. "Don't call me that."

"Right. Sorry. Kitty." She rolled her eyes while the other two women *tsk*ed.

For Mother's Day, Annie had offered to take her mother out to brunch, just the two of them. It had turned into brunch at The Ivy, no less, so they could do some celebrity spotting (her mother's favorite pastime) and her mother's best friends had shown up as well. Now they were all in the process of getting day-drunk and well, Annie couldn't really complain. They were all mothers, after all, and it was Mother's Day. So she was now picking up the tab for three soon-to-be-soused women at a restaurant that was more than she'd budgeted for. But that was okay.

Funny how not a lot mattered when you were depressed.

Six weeks had passed since she'd run away from Painted Barrel. She'd been in hiding, avoiding her phone, avoiding email, avoiding Facebook, until enough time had passed that Dustin'd stopped contacting her. Of course, then she was just hurt that he'd stopped altogether, which was silly of her. She told herself that she'd gather her thoughts in LA for a week or two, find Spidey a new home, and then fling herself into her next movie, training her new project and forgetting all about a cowboy with a laughing smile and fantastic shoulders.

Then, her next movie was canceled a week before she

was supposed to acquire her newest dog. In a way, it was a blessing. She hadn't yet found a home for Spidey. It wasn't for lack of interest—he was an adorable Boston terrier and she had the names of several families that were looking for a well-trained family dog to add to their home. But Spidey was sweet and loving and he understood that she was sad. He curled up next to her and slept so sweetly at her side that she spent most nights hugging him (and crying a little). If she didn't have to give him up, that was all the better.

Her mother didn't understand, but Kitty rarely understood these sorts of things. Her life (and that of her two best friends, Honoria and Vivian) was entirely focused around Hollywood and movie roles. All three were well-connected enough that they got walk-ons in all sorts of movies, just enough to make ends meet. They hustled. They schmoozed. They networked. And when one found a good lead, she made sure to share it with the others. They'd all had so much plastic surgery that they got roles for women ten to fifteen years younger than they actually were. Kitty was pushing fifty but liked to think she could get parts for "soccer mom" or "office professional" or even "aging hooker" as long as no one looked too closely. All three friends had their faces plumped with so much filler that they had apple cheeks and plastic expressions and they were the epitome of Hollywood clichés . . . but they were happy, so who was Annie to complain?

"Darling," Vivian cooed at Annie. "If you need work, my daughter's friend is in one of those period pieces. The sixties. They're going to be shooting a Woodstock scene and I'm sure you'd work for 'hippie number three' or something along those lines." She gave Annie a beaming smile and finished her martini.

"I'm fine, thanks. I think I'm just going to take a bit more time off work and figure out what my next steps are."

They all three stared at her like she was growing another head.

"Next steps?" Honoria asked, with a little shake of her purple hair. "What next steps are these? You need to stay in the game. Do you need a new agent? I can get you in touch with someone."

"No, I'm fine. Truly." The waiter arrived with their lunches, saving Annie from having to make excuses. They didn't understand wanting to pick projects, not when they chased down every movie they could. It was less about the money for them and more about the glamour of seeing yourself on camera for those rare fifteen seconds or so. Annie wasn't sure if she envied them or pitied them. They loved their lives, after all. They were living their dreams. So what if it seemed like a messy nightmare to her?

The waiter set down Annie's eggs in front of her, and suddenly the smell hit her like a wave. Next to her, Kitty had a bowl of fresh fruit, and the scent of bananas and cantaloupe seemed overwhelmingly powerful. It mingled with the eggs, and a cold sweat broke out on her brow.

Oh no. She was going to vomit.

Annie bolted from the table, her hand clapped to her mouth, and wove through the crowded restaurant. Luckily, she made it to the bathroom before puking her guts up. After a few rounds of dry heaves, she felt better. She washed her face, composed herself, and went back out to the table with a faint smile on her face.

All three women were staring at her. Kitty and Vivian were looking at Annie with horror, and Honoria had a knowing smirk.

"Sorry," Annie said, sitting back down and pushing her eggs away. "I think there was something in the orange juice that upset my stomach."

"It's not the orange juice, honey." Honoria cast a smug

look at Kitty. "I used to get sick at the smell of eggs all the time when I was pregnant with my Carmen."

"Oh, I'm not pregnant," Annie said quickly.

"Have you had sex, darling?" Vivian asked.

Annie blinked. "I . . . I don't know that it's anyone's business."

Kitty gasped. "Oh, Annie. Was it a director? Sloane?" Her eyes widened. "Is he cheating on his wife? This is wonderful. He's got another movie coming up and I bet we can all get roles in it—"

"Mo—Kitty, no," Annie protested, shuddering in horror at the thought of sleeping with Sloane. "I didn't sleep with anyone in the film crew. Jesus."

"A local, then," Honoria said. When Annie's cheeks grew hot, Honoria gave a smug nod. "Told you both."

"Oh Annie, you didn't." Kitty looked disappointed. "Locals are just a mistake."

Boy, she knew that. "I'm really not pregnant, everyone. I promise."

Honoria reached into her purse and pulled out a box. "Here. I've got pee sticks. Go take one in the bathroom. It'll tell you if you're pregnant."

Vivian snagged her newest martini from the waiter before he could set it on the table. "Darling, do we need to ask why you're carrying around pregnancy tests in your purse? You're pushing forty-seven—"

"Shhh," Honoria snarled, a dangerous look in her eyes. "And I'm seeing someone." She shrugged. "He's a casting director."

Their attention suddenly went to Honoria. "You don't say," Kitty leaned in. "Tell us more."

"It's a small, independent film company," Honoria began.

Vivian snorted, taking a deep slurp of her drink. "Porn."

"No! It's legit. They do found footage types of movies

for Netflix. I promise it's not porn. Anyway, he's very nice and he has a lot of money." She looked smug. "And he's going to cast me in *The Paranormal Castle*. He said so."

"Oooh, a horror flick." Kitty's plastic face was full of longing.

Annie eyed the pregnancy test on the table. This was ridiculous. And yet . . . before she could overthink it, she snatched the kit from the table and headed back to the restroom.

There was no way she was pregnant. So she was a little sensitive to smell today. So she'd missed having her period. She'd taken a morning-after pill. That took care of things, right? She wasn't pregnant. They'd used condoms.

But one of the condoms had broken.

Another cold sweat broke out over her body and this time, Annie was prepared for the vomiting.

Round two of puking was terrible, especially because there was nothing in her stomach. But that just meant she had food poisoning, right? She clung to the toilet for a little, trying not to think about how dirty it was because she could only handle so much this morning. Then, when everything settled, Annie got to her feet, opened the box, and used one of the kits.

Five minutes later, she used the other kit in the box, just to be sure. It had to be a mistake.

Both read "pregnant."

Tears threatened to flood her eyes. How? How was it possible?

The bathroom door opened and Annie winced when she heard Vivian's voice. This was not what she needed at the moment. Maybe if she was quiet, Vivian would go sit down again.

"Darling?" Kitty said, and Annie bit back a groan, picturing all three women with their drinks huddling in the bathroom outside her stall.

"I'm here," Annie managed.

"Well?"

"Pregnant," she admitted. "I don't understand. I took a morning-after pill."

"Those don't work if you're ovulating," Honoria volunteered.

"How would you know?" Vivian demanded.

"I have five kids. Of course I know," Honoria snapped.

"*Hmph*. I thought you were getting pregnant for roles."

"Oh please. No one gets pregnant just for roles."

"Darling." It was her mother again. "I know a good doctor in Malibu. We can get you fixed right up."

"Or you can get a few pregnancy roles," Vivian suggested. "And I hear there are people that pay for babies in foreign countries, so there's that."

"You're drunk," Honoria told Vivian in disgust.

Annie laughed. What else could she do? Hysterical, she just laughed and laughed, burying her face in her hands. She laughed so long and so hard that at some point it turned into sobbing.

"Oh honcy," her mother said softly. "Happy Mother's Day to both of us."

CHAPTER TWELVE

Six Months Later

You sure you're okay, honey?" Kitty asked as she rushed around the house, fixing her makeup last minute and then scrutinizing her beaded handbag. She was dressed for a cocktail party despite the fact that it was seven in the morning, because she had a walk-on role and needed to head to the set. "You don't need another pillow?"

"I'm good," Annie told her. She had a pillow behind her lower back and one next to her, just in case. "Go enjoy yourself. Maybe they'll give you a few more lines."

"They have to be good ones, you know," Kitty told her, putting in a hoop earring. "Viv said that she spoke on her last movie and the director made them reshoot it so he wouldn't have to pay her scale. Cheapasses."

"Super cheap," Annie agreed.

"You want me to bring you home anything? In-N-Out maybe?"

Annie patted her enormous stomach. "No. I think I'm going to skip the milkshakes and burgers today."

"It's probably a good thing," Kitty said, looking over at her daughter with a faintly puzzled expression. "I don't recall porking up like you have when I had you, but then again, I do try to watch my figure. I can give you a good laxative—"

"Bye Mom," Annie said pointedly. "Have fun."

"All right, honey. I'm leaving!" She hesitated, grabbed her beaded purse and put her wallet into the discarded purse, instead, then rushed out the door. "Call if you need anything!"

"I won't," she called back. She waited until the door shut and then breathed a sigh of relief. Annie loved her mother. She really did. But Kitty was difficult to live with at times, and they got along best when they weren't in each other's hair constantly. Given that Annie had lived at home for seven months straight with no breaks for a movie—something that hadn't happened in years—they were getting sick of each other. She was going to need to find an apartment when the baby came, she knew. Her mother's house was a good size for Hollywood—twelve hundred square feet— but it felt tinier every day.

Of course, Annie needed steady work before she could get an apartment. Her savings were dwindling and apartments in Los Angeles were an arm and a leg. With a sigh, she picked up her laptop and gave the dog's head a pat before resting the computer on her belly. Tucked against her other side, Spidey gnawed on one of his chew toys, happiest when he was next to her. She'd kept the dog.

And she'd kept the baby.

Her mother hadn't understood either choice. It wasn't her choice to make, though. Annie loved Spidey, and after she'd had a few weeks to weep through her feelings, she loved the baby, too. It didn't matter that Dustin was a jerk or that he'd used her. They'd made a life together and she wasn't going to get rid of it because it was inconvenient.

Hadn't Kitty raised Annie all on her own? She'd never known her father—her mother just said that he was a guy she'd met on set and that was the end of that. Two generations of Grissom women were going to be single moms, then It happened. She'd make the best of it. And her mother had loved her and raised her well, so she was going to do the same for her baby girl.

Or baby boy. Whichever. It didn't matter—she'd love the little one just the same.

She reached down and stroked Spidey's ear as the dog happily snorted, licking peanut butter out of his Kong chew. Maybe she'd see if there was another dog movie that needed a Boston. Sometimes that happened—they didn't care what breed the dog was as long as he was trained and listened to commands. But it hadn't happened lately, and Annie's agent hadn't been able to line anything up for her at all.

She knew some of it was that she'd bickered so much with Sloane on the last movie, and because the industry was small, word got out. A few jobs had popped up, but a lot of them had involved traveling to other countries and with Annie's heavy belly, that was out of the question. When she had a baby, those jobs would be impossible unless she schlepped her kid off to someone else for months on end, and she refused to do that. She sure couldn't leave the kid with Kitty. Her poor baby would end up on every casting call for infants known to mankind, and she didn't want to do that to him or her.

Maybe it was time to get out of the movie business entirely, she realized. Start something new. She could contact a few local pet places, see if they had openings for dog trainers. Heck, she'd run a cash register at a pet store if it'd give her some cash coming in and steady work. If she could rebuild her savings, she could think about the next step— like running her own dog training business.

Until the baby came, though, it was best to think in small steps.

With a sigh, she shifted on the couch, ignoring the twinges in her lower back. Balancing the laptop, she checked her email. Sandwiched in the usual junk emails was a notice from her agent.

She opened it . . . and her heart sank.

The Goodest Boy was going into reshoots. Annie needed to be in Wyoming in three days.

Reshoots were a fact of life in filmmaking. It was when the director decided that he needed more footage or needed a scene redone, and so everyone had to go back out on location. Reshoots were expensive and usually you weren't paid for the extra time, but they were in the contract you signed, so it was expected.

Annie had forgotten all about reshoots for *The Goodest Boy.*

That meant going back to Painted Barrel.

That meant she might see Dustin Worthington.

And his girlfriend. Or wife. She didn't know which one it was, just that Annie was the "other woman."

Well . . . shit.

She rubbed her pregnant belly, thinking. She couldn't exactly bail out of reshoots, given that Spidey was one of the stars. She had to go. Getting there wasn't a problem, really. She'd rent a car, squeeze her big belly behind the steering wheel, and drive up there again.

But her stomach churned with dread at the thought of seeing Dustin—or his blonde girlfriend—again. She didn't know what to do.

She had three days to figure something out.

Annie went to the laundromat to wash her clothes, because she would need them for Wyoming. She went to the dry cleaner and picked up her mother's clothing just because she was out, and then went to the pet supply store and bought an obscene quantity of training treats so she could brush Spidey up on some of his tricks. Hopefully the reshoots wouldn't be too painful. She kept the day busy with errands so she wouldn't have to think too hard about Dustin.

She did anyhow, of course.

She wondered how he'd react to the thought that she was pregnant. Not just slightly pregnant, but starting-to-waddle, really-big-in-the-waist pregnant. Even her lips had puffed up, as if in solidarity with her ankles, which were permanently swollen at this point. Being pregnant was probably sexy for some people, but she mostly just felt ungainly and awkward.

Not that she wanted to be sexy around Dustin. Still, if she did run into him, it would be nice for him to be bowled over at how beautiful she was, how he'd messed things up between them. She entertained ideas of him groveling, begging for forgiveness only for her to turn her nose up at him and declare that he'd destroyed everything they might have ever had.

In reality . . . she wasn't sure she wanted to tell him she was pregnant.

She could hide it, mostly. Sure, she was poking out in the midsection, but a big bulky sweatshirt or an oversized wraparound sweater would probably hide the worst of it. She could avoid going out into Painted Barrel and stick to her hotel room. They were only going to be doing reshoots for a few days, after all. She might not see him. She might not need to tell him that he was going to be a father.

But that struck her as . . . kind of wrong.

Shouldn't he know? No matter how bad of a person he was, or how big of a user, didn't Dustin deserve to know he had a child coming into this world? Didn't her baby deserve to have a father or to at least know of him? Child support aside, she'd often wondered about her own father growing up. As an adult, she didn't care as much anymore, but with a baby on the way, she was remembering all of the times that other children'd had father figures and she'd only had her movie-obsessed mother.

Well, and her mother's equally obsessed friends. And their plastic surgeons, who sent holiday cards to their favorite repeat clients.

Annie's childhood hadn't been all that normal, and the closer she got to her due date, the more she wanted her baby to have everything.

Everything.

So . . . it was a dilemma. Did she tell the rotten cowboy he was going to have a wonderful, magical child that she was growing in her belly and that he couldn't be in the baby's life unless the baby wanted it? Or did she let it slide and pretend there was no baby until she was safely back home again?

Annie pondered it late into the day, even as she packed her clothing and dug out every oversize tunic and sweatshirt she possibly could and stuffed them into her bags. Her mother eventually returned home, slightly frazzled and smelling like booze, but beaming. "I had four lines today, Annie! They let me flirt with the bartender in the scene, and the director even said it might stay in the final cut!"

"That's great, Kitty." Annie folded a cream-colored dog sweater and stuffed it into the bag. It was sticky with unseasonably warm weather here, but the mountains would be colder. Spidey would need to make sure he had warm clothing.

"You're packing?" Kitty flopped into Annie's bedroom and sat at the foot of the bed. "What's going on?"

"Reshoots for *The Goodest Boy*. I have to be in Wyoming in three days."

Kitty groaned. "Reshoots. As if they think everyone's

made of money and can just drop everything. They don't even pay for reshoots!"

"It's in the contract." Annie shrugged. "I'll do it. I have to. I'm just not looking forward to going back to Wyoming."

Kitty made a sound of agreement, pushing her bleached hair back off her face. "I imagine it's hell on your complexion."

Annie frowned at her mother. "I don't care about my complexion—"

"Well obviously, darling. You should have had those freckles lasered off years ago like I did."

"I'm talking about the cowboy, mother. You know, the father of my child?" She patted her stomach, and as if responding, the baby shifted and kicked. She smiled to herself, rubbing. "This little guy is coming in ten weeks and I'm trying to figure out if I should tell the father he exists."

"*Ugh*, why?"

"Because he's going to be a parent?"

"Not if you refuse to put his name on the birth certificate."

"Mother."

"Don't call me that."

"Fine then. Kitty."

Kitty shrugged. "You got on just fine without a father."

"I know. But I want to make sure it's the right choice." Annie stroked her rounded belly absently. She was constantly touching it now that she'd started to show, as if caressing her own stomach would somehow tell the baby inside how excited she was for him—or her—to arrive. "You never told my father about me, did you?"

"Oh, I did," Kitty said breezily.

"You did?" Annie stared, shocked.

"Yes. I believe he told me that I was a whore and he gave me two hundred dollars to fix my problem."

"Wow. What a winner."

Kitty shrugged. "We Grissom women can pick them, it seems."

Boy, she was not wrong. The thought was depressing. "But you did tell him."

Her mother nodded. "At the time, I thought he should know. Be a father and all that. But I was much younger then, and stupider. Men don't want to be a father unless it's their idea."

Annie's stomach hurt, acid burning in her throat. Heartburn, she told herself, though it was most likely nerves. Her mother's words had brought up a memory of her time with Dustin. Of him talking about his father, and how he'd had to marry Dustin's mother after he got her pregnant and stayed home, running the family business. How Dustin had never wanted that.

Wasn't this the same scenario? Wouldn't she be forcing this onto him? *Ugh*. Annie swallowed hard.

But no, this would be different. She'd be letting him know about the baby . . . and that was it. She didn't want child support. She didn't want him to have any claim on her baby. Just because she was going to do the right thing didn't mean that he had to.

She realized that her mind was made up. For her baby's sake, she'd tell Dustin about the child. What Dustin chose to do with that information was up to him. She didn't need—or want—him in her life. He could tell his blonde girlfriend . . . or not. It didn't matter if the baby caused problems between the two of them.

Dustin should have thought of that before he'd slept with Annie, after all.

And really, Annie did best without secrets. She was an honest person and couldn't live a lie, even if Dustin was okay with it. That wasn't who she was . . . and she wasn't going to change for him.

* * *

Dustin's address was easy enough to find. She found his profile on Facebook (and okay, she might have hate-stalked it a little, but just a little) and then looked up the Price Ranch. It was apparently a big cattle ranch tucked into the mountains near Painted Barrel. While the website was outdated, she recognized the ranch's "brand"—the symbol she'd seen on Dustin's belt. That had to be it.

Once she'd rented a car, kissed her mom goodbye, and loaded up with snacks for both herself and Spidey, Annie headed off to Wyoming.

Driving across several states was a different experience when you were seven months pregnant. For one, she had to stop constantly to pee. Since she was by herself, every time she got gas or a snack, people gave her pitying looks, as if it were abnormal for a pregnant woman to be by herself. It irritated her—but then again, it could have been hormones causing that, too. Either way, she was in a rather pissy mood by the time she got to Wyoming, and when she found the turnoff for the Price Ranch, she was ready to get out of the car and confront someone.

The ranch itself looked rather idyllic. It was tucked deep into a valley in the twisting mountains, and the pass she had to take to get up to it was a little dangerous-looking, but it seemed safe enough. There was a light snow on the ground but the road itself was clear enough. She hoped the snow wasn't going to be a big problem for the reshoots. Stupid if it was going to snow the entire time, but then again, she wasn't the director. No one asked her opinion. There was a big gate with a grate of some kind across the front to keep the cattle from leaving, and when she turned down the road, she saw an enormous house that looked like a log cabin in the middle of the wilderness. There was a big barn off in the distance, rail fences as far as the eye could see, and cattle speckled over the rolling hills. It looked very pastoral.

"It's pretty, isn't it, Spidey?"

The dog ignored her, gazing at his now-empty Kong, hoping for a peanut butter refill.

"You can have that later," she promised him. She drove up to the house itself, wondering if there was an appropriate place to park, and then laughed at herself. What was the appropriate sort of parking etiquette for showing up on someone's doorstep pregnant with their baby? Parallel? Crossways? Cut off any exits just in case of a runner? Chuckling to herself at the joke, Annie got out of the car and wrapped her sweater tightly around her bulky midriff, then moved around to the back to get Spidey out of his seatbelt harness and into a leash harness. Once that was on, she put on his little winter coat and booties, because it was rather cold outside, the wind tearing through her clothing. Definitely colder than California, that was for sure. Shivering, she let Spidey climb down out of the car—she wasn't really able to carry him at this point—and then they waddled up to the door together.

The house had a covered front porch, with a couple of wooden rocking chairs. Off in the distance, she could hear the sound of chickens, and she thought she saw a horse on the horizon. Was Dustin here? Goose bumps covered her arms and she felt a prickle of dread.

She'd never done this before—confronting an ex-boyfriend. She had a feeling it was going to go badly. Really badly. For a moment, she wanted to turn around and get back into the car. Hesitant, Annie put a hand on her stomach. "Give me a sign if you want this, baby. If not, I'll turn around and leave and no one needs to know."

The baby kicked, just under her hand.

Drat.

With a sigh, she headed for the house, Spidey at her heels.

Annie headed up the steps, glancing at the trucks nearby. There were several under a carport off behind the house, and she caught sight of Dustin's familiar red monster of a truck. Yeah, this was where he lived. She didn't know if that made her feel better or worse. It didn't matter. It was something she had to do. Steeling herself, Annie took a deep breath and then tapped the doorbell.

"Coming," a female voice called out. Annie waited on the porch, trying not to fidget. It seemed to take the woman a long time to get to the door, and she started to wonder if there was a problem. Finally, the door opened and the woman gave her a confused look. "Hello? Can I help you?"

If possible, the woman in front of her was even more pregnant than Annie was. She had dark, curly hair that she wore in a tail over one shoulder and had on a man's plaid shirt over a long skirt, her belly straining the buttons. At her side, a big white dog wagged its tail happily.

"Hi, um, does Dustin Worthington live here?" Annie touched her belly.

The woman's eyes went wide. "Oh. Oh, you're Annie. Oh my goodness." She sagged, and Annie immediately moved forward to try and help her.

"Wait!" Annie cried out, trying to hold her up. She was in danger of falling over herself. "I don't think I can carry you!"

"No, I'm fine," the woman panted, and they somehow managed to wobble over to the nearby couch together before both of them collapsed.

Wheezing, Annie rolled onto her back, her hands supporting her stomach. The other woman did the same. "That . . . was a close one," Annie told her. "If you'd gone to the floor, I don't think I could have helped you up."

"Like a turtle on its back," the woman said, still panting.

"Or two beached whales," Annie agreed, picturing it. A horrified giggle burst in her throat.

The other woman looked over at her. Giggle-snorted.

And then they were both laughing. It was just too funny and horrific, two helpless pregnant women depending on each other for support and hoping the other had the strength. Once she started laughing, Annie couldn't stop, either. She just kept picturing it and how funny they must have looked.

"Stop, stop," the dark-haired woman howled. "I'm peeing my pants. My . . . bladder . . . baby's right on it . . ."

Annie wiped tears from her eyes. "Mine too," she giggled. "So awful."

"The worst. Pregnancy sucks. They all lied to me," the brunette managed, and then burst into a fresh round of laughter.

"I don't know why I keep laughing," Annie said, unable to stop. She just kept giggling, as if it was the funniest thing on earth.

"Hormones," the other woman agreed between chuckles. "It's either that or weeping."

Oh gosh, and Annie really wanted to weep, too. Suddenly the laughter turned to tears and she started to cry.

"S'okay," the other woman managed, staggering to her feet. "If you wet your pants, I have some extras."

"This is a nightmare," Annie said. She pressed her hands to her face. "All of this."

"Oh, honey." A moment later, a tissue was pressed into her hand and the other woman gave her shoulder a squeeze. "If you want to leave, I won't tell Dustin you were here. It'll be a secret between us beached whales."

A hysterical laugh bubbled inside her again. "How did you know I'm Annie?"

"The red hair and freckles." The woman patted her stomach and then eased herself onto the couch next to Annie again. "Though I admit the baby bump is a bit of a surprise."

"More like a baby mountain," Annie admitted. "We're practically the same size and I'm only at thirty weeks."

"Thirty-seven here," the other woman said, her hand going to the small of her back. "Ready for this to be over. I'm Cass, by the way. Eli's my husband."

Annie swiped at her face. "I remember Dustin mentioning you. Hi. Annie."

"Movie girl. Dog girl. I know." She leaned back on the sofa and closed her eyes. "That was enough cardio for me today. If you don't mind, I'm going to sit here for a moment longer so my stomach settles."

"Is there anything I can get you?"

Cass waved a hand in the air. "I'm all right. I just get winded easily. Huge baby crushing my lungs and all."

Gosh, Annie understood how that felt. She waited a few moments and then said, "Thank you."

"For?"

"For offering to not tell Dustin I was here. I wasn't sure if I should come."

"I get that, considering you broke his heart and all."

Annie frowned, toying with her tissue. At a slight jingle, she looked over and Spidey was politely sniffing the room, exploring an enormous dog bed that was near the fireplace. Right. They had a lot of dogs here. The white fluff monster that was Cass's dog was busy sniffing Spidey's hindquarters, but her dog was ignoring him, used to strange animals. She should call off the other dog so Spidey didn't get nervous, but then she realized what the other woman said. "I'm sorry, did you say that I broke Dustin's heart?"

"Well, yeah. Told us all about you for a week and then said nothing at all for the next six months. Eli and I connected the dots. It's not like Dustin to be silent, you know. We figured you hurt him pretty bad."

Something didn't make sense. She tore at the tissue, anxious. "You mean he hurt me," Annie gently corrected. "By not telling me that he had a girlfriend."

Cass opened her eyes and squinted at Annie. "What girlfriend?"

"I know he has a girlfriend." Her stomach was starting to hurt, and the baby did a somersault inside her, adding to the dizzy, spinning sensation.

"Dustin? Dustin Worthington? Mister Flirt And That's It?" Cass shook her head, her curls sticking to her sweaty brow. "Dustin never sees a girl more than once. That's why we all knew your name. He wouldn't shut up about you. Well. At first." Cass gave a little grimace.

Annie was pretty sure she was going to be sick. "The woman in town told me she was his girlfriend."

"What? Who?"

"The blonde in the pharmacy. Red lips. Really pretty. Big hair. I forget her name—"

"Theresa?" When Annie nodded, Cass rolled her eyes. "She's a one-woman crazy train. Also known as 'stalker.' He dated her once, I think, but she decided she deserved more. Dustin didn't agree. She makes herself a pain in the ass every now and then and reminds him that she's alive, but he's not interested. Never really has been."

"Oh no," Annie moaned. Now she was the one that needed to lie down on the couch. She leaned back and pressed a hand to her forehead, feeling faint. "This is even worse than I thought." No girlfriend? No wife? Just a crazy ex-lover? Or shoot, if they'd only gone out once, that didn't even mean they were lovers. Not really. A vivid memory flashed through Annie's mind—of Dustin checking the expiration date on the condoms. *You never know*, he'd said.

Because he'd had them for so long?

That meant . . . there was no other woman. He'd really wanted to be with Annie.

And she'd ghosted him. Acted like a jerk for seven months, convinced she'd been wronged.

Now she was the bad guy.

"I'm going to throw up," Annie whispered.

"Please don't puke or I will, too."

She wanted to say it was too late, but she couldn't, because lunch was coming up and she barely had time to lean over the couch and lose the contents of her stomach. A moment later, Cass heaved, and then both women were sick.

It would have been funny if it wasn't happening to her.

Instead, she just started to cry again.

Stupid hormones.

CHAPTER THIRTEEN

Dustin chewed a toothpick and gazed up at the sky. Despite the fact that it was cold outside and a fresh dusting of snow lay on the ground, it was a nice day. The sky was blue, the cattle were healthy and behaving. The fences were mended and his horse was in a high-spirited mood.

Should have been a good day. He should have been thinking about the upcoming winter, of all the things around the ranch that would need doing as the cattle got fatter, readying to have their calves in the spring. Thinking about how much hay they had, and if it would last them the winter or if they'd need to purchase some from a neighbor. If they were going to breed one of the horses this year or wait until next year. If the farm equipment needed a tune-up. A cowboy had to do a dozen tasks a day of any and every kind, and normally his head was full of a to-do list that kept him busy but never bored.

He was bored now, though. He looked at the mountains in the distance and didn't feel pleasure at the sight of them.

Instead, he wondered if he should cash out his savings and buy that boat he'd been thinking about. He had a call in to a salesman down in Florida, but he hadn't pulled the trigger yet. Hadn't felt like the right time, but as every day crawled past and Dustin couldn't concentrate, he figured that time was getting closer and closer.

Eli rode up next to him, eyeing the cattle that were churning up the thin layer of snow. "You look like you're a million miles away."

He only nodded. "Just thinking about the spring."

"Gonna be a busy one. Herd's bigger than ever." He held his reins lightly, watching the cattle.

"I know." They'd talked with the owner of the ranch last spring, held back some of the heifers from sale because with four cowboys on the ranch—Dustin, Eli, Jordy, and Old Clyde—they could handle more, bring up profits. Price told them that if they got the ranch in the black, there'd be a healthy bonus for them come next summer, and it was something they were all looking forward to, even if it meant they were edging close to five hundred head of cattle right now.

"Meant to talk to you," Eli said slowly, guiding his horse alongside Dustin's high-stepping one. "Jordy wants to go into the navy after calving in the spring. Said he wants to see the world."

Dustin grunted. "He's a good kid."

"He is. But that's going to put us short one trained ranch hand, and you've had a restless look in your eyes. I'm wondering if I need to make plans for both of you leaving." Eli gave him a piercing look. "Me and Clyde can manage if we have to. Hire one of the local boys to help out if we need, for a time. Just letting you know so you don't feel trapped."

"I haven't decided," he admitted. But he'd called about the boat last week, and he'd been looking up beaches in Florida for a while. He wasn't quite decided . . . not entirely. "I'll let you know."

Eli nodded and rode away. That was Eli. Didn't mince words, didn't ask a friend to stay. Didn't complain that they'd be shorthanded. He just told things how they were, and if it meant more work for him, then he'd just knuckle down and handle it. He didn't mention that Cass would also have a new baby and that would eat into his time. Eli would just handle it, like he did everything else.

Still, Dustin wasn't sure if he wanted to stick around if the only people at the ranch were him, Old Clyde, and the loving couple and their new baby. Be damn awkward, especially because Dustin suspected Old Clyde didn't have many more years of ranching in him. Clyde knew everything forward and backward, of course, but he ached most mornings (even if he wouldn't admit it) and was slower to mount and dismount his horse.

Dustin knew he was needed on the ranch . . . didn't mean that Florida wasn't mighty tempting, though.

Might be time for him to move out. Wyoming didn't hold much for him anymore.

They were heading in at sunset when Eli checked his phone and then kicked his horse into a gallop, dashing toward the house. Uh-oh. Dustin followed behind at a swift trot, worried. Eli usually ignored his phone, but the closer Cass got to her due date, the more he checked it just to make sure that his wife was all right.

Either Cass was in labor, or something was wrong.

When he rode in, he saw that Eli had abandoned his horse at the hitching post in front of the barn, and Dustin took both horses inside, then unsaddled and brushed them down. If Eli needed help, he reckoned that he'd call or text, or at least come out to the barn. If Cass was having her baby, he'd let them have a few minutes alone. Once the horses were taken care of, he glanced down at the empty stalls. Jordy and Old Clyde were still out, most of the dogs with them, but they'd be coming in soon for dinner.

Well, if Cass was feeling poorly, Dustin supposed he could make dinner, too.

He headed inside, and took off his boots in the mud-room, then hung his hat. From the living room, he could hear Cass sobbing, and Eli calming her. "No, baby, it's all right. I won't let her eat it."

"She's a dog!" Cass wailed. "That's what dogs do when someone's sick! I'm sorry!"

"Ain't your fault. Now, stop crying and hush," Eli comforted. "I'll clean it up."

Ugh. Dustin could guess what that was about and he didn't want to picture it. Eli had the patience of a saint with all of Cass's crying lately. He said it was just hormones, and he took it all like a champ. Dustin, well . . .

Wait.

There was more than one woman crying in the living room?

Puzzled, he headed out of the kitchen and poked his head out.

Cass stood in the middle of the living room, her face blotchy from crying as she wrung her hands. Joy—Cass's big dog—wagged her tail happily at her owners' feet, and Eli had his hands on his wife's shoulders, trying to calm her. Watching Dustin from the middle of the room, a blue harness on him, was a familiar-looking white Boston terrier.

That meant . . .

His heart squeezed in his chest. He stepped out of the kitchen and into the sprawling living area, looking for familiar red hair. There, by the window. He'd been unable to see her from the kitchen itself, and right now she had her back turned to him, her face practically pressed against the glass of the front window as she held on to the curtain. She wore an ugly, bulky brown sweater that she practically swam in, but he didn't care.

She'd come back.

And . . . she was crying?

His heart squeezed in his chest again as he stepped forward—and Eli put a hand out. "Watch it, man. There's been . . . ah, an accident."

Dustin glanced down. It looked like there had been several accidents all over the rug, which explained why Cass was crying. It was hard being sick and pregnant. He sidestepped the worst of it and moved to the window. "Annie?" This had to be a dream, he thought. He was imagining the soft red hair that fell in waves to her shoulders, the pale, freckled skin.

But then she turned around and looked at him.

It was her—and he drank in the sight of her face as if he'd never seen a woman before. He drank in every freckle, every pale eyelash, the full pink lips, the sad green eyes. She'd been crying, too, and he wanted to hug her and let her know that everything was all right.

It didn't matter that she'd abandoned him, had cut him off without a word.

She was back. She was going to explain everything, and then it would all be okay. He could forgive and forget.

But as he moved forward, she shifted. She turned to face him and her hand went on top of her sweater, outlining a very large stomach.

A pregnant stomach.

Dustin stopped. Stared.

Annie burst into fresh tears.

Oh, hell. "Hey, hey," he murmured, moving to her side. "If you're not happy to see me, just say so." He hoped the joke would earn him a smile.

Instead, she only sobbed harder, her hands covering her face.

Behind him, Cass gave a choked little sound, as if she was about to start crying, too. "Dustin," Eli warned.

"Right. Come on, Annie. You and I should go talk." Before she could protest, he slid an arm under her knees and around her back, hauling her against him. Jesus, she definitely weighed more than he'd imagined, thanks to the pregnancy. He didn't stagger, though, and he wasn't about to put her down, no matter the little sounds of protest she made in her throat as he held her.

Spidey barked at him, his leash dragging behind him.

"Come on then, Spidey. You too, Moose." He headed down the long hall to his room. Naturally it was the furthest from the living quarters, but he managed to open his door and carefully deposit Annie on his bed. Even as he did, he winced at his room. It wasn't very tidy. He had clothes everywhere, and the bed wasn't made. Then again, he wasn't expecting company, so he couldn't be blamed for it. Even so, he flicked an old T-shirt off the foot of the bed and fluffed the pillows for Annie. "Lie down."

"S-stop being so n-nice to me," she cried.

He noticed his boat pamphlets sitting on the nightstand and swept them into the drawer, then slammed it shut. "What are you talking about?"

"You're being n-nice to me and I ghosted you," she sobbed. "You should hate me."

"I might hate you," Dustin agreed, gazing at her huge belly. "First tell me if that's mine."

She gasped, glaring up at him through her tears. Her eyes were brilliant green, and he wanted to smile at her indignation—and the pillow she tried to launch at him. "You ass! Of course it's yours! Would I be here if it wasn't?"

"I don't know. You tell me. I didn't think you were the type of girl to run out of town after we had sex, but here we are."

Annie tried to sit up, swinging her legs over the side of the bed. "This was a mistake," she muttered. "I'm leaving—"

"No, you most certainly are not," Dustin told her, grabbing her ankles and putting her feet back up on the bed. "You need to relax and stop crying, and then we can have an adult conversation about what the hell's going on and why there's so much puke in the living room." *And why you're pregnant*, though he didn't add that last part. She was a little prickly at the moment.

Her hand went to her brow, and he noticed there was a greenish cast to her pale skin. *Uh-oh.* "I got upset, and when I get upset, with the baby pressing against my stomach, it all sort of comes up." She grimaced, fluttering her other hand over her rounded belly. "And then I threw up, and that made Cass sick, which made me sick again and . . ."

"Right. Well, don't worry about it. I'll get it cleaned up. Do you need some water? Something to eat?"

She gave him a miserable look. "No."

"Can you stop crying long enough for us to talk, or should I leave you alone?"

Two fat tears slid down the sides of her face. "No."

Dustin heaved a sigh. Her weeping was tearing at his chest, making the burning anger he'd been carrying for the last few months dissolve. Yes, he was still mad, but it was hard to yell at a crying pregnant woman. "No, you don't want me to leave, or no, you don't want to talk?"

"I'm not sure what I want," she admitted.

Yeah, well, that made two of them. "You want to tell me how this happened, then?" He gestured at her belly.

She sat up in bed, her eyes narrowing in anger. "Are you serious?"

"Yep."

Her jaw clenched before she answered. "Well, when two people start to kiss—"

"You know what I meant." He liked her sass more than her tears. His mouth twitched with amusement.

"Probably when the condom broke."

"I thought you got a morning-after pill?"

"I did. It didn't take. Apparently they don't take if you're ovulating." Annie's hands slid to her belly and she caressed it. "I never thought about the ovulating thing. A couple of weeks after I got home, I started to get sick. Strong smells bothered me. Took a pregnancy test and . . . yeah." She shrugged and gave him a defiant look. "And I'm keeping it."

"I figured that much." Her belly was enormous and he tried to count back in his head. "How far along . . ."

"Thirty weeks. Ten more to go, more or less." She shifted on the bed, clearly uncomfortable.

Dustin moved to her side, adjusting pillows and fluffing one so she could put it behind her head. She lay back, sitting up and propped up by the pillows in his bed. She was beautiful. Pregnant as hell, but still beautiful. Fierce longing shot through him, mixed with pleasure. She was pregnant with *his* baby. His woman. His Annie. And she was carrying his son . . . or his daughter.

The thought humbled him and filled him with joy all at once.

This was what he wanted, he realized. More than any boat, more than escaping the mountains or seeing the world. He wanted Annie in his life, and he wanted their baby. He'd never wanted anything so fiercely in all his life, and the thought staggered him.

Was this how his father had felt when he'd married his mother after getting her pregnant? Suddenly he understood.

And Dustin wasn't going to let Annie get away again. "So what happens now?" He kept his tone casual, easy. If he pushed too hard too fast, she'd go running again.

Annie's brows drew together and she gave him a funny

look. "What happens now? In ten weeks, I'm having a baby, that's what happens."

"I meant, what about us?"

She looked worried. "Dustin, there is no 'us.' Whatever we had died when I left Wyoming." A flash of guilt crossed her face and she seemed sad. "I wanted to tell you about the baby just to be nice. You don't have to be in our lives. I'm not asking for child support. I'm not asking you to put your name on the birth certificate. I'm not asking for anything, but I thought you should know that there will be a baby."

Not be involved? Not be with her? That wasn't what he wanted at all. He crossed his arms over his chest. "And what if I want there to be an 'us'?"

Annie's expressive eyes grew even sadder. "After what happened, I don't think there can be an us."

He moved to the bed, took her hand in his. "Thing is, I don't know what happened. You left and wouldn't talk to me. You want to tell me what it was so I know how to handle it when it comes up again? So I can fix it for the future? Because I don't want you running off again. I want you to stay so we can figure this out."

She bit her lip, gazing down at their joined hands. For a moment he thought she was going to pull away, but she only sighed and looked up at him, leaving her hand in his. "So after you left . . . that night . . ." Her cheeks flushed bright red. "I went to the pharmacy to get a morning-after pill."

"Okay." He waited.

"And then I met some woman there with big blonde hair who called me a skank and told me that she was your girl-friend." Annie's look turned accusing.

"What?" He did a double take. "Theresa? Seriously?"

"Yes, seriously. And I was feeling vulnerable and . . ." She spread her hands. "All of these things just added up and I thought I'd been lied to."

"Wait wait wait. What things added up?" Dustin jumped off the bed, pacing, because he was getting pissed all over again—not at her, but at Theresa. At the situation. Hell, at the world. "What are you talking about?"

She wrung her hands again. "The looks people were giving me in town. The fact that everyone that knows your name smirks and talks about what a Lothario you are."

"A Lothario . . . and you believed them?" He shook his head. "Annie, I've never done more than a date or two with any girl around here. I certainly never slept with any of them."

"Yes, but how did I know that? And everywhere I went, people were telling me what a manwhore you were. Everyone was warning me about you and how you were going to use me. I freaked out." She kept twisting her hands. "I'm never the girl anyone pursues. I didn't think you liked me for me, and I felt stupid."

"And you didn't think to ask me about this?" He crossed his arms over his chest, trying not to get angry.

"It was a vulnerable moment," Annie said defensively. "And Theresa was beautiful. Just your type."

"My type," he said, voice flat. "Blonde and loud?"

"Like I said, it was a mistake. Cass corrected me." She tucked a strand of red hair behind her ear. "And I realize I was a jerk to run off."

"Yeah. Double jerk for deciding not to tell me about the baby until now." He couldn't decide if he was pissed or relieved that he hadn't done something wrong. Either way, he'd lost eight months he could have spent with her, watching her belly grow, sharing those moments with her . . . and sharing a bed.

When she buried her face in her hands again, though, he felt like an ass. This couldn't be easy for her, either. Dustin moved back to her side and sat down on the bed next to her, hugging her against his chest. She was back, and that was all that mattered. "I'm sorry."

"You have a right to be mad," Annie told him. "I shouldn't have acted the way I did."

"In a way, I understand it. A little. Though I'm still frustrated that it took eight months to bring you back."

"Reshoots," she told him, straightening a little and wiping her face.

"What?"

"I'm here for three days because of reshoots for the movie. After that, I'm going back to Los Angeles."

His entire body stiffened in angry frustration. "So you didn't come back to see me or tell me about our child. I'm just an afterthought in your career."

"That's not how I meant it," she said softly. "I was hiding—I admit that—and being forced back here forced me to be brave." Annie turned toward him, her eyes big and sad. "I don't want you to feel obligated about any of this. We used a condom. You don't have to be part of the baby's life. I know you don't want to end up like your father."

"I'm not thinking about my father right now. I'm thinking about you and me. Are you going to give me a chance?"

"A chance for what?" She looked genuinely confused.

"A chance to show you that I care for you? That how I feel for you doesn't have anything to do with my father, or Theresa, or the baby, or anyone else? It's how I feel about Annie Grissom?" He took her hand and placed it over his heart. "This has been broken for eight long months."

Her eyes went soft, her expression so sad that it made him ache all over. "I'm sorry I hurt you," she whispered.

"Then make it up to me. Give me a chance to get to know you again."

She bit her lip. "All right. When I get my room number in town, you can—"

"Nope," Dustin told her quickly. "You can stay here with me. My bed's more comfortable than the hotel room and this will give us a chance to spend time together. And I can take care of you." When she hesitated, he brushed a sweaty lock of hair back from her face. "You were sick earlier. You're tired. I can see circles under your eyes. Let me take care of you, Annie. You and our baby."

Her gaze slid to his mouth, as if she was thinking about kissing him. "I need to be at the hotel at six in the morning so the crew bus can take me out on location."

"Not a problem. I'll pick you up, too."

"And is it okay if Spidey stays, too?"

He chuckled. "As if I'd part you two. I'm surprised you still have him."

"I couldn't give him away. He's my buddy." She smiled, the expression tentative, and it broke his heart. He wanted to hug her all over again. She hesitated. "Are you sure it's all right if I stay with you?"

"Of course." He didn't add that he wanted to tackle her if she thought about leaving. He didn't want her to leave his sight at all. Not until he'd convinced her that she belonged at his side.

Annie nodded. "Do you mind if I lie down, then? I'm tired and I'm not feeling so well. Being pregnant means I get tired easily."

Immediately he felt like an ass. Of course she didn't feel well. She'd been sick in the living room and here he was, grilling her about their relationship. "You lie down and I'll get you some crackers and hot tea."

"Decaf, please," she told him, and he nodded.

He helped her get adjusted in the bed, tucking her under the blankets. She looked small and fragile despite her belly, and it made him want to protect her, to keep her safe from anything that might upset her.

She had to let him help her, though, and that was going to be the sticking point.

When he was satisfied that she was comfortable, he went out into the kitchen and put on the kettle. Eli was in the living room, and Dustin could hear the carpet steamer running. He dug around for crackers, found some, and then headed over to Eli just as the man was wrapping the cord, his task finished.

"Just so you know, Annie's going to stay with us for a few days," he told Eli.

The other cowboy just nodded.

"And I'm gonna need to take care of her. Driving her to her shoot and picking her up and all."

"You do what you need to do," Eli told him. "Ain't a problem."

"Thanks, man."

Eli studied him. "You want me to clean out the baby's room so she has somewhere to stay?"

The baby's room? With Cass's delivery date so close? The ranch's bedrooms were all being used except for the small office, and Eli and Cass had recently painted it and converted it to a baby's room, complete with crib and white, lacy blankets and stuffed animals. It was ready for the baby. Cass wouldn't mind, though. She had a big heart. And Annie would probably find it adorable . . .

But he wanted her with him.

"No, she's staying with me," Dustin said. When Eli opened his mouth to speak, Dustin cut him off. "If anyone asks, there's no extra room in the house. None at all. She stays in my bed."

"You want me to lie," Eli said slowly.

"Yes."

"All right then." He smirked.

He went back to the kitchen and waited for Annie's tea. Damned thing seemed to take forever, and he was impatient to get back to her. While he waited, he went and found her car keys and moved her car to the carport, getting her luggage out of the back so she'd have something to change into. As he crossed the living area, he noticed that Moose was curled up in the big dog bed by the fire, and Spidey was a little bundle at his side, still wearing his leash and harness. He snapped his fingers. "Come on, boys. You can come lie down, too."

The dogs got up, trotting over to him. Moose's fluffy tail wagged so widely that he nearly knocked down Spidey, who just watched him with his big, dark eyes. He scratched Moose's head and then bent down, unharnessing Annie's dog before heading on to the bedroom, pets at his heels.

Crackers. Tea. Right. He set the suitcase inside, made sure the dogs were settled, helped Spidey into bed with Annie (who was sleeping), and then went back for the tea and crackers. When he returned to the room a moment later, though, she was sitting up, trying to reach one foot.

"Here," he told her. "I'll get that." Dustin set the beverage and snacks down on the nightstand and then knelt in front of her. Her boots were loose, soft, fuzzy things, but when he pulled one off, he saw that her entire foot itself was swollen. "Is this normal for pregnant ladies?" he asked, a little worried.

"Unfortunately, yes," she told him between yawns. "Happens every time I'm on my feet for longer than five minutes."

"Well then, I'll make sure you stay off of them." He tugged her other boot off and then rubbed her arches. When she gave a little moan of pleasure, he gritted his teeth, because his cock didn't seem to understand that she was pregnant. "You just relax and I'll rub your toes for you. Maybe we can make the swelling go down."

"You're so nice to do this for me," she told him, sighing. When he said nothing, she added, "I'm sorry I was so awful to you. I was . . . scared."

"Scared?" He had to ask. He'd told himself that he wasn't going to push her, but some things you couldn't let lie. "Scared of what?"

"You and me, I guess." Spidey pushed himself into her

arms and she held him close, lying back on the blankets with him tucked against her side as Dustin rubbed her feet, flexing and massaging each toe to try and make her comfortable. "I've always been the dumped, never the dumper. It's hard to date in Hollywood or in the movie business when you don't have breast implants or hair extensions or any of that. Guys expect a certain look. My mother aggressively pursues that look. I . . . don't. And of course, there's the fact that my father told my mother that she should abort me when he found out she was pregnant." She toyed with one of Spidey's ears. "I saw Theresa, and heard her words and . . . I just assumed the worst."

"Yeah, you did." He gently propped her feet up onto a pillow, then pulled the blankets close to her. "You could have talked to me."

She kept fussing with the dog's ear, avoiding eye contact. "I just thought I'd been stupid. You never wanted me to come over, remember?"

"Just because I figured we'd have more privacy in town. Guess that was wrong."

"*Mmm.* That didn't help things, though. I felt like I'd ignored all the warnings everyone gave me about how much of a player you are."

He'd never paid much attention to his reputation around town. Never thought it'd be a bad thing to be known as a flirt and a player—after all, it'd keep the expectations in check. If no one figured he was much for a relationship, there shouldn't be any hurt feelings when the inevitable split came. But now he saw that it was a problem. Now that there was Annie in his life—and a baby on the way—it was time to fix things.

"Maybe after you finish the movie reshoots," Dustin began slowly, "you could stay with me for a while."

"Why?"

"So we can get to know each other. So we can see how

we want to tackle being parents together." When she didn't say anything, he decided to try and sweeten the deal. "I mentioned a while back that Cass ruined the ranch dogs. They beg all the time now, wanting scraps. It'd be nice to have them trained properly, especially the young ones. And I'd take care of you, of course."

"I'll think about it," she murmured.

"You do that," he said. "Now drink your tea."

After he managed to get half a cup of tea and some crackers into her, he noticed that she was starting to droop, her eyelids closing. Dustin helped her undress, avoiding looking at her body so she wouldn't feel uncomfortable. He managed to get her into one of his shirts, and it hung loose all over her except across the belly, where it was tight. He still liked the sight of it, though. Then, she crawled back into bed and was asleep in moments.

He set the alarm for early—not that he needed it, but she might—and then slid into bed next to her. She immediately turned and snuggled against him, tucking her body against his. Dustin cautiously put his arm around her, touching her belly.

His child was in there. They'd made that together.

He'd lost so much time with her already. He wasn't going to lose another minute, he decided.

CHAPTER FOURTEEN

His Annie was not a morning person.

Dustin woke up before the alarm and made breakfast—peanut butter toast and oatmeal—and poured a glass of milk, then set it on a tray and brought it into the room. The dogs thumped their tails eagerly, but he shooed them out. This was for his woman . . . and his baby. He touched her arm gently to wake her up. "Hey, Annie?"

"*Mmm*," was all he got. She pulled the pillow against her face and went back to sleep.

He bit back a laugh—to think that last night he'd been afraid of waking her up by holding her. The woman could saw logs with the best of them. He pulled the pillow out of her arms. "Breakfast time. I made you something to eat."

She cracked an eye open. "I *am* rather hungry, but it's too early."

"Five a.m. Ain't all that early."

Annie groaned as if in pain. "Says you." But she woke

up. After he made sure she ate breakfast, he left the room so she could shower and change in peace. He let the dogs out, fed 'em, and cleaned the kitchen before harnessing Spidey and packing a lunch for her. So damn domestic—Cass would laugh her ass off at him. He didn't care. He liked the thought of taking care of Annie and his baby.

My baby. Even just thinking that filled him with so much damn pleasure.

When she was ready to go, he drove her into town. Sure enough, there was a crowd of movie people waiting to load into one of the plain white buses they used to trek out to the filming site. They gathered in front of the main hotel, and Dustin glanced over at Annie. Her face was tight, her expression thoughtful. She didn't look as if she were thrilled to be rejoining them.

"You don't have to do this," he began.

She shot him a look. "I do unless I want to be sued by the movie production."

"Okay, fair enough. Is there anything I can do to help?"

A hint of a smile curved her mouth. "No. Just offering is nice, though. I appreciate it."

He parked across the street and helped her out of the truck, then handed her Spidey's leash. With his arm around her waist, he led her toward the bus. It was cold out and she was only wearing a sweater, which he didn't like. "Here. You take my jacket," he told her as they stood in front of the bus. "Better too warm than not warm enough."

"I'm not sure if it'll fit," she protested, but let him ease it onto her shoulders. Once it was on her, though, it was clear it was entirely too big for her small frame. She looked adorable.

Dustin handed her the lunch he'd packed. "Have a good day at work, honey." And he leaned in and hugged her in front of everyone.

* * *

In a daze, Annie got on the bus with Spidey and watched as her cowboy crossed the street. She stared at his wide shoulders, the cocky slant of his hat, the tight backside, and her throat went dry.

He'd slept next to her last night.

He wasn't angry.

He'd kissed her in front of everyone. Held her close and made it obvious that she was with him.

Katherine immediately sat down next to Annie, giving Spidey a smile. "So what's going on with the cowboy?" she demanded immediately.

"I wish I knew," Annie told her.

Reshoots were not the most thrilling part of a picture. Everyone was in a bad mood because they'd already been paid, and this was extra work that no one wanted to have anything to do with. It happened on a lot of movies, but Annie couldn't remember ever dreading a reshoot like this one.

Luckily for her, Mr. Sloane was more focused on working with Chad Weathers than with anyone else. He'd cast a few looks at the dog, frowned at Annie, and then went back to talking with his star. *Good.* Maybe he wouldn't need them for much of anything. She crossed her fingers and hoped. Just being around Sloane was making Spidey act up. He was nervous and snappish, and so she went over some of his basic tricks with him to make sure that if he was needed, he'd be ready.

She understood, though. She was feeling a little snappish herself.

Her feet ached and since she had to be on the cold, cold

blustery fields, she sat under an umbrella and hugged Dustin's jacket against her, thankful for its warmth. Katherine joined her, shivering, and they both huddled and watched as the actors choreographed an outdoor fight scene. They weren't needed, of course, but it didn't mean that they could go home.

"So . . . that's a surprise," Katherine said at some point, and Annie found herself spilling the beans about all of it. How she and Dustin had slept together and how she'd thought it was something special. How Theresa in town had told Annie that she was Dustin's girlfriend, and how she'd believed her. How she'd run home to Los Angeles and found out about the pregnancy, and then returned and confronted Dustin only to realize that she'd been wrong all along.

"*Hmm*," was all Katherine would say.

Annie poked her in the side. "What does that '*hmm*' mean exactly?"

"It means that I don't know if I believe him," she told Annie. "I mean, it's awfully convenient that you show up and it's all as perfect as he says. Did you talk to the other woman yet? Theresa?"

"No," Annie admitted. "I just got in last night. Got sick, and then I went to bed early. He took care of me, though."

"Of course he did. You're as cute as a dumpling with that belly of yours. You're glowing. You look adorable pregnant." Her friend smiled. "But you've also got the right to be a little concerned. I'd say go meet this supposed sidechick and have a talk with her. Find out what she thinks her side of the story is, and compare it with Dustin's. You don't have to accuse anyone of anything. It's just called being safe."

Katherine made it sound so very logical. "I guess I should. It's funny," Annie said, watching as Spidey chewed on his little jacket and shoes nearby. "Every time I think I have my mind made up about how things should go, something changes. I thought I should cut Dustin out of my life, but then I see him again and it's all different than how I pictured it. So then I think maybe we can give things a shot again . . . and then I talk to you and wonder if I'm being too trusting once more." She smiled faintly and looked over at her friend. Katherine always seemed to know exactly what she wanted. "If you were me, what would you do?"

"Oh no." Katherine laughed. "I'm not falling into that trap. You have to make your own decisions. I mean, we are different from step one. You're keeping the baby, right?"

"Yeah." She touched her belly. Just thinking of the life inside—the one that she'd made with Dustin—made her so happy. "There's no way I'd ever give him—or her—up."

"See, I would. I'd give my baby up for adoption because I know I can't give him or her the life that I want. I'd rather hang around on movie sets and party, you know? I'm not ready to settle down and make a family, and that's not fair to a kid." She shook her head. "So does that mean you're done with movies? I thought you were going to New Zealand for your next flick."

"Things changed. The movie was canceled before production started." The baby kicked, and Annie smiled to herself. "I think I'm pretty done anyhow. I don't want to travel with a baby, and I can't imagine Kitty pitching in."

Katherine shuddered. "Kitty would only pitch in if the baby would hold her martini shaker instead of a rattle."

Annie giggled at that, because the mental image was too crazy—and yet too realistic. "So yeah, I think I'll try something different for a while."

"Please, please tell me you're not going to give up all your aspirations of a career."

"No. I imagine it'd be fun to stay home with the baby for a while, but I'll need to do something with myself. Something with animals. I still like what I do." She looked thoughtfully at Spidey, and then reached out and fixed one of his little booties that he'd nearly bitten off his paws. "Maybe boarding, or training. Vet school. Something."

"Good," Katherine said emphatically. "Keep thinking along those lines. You are a strong, beautiful woman who just happens to be growing another person inside her." And she shuddered.

Annie laughed. It felt good to be happy again. To be light and carefree. So what if she was pregnant and not married? It was modern times. She didn't need a man. She had her own money, and even if it was dwindling, she had a fantastic résumé and she could get more work with animals easily.

All she had to do was figure out what she wanted. Piece of cake.

Several of the big scenes in the second half of the movie were reshot. She noticed as she reviewed the script that Spidey (and therefore Annie's work) was being cut out of scene after scene. Conversations were cut, dog tricks were removed, and a lot of the shots of Chad Weathers were done from the waist up. Annie should have been annoyed, but she was just relieved. It meant less arguing with Sloane, and it meant they were one step closer to done.

The set was chilly, the wind ripping despite the windbreaks that assistants held up so the actors wouldn't be affected, and at one point, Spidey crawled into her lap and tucked himself against her under her coat, shivering. When snowflakes started to drift from the sky and the director wrapped things early, she was relieved.

Time to go home.

Of course, home wasn't the hotel, or the house she shared with her mother. It meant going back to the ranch with Dustin, and she worried that she'd be overstepping. That in some way she'd misread things and she wasn't as welcome as she'd hoped. But when she got off the bus, Dustin was waiting on the curb with a thermos and a warm blanket, and she could have kissed him with gratitude.

"Hi," she said breathlessly as he took the leash from her. "What's all this?"

"It's a nasty day. Thought you might want some hot cocoa." He wrapped the blanket around her shoulders.

"Shoot, I need to find myself a cowboy," Katherine teased as she sauntered past. "See you tomorrow, mami."

"Bye." Annie smiled at Dustin and took a sip of the cocoa. It was amazing and yummy and so very thoughtful of him. When she'd texted him to pick her up, she hadn't asked for this. It was all him, and it was so sweet. "We heading home?"

"Not yet. I thought I'd take you out to dinner."

"You did?" She was surprised. "Why?"

"It's called a date." He hefted Spidey into his arms. "This little guy's freezing."

She grinned as Spidey took that opportunity to start licking Dustin's chin. "Bostons don't have long hair to keep them warm. That's why he's got that coat."

"I just thought you liked dressing him up," Dustin admitted, and she chuckled. "He can chaperone our date. Wade, who runs the bar, doesn't mind if a dog comes in as long as he stays out of the way. Says they're all service dogs in his eyes."

"The bar?" She patted her rounded belly. "You sure you want to take a pregnant lady there?"

"Well, it's either that or the mini-mart, and I'm not sure you should be eating hot dogs from there. Rumor has it that they've been around since before the Grand Canyon." His smile flashed. "And the bar has some good eats."

"All right, then, if it won't be a problem."

"It's not." He took her bag from her and slung it over his shoulder, made sure the blanket was tucked around her shoulders, and then took the thermos so she could walk with her hands free. Well, waddle. Her hips were spreading and her movements were getting less graceful by the day, but she didn't care. Every day she was one day closer to her baby being born.

They went to the bar and Dustin waved at the bartender, then pulled a chair out for Annie at one of the tables. She felt wildly conspicuous, since the place was crowded with a mix of movie people and some of the locals, but Dustin was at her side and pulled his chair next to hers, and she supposed it didn't matter. They were together.

He pulled in a chair and tapped it, and Spidey jumped into it, sitting as if he was a human. She laughed, loving the mischievous look on Dustin's face. "You're going to get us in trouble."

"For seating my son? Never. Isn't that right, son?" He rubbed Spidey's round head. "Why's he called Spidey anyhow?"

"I don't know. I got him from a shelter and that was his name. I figured he'd be easier to train if I kept it, but I've always wondered myself."

"A shelter, huh?"

"Yeah, he's almost entirely white, and that's not a desired look for Boston terriers, unfortunately. Most people want the traditional black and white markings. The off-color ones sometimes get dumped."

"People are jerks," he said, rubbing the dog's head affectionately. Then, he leaned over to her and gave her a quick kiss. "Wade keeps the menus at the bar. Let me grab you one."

"Okay." She watched as he got up and crossed the room, bigger than life in his cowboy hat and his easy stance. He was the most attractive man in the room and she noticed people watching him. It's a small town, she told herself. People get in other people's business. It happens. When he came back to the table, he smiled widely at her and offered her the menu. "You want a drink of some kind? Water? Hot tea?"

"I'll just drink my cocoa. It's my favorite food group."

"Chocolate?"

"Exactly."

He laughed. "Will it bother you if I get something big to eat? I'm starving."

"Only if you judge me for eating almost as much as you." She patted her belly. "My appetite's up lately."

Dustin reached over and patted her stomach. "That's fine with me." He froze and then looked at her. "Is it okay that I touched you?"

"It's fine," she told him. "I'm getting used to everyone thinking my belly is fair game." When he looked chagrined, she patted his hand. "Really. You're allowed to touch it anytime, I promise."

"I'm going to take you up on that offer," he murmured, and for some reason it sounded sexy and delicious, and then she was blushing. Gosh, her mind went straight to the gutter around him, which was probably unfortunate because she was really pregnant and he probably didn't find that sexy compared to how she'd looked the last time he'd seen her.

She wished he would kiss her. Not the quick peck he'd given her so far but a real, honest-to-goodness, toe-curling kiss like he had before.

But then he reached across the table and held her hand, and however slow they took things, she decided that would be fine, too.

Despite the fact that they were in a bar, dinner was surprisingly lovely. She had a grilled cheese sandwich and fries, and Dustin had a huge burger that he kept trying to give her bites of. It was cute that he wanted to feed her, but it made her shy. Neither of them drank alcohol, and she was relieved that no one seemed to be looking at her oddly for being in a bar despite the fact she was eight months pregnant. She guessed it was like he'd said—this was the only restaurant in town. Funny how she'd never really paid attention to that before. The two months that they'd been shooting here previously, she'd mostly ordered stuff on Amazon and had it shipped to the hotel, or grabbed snacks from the mini-mart. It was nice to go on a date.

And Dustin made it clear to everyone that it was a date. They talked, and he paid attention only to her. He held her hand. He tried to give her bites of food and stole the occasional fry from her plate. When they got up to leave, he stood up and helped her to her feet, and then put his arm around her waist.

He was making it clear to everyone in town that she belonged to him.

Annie loved it. Maybe she should have been all rah-rah independent woman like Katherine told her to be, but after eight months of being pregnant and solo, it was nice to have someone to lean on when she was tired, or for someone to carry her purse and the dog's leash when her back was hurting. Dustin didn't seem to mind any of this, and it made her surprisingly weepy.

Well, the weepy part wasn't all that surprising. She seemed to cry all the time now, just one of the many perks of being pregnant.

As they rode in the truck back to the ranch, she noticed another "perk" of being pregnant was rearing its ugly head. Dustin kept giving her these sexy little smiles as he looked over at her, as if he was just thrilled that she was with him. And every time he did, she couldn't help but notice his strong jaw, his tan, his big shoulders . . . and then she remembered sex with him.

She also remembered how long it had been since she'd had sex.

Annie knew that being pregnant was going to have its

ups and downs. Her body would change, things would make her sick, and her breasts would ache. No one had told her, though, that she'd be really, really turned on at the drop of a hat. Just thinking about Dustin and his arm around her waist made her feel squirmy with need.

Ironic that she was turning into a horndog when she'd never felt less attractive in her life. *Thanks, pregnancy.*

Now that she'd turned her mind to sex, though, she couldn't stop thinking about it. Even when they got back to the ranch and she met the others. Jordy, Old Clyde, and Eli were all very nice. Cass smiled at her and gave a wink like they'd shared a secret pregnancy moment yesterday. Their dogs were wonderful, and even Moose looked like he was thriving in the group, though he didn't come out to greet her. He was content to stay by the fire, but his tail thumped against the floor when she called his name. That was a good sign.

Really, the ranch was lovely. Everyone there was lovely. If she wanted to stay for a bit, she suspected it would be perfectly fine, and Cass had hinted that Annie could help when Cass's baby arrived, and that it'd be practice for her own upcoming baby. It sounded wonderful.

But Dustin had to want her here. Right now he was being polite and attentive, but he still hadn't kissed her. They'd had several times when they'd been alone together since she'd arrived yesterday. Not one toe-curling kiss.

That kiss was becoming more and more important by the moment.

It shouldn't matter, she knew. They could be friends and all of the chaos of their relationship could be in the past. She'd go back to LA and raise the baby and forget all about sexy cowboys and their wicked smiles. But if he wanted her to stay here like he said . . . he needed to show her. She needed him to want her.

Friends could raise a baby as easily as lovers could. If

she was going to be with him, she wanted it all. She knew the sex was great and right now, her fired-up brain wanted that as a requirement for a relationship going forward. Plus, her tender ego needed the reassurance that Dustin liked her, truly liked her. That he wasn't just doing this song and dance because she was pregnant.

So she waited for the right opportunity for him to kiss her. When she yawned and hinted that she was tired, he took her to his room and offered to help her undress. She took him up on that . . . and then was disappointed when he didn't even look at her body. Not once. He disappeared to feed the dogs and check in with the others for tomorrow's work, and she was left to her own devices in the bedroom. Annie lay in bed and tried not to scowl as she got comfortable.

Maybe she needed to hint.

But if he really was attracted to her, would she need to hint at all? Shouldn't he just be overcome with lust and the need to touch her?

It was frustrating.

Dustin returned a little later and she closed her eyes, pretending to be asleep like a coward. When he brushed his teeth and got ready for bed, though, she felt a little stab of despair.

Was this a sleepover only? Had he invited her to stay with them just so he'd be her buddy and that was it? She clenched her jaw, desperate not to cry again (stupid pregnancy hormones) because a crying pregnant woman was even less sexy than a regular pregnant woman.

Dustin turned off the lights and climbed into bed next to her. It was only a full-size bed and he was a big guy, so he moved close to her, his body brushing against hers, and then he kissed her shoulder.

"Night."

That was it.

Annie stared up at the ceiling and wondered if screaming would be inappropriate.

This was going to kill him, Dustin decided.

He loved that she was back. He loved that she was in his bed, her body pressed against his. He loved how warm and soft she was.

He hated that he couldn't touch her. His dick didn't understand that she was pregnant and probably wasn't in the mood for anything. It only knew that she was here and in his arms and so it was as hard as a rock. His body ached with how badly he wanted to caress her, to sink his fingers into that bright red hair and kiss every freckle on her skin.

But he had to be patient. Ten more weeks, she'd mentioned, before the baby was born. And he didn't know much about babies, but hopefully they could have sex a few weeks after that.

Maybe he needed to read one of those baby-on-the-way books and find out more. Yeah, reading might distract him from the raging hard-on he'd had all day and would probably have for quite some time if she stuck around. He didn't know how it felt to have a baby inside you, but he imagined it meant she wouldn't be interested in much other than sleeping for a long while.

He was just gonna have to suck it up and endure.

CHAPTER FIFTEEN

The next day was actually pretty nice, all things considered. The weather was warm(ish), the scenes being reshot weren't painful to experience, and Sloane wasn't screaming. Maybe it was because the director was far more focused on the actors and the choreography of the fight scene to really focus on his nemesis Annie, but overall, she had a good day. There were no complaints, and when things wrapped up that night, Dustin was waiting to drive her home, and he'd even brought her donuts since she'd mentioned them that morning. She knew she was taking him away from his work on the ranch, but he said not to worry about it, so she wouldn't.

That evening, they had a wonderful dinner with the rest of the ranch crew in the big, rustic kitchen. Eli had made chicken and dumplings (since Cass was still figuring out cooking despite being the "cook" at the ranch), and it was delicious. The company was so much fun—as an introvert, she wasn't really all that sure how she'd handle staying at the ranch when so many others lived there, but she could tell already that Cass was going to be a friend. Eli was silent but clearly doting on his wife, and Old Clyde and Jordy were a hilarious pair. They had her giggling into her spoon as Old Clyde shared the story of the first time Jordy had to help deliver a calf, and she swore her entire body ached by the time he was done. Dustin had rubbed her back and grinned at her pleasure, as if he liked her quiet inclusion into the group.

Dustin. She knew she should have been more open, more affectionate. It was clear he was trying to establish with the others that he was with her, and she loved it. But she was also scared. She'd hated him for eight months, and it was hard to get past the feelings of betrayal even if he was awesome now. He'd been wonderful for a few days, but she needed longer to trust again.

It also didn't help that while he held her hand and touched her back and shoulder repeatedly, he never made a move to kiss her, really kiss her. It made her wonder if everything was just for show. Did he want to be part of the baby's life and that was why he was pretend-romancing her? Or had his feelings cooled off in the months they were apart and now he didn't know how to extricate himself? She wished he'd just tell her.

Or kiss the hell out of her.

Either one would be good, really.

She didn't sleep so well that night despite being exhausted. Her dreams were full of Dustin, but every time she reached for him, he faded into the distance and all she grasped was smoke. She chased him through the rolling fog, but when she finally got to him, he had his arms around Theresa.

That didn't make her feel better. She woke up cranky at the world.

Day three of the shoot was a foul one, and Annie was tense as they shot a scene involving Spidey and one of the horses. It was supposed to look like the two were communicating so dialogue could be dubbed in later, but the horse kept flicking his head and prancing, and the scene had to be shot several times before one take was good enough. The entire time, Sloane kept shooting Annie irritated looks as if she was causing the problems, which just made her mood even worse.

On top of this, Dustin was solicitous and kind and funny, and basically the perfect boyfriend.

That was partially why she was so frustrated—he was utter perfection and she'd been the jerk that separated them. She wished, just a little, that he wasn't as perfect as he seemed. That he had flaws. That he'd show a flash of short temper and she could say "Aha!" and then disappear back to California because that would be so much easier than figuring out what she wanted.

That evening, she showered and considered shaving her legs. Granted, she couldn't really reach them, but maybe if she flashed him a bit of naked, sexy leg he might jump on her and passionately kiss her until she spontaneously combusted. Or something. Anything would be preferable to the neutral friendship that seemed to be setting the pace right now. Not that there was anything wrong with friendship.

She just seemed to be one of those needy pregnant ladies that were constantly turned on. It wasn't a problem until she was around him.

Now all Annie thought about was sex. She thought about it when he gave her a quick peck goodbye in the morning. She thought about it in the shower when she got home from a day of reshoots. She thought about it during dinner when he put his hand on her knee as if they were an old married couple. She thought about it when Eli and Cass gave each other sweet looks throughout the evening. She thought about it when she climbed into their completely chaste bed for another night of sleep and nothing more.

So yeah, she was considering shaving everything in the hopes of enticing him into making a move of some kind.

Something.

Anything.

But when she picked up the razor and tried to angle a way to run it along her leg without falling over, she realized how futile it was. There was no shaving anything this pregnant. With a sigh, she turned off the water and tugged a towel most of the way around her body, her belly sticking out from the soft terry cloth. She studied her reflection in the mirror. Her lips were a bit fuller due to the pregnancy, and her face was a little puffy from the extra weight she was carrying. Her breasts were definitely bigger (and some days downright uncomfortable) but her belly was the most noticeable part. It was enormous, with stretch marks along the lower curve no matter how much she lotioned the bulge of it. It was silly to compare pregnancy bellies with another woman, but Annie had definitely noticed that Cass was a daintier pregnant than she was, and that sucked.

Cass probably had sex, darn her. She and Eli probably had pregnant sex all the time, and the thought made Annie wistful. She brushed her teeth and flossed, lotioned up her belly, and then slipped on her nightgown. Then, she stared at her nightgown. Maybe it was the problem. Maternity wear wasn't exactly the sexiest gear. Her nightgown was sleeveless pink-and-white floral and hung like a sack off her body. *All right, that probably isn't helping in the sexiness department.* Frowning to herself, she left the bathroom and headed for her suitcase, picking through her clothing.

"Something wrong?" Dustin asked as she emerged. He was sitting in the rocking chair in the corner of the room, tugging his boots off and looking just as deliciously sexy as ever, damn the man.

If he could fling her down on the darn bed and kiss the

heck out of her, that would be great. Damn him for looking
so mouthwateringly delicious. She tore through her suitcase
with new enthusiasm. Surely there had to be something
even halfway sexy—well, sexy-ish—in here that she could
sleep in? He put his arms around her and slept against her
every night, but she needed something to entice him into
nibbling on her neck.

Of course, just thinking about neck nibbles made her entire body flush with need. Biting back a moan of frustration,
Annie pulled out an old T-shirt and then discarded it. A bra
and panty set? No, the ones she'd bought were hideously
functional and not much else. *Shoot.* This was tricky.

"Annie?"

"I'm uh, looking for something." Something slinky . . .
which didn't exist, apparently. "Never mind."

"Can I help?"

Her cheeks flushed bright red as a thousand filthy thoughts
sprang to mind. "Nope! I'm good. You can go shower."

Dustin gave her another puzzled look before heading off
to the attached bathroom and shutting the door behind him.
When the shower spray started, she lay back on the bed and
sighed in frustration, staring up at the ceiling. She was just
a mess. Why had no one told her that being pregnant would
also mean that she would be constantly turned on while
feeling incredibly unsexy? Life was so unfair.

The baby turned in her stomach, and she rubbed the
bulge. "Sorry, baby. You're wonderful. It's just my hormones
that are making me crazy."

Really, all he had to give her was a sign. Just one tiny
sign that he found her appealing still and she'd be all over
him like green on grass.

Of course, she could make the leap herself. She could
snag him by the collar of his shirt and haul him against her
for one of those delicious, tongue-tangling kisses like they

used to share . . . but she needed him to be the one to make the first move. She already felt wildly vulnerable. He was so perfect and she was the heavily pregnant woman who'd thought he was the devil for the last eight months and had nearly cut him out of the baby's life.

So yeah, "vulnerable" was a good word for it.

Lost in thought, she didn't notice that Dustin was done with his shower until the door opened and he stepped out in nothing but a towel. "Oh." Annie propped up on her elbows, startled at the sight of him nearly naked. His tanned skin was glistening with droplets of water and how had she never noticed those two dimples at the base of his spine? Gosh, she wanted to lick them . . . among other things.

"Sorry . . . is this uncomfortable for you?" He froze, glancing over at her. "I figured since we'd both seen each other naked . . ."

"It's fine. I was just surprised, that's all." Tearing her gaze away, Annie pretended to fluff her pillow and then lay on her side. Left side, always, because pregnancy had all kinds of rules about how you could and couldn't lie down. It was just another one of those things that made her feel like a balloon ready to pop, and the fact that Dustin seemed to only like her in a platonic way now was just the icing on the cake.

Just one real kiss. That was all she asked. One kiss that would show her nothing had changed between them.

Dustin turned off the light and she heard the sound of rustling fabric as he pulled on some clothes. He got into bed next to her, and then tucked his long body along her back, spooning her against him. "Night."

Annie scowled into the darkness.

Hormones thwarted once more. She bit back a sigh, reminding herself that despite having sex, despite being seven months pregnant with his child, they were still strangers.

They didn't know each other as well as most couples did, so of course there'd be miscommunications and missed signals. It happened. If she wanted something, she should just say it.

But she'd always been a shy, private person. To open her mouth and demand that a sexy man kiss her . . . it wasn't something she could do. What if he just wanted sex for the sake of sex and she mistook that for love? It would break her all over again.

Better to just take things slow and hope he'd realize he wanted her as desperately as she wanted him.

The baby kicked in her stomach, as if agreeing with that sensible thought.

She felt Dustin's big body twitch in response. "Was that . . ."

"The baby? Yes." Then, she couldn't stop the giggle that threatened. "What else would it be?"

"I don't know." Annie could hear the amusement in his voice. "Bad gas?"

"Gee, thanks. No, it's the baby. He—or she—tosses and turns all day long. You want to feel?" It occurred to her that he hadn't really asked to touch her stomach. Oh sure, he'd brushed against it at the bar, but he hadn't experienced what it was like to feel the baby moving and wriggling inside her. "He's a real gymnast."

"Do you mind?" His arm slid around her, moving lower and his hand splayed over her belly, just above her navel.

"Of course not." She even hitched up her ugly, unattractive nightgown and pressed his big hand to her bare skin so he could experience it as closely as possible. They waited. For a long moment, she wondered if the baby was going to calm himself and make a liar out of her, but after a few seconds, he began to do his usual flipping and kicking, as if protesting bedtime.

"Holy smokes," Dustin murmured, awe in his tone. His breath fanned hot against her shoulder and a moment later, his chin rested against her arm, and she loved his response. "He's really moving. She's really moving. Whichever. You don't know if it's a boy or a girl?"

"Oh, my doctor knows. I asked him not to tell me. I want to be surprised." She rubbed the lower curve of her belly. "Sometimes I think it's a boy, though. I'm carrying low, which all the old wives' tales say is a boy, but beyond that, it feels like a boy to me. Just a hunch I have."

"A boy," he murmured, and his fingers lightly rubbed her skin, sending little jolts through her body. "That's amazing. I'd be happy with a girl, too."

"Same. I'm just ready for him or her to show up."

"You pick out a name?"

She bit her lip. "I was thinking something gender neutral, so it wouldn't matter what the sex is. I like Morgan and Lee and Dakota. I guess I should have checked with you first, though."

"You didn't know," he said easily, and chuckled when the baby turned in her stomach again. "I like all of those names. You have good taste."

Funny how hearing that would make her glow with pleasure just five short minutes after she'd been wondering if he wasn't attracted to her anymore. She supposed if he was a good dad, she couldn't ask for more.

Could she?

He felt the baby move for a bit longer, then slipped his hand away. "I should let you sleep."

She wanted to tell him that she wasn't all that tired, that she wanted him to keep touching her, to caress her and kiss her and tell her that he still found her beautiful, that nothing had changed from that kiss-filled week back in the spring.

But all she said was, "Good night."

* * *

All right, people, that's a wrap." Sloane waved a finger in the air, indicating that they were done.

People cheered. Some clapped. Annie yawned. Not that she wasn't grateful for the movie to be done, more or less, but the baby made her sleepy in the afternoons, and today was surprisingly warm for Wyoming in the fall, and with the sun shining down on them, it made her think of naps more than anything.

At her side, Katherine elbowed her, clapping. "Show a little enthusiasm, the boss is looking this way."

Annie clapped excitedly at that, and she beamed at Sloane as he looked in their direction. She didn't miss Katherine's little snort of amusement. "Thanks for the warning."

"Yeah, well, you're already in the dog house, no pun intended. Didn't want you to make things worse for yourself."

"It's the baby," Annie admitted, glancing over at her friend. "That and I haven't been sleeping so well."

"Only nine hours a night?" Katherine teased, bending down to pick up a stray piece of equipment. "Your ability to sleep through anything is legendary."

"I found something that causes me to stay awake," Annie said. "A big cowboy sleeping next to me."

"Oooh, spill."

Around them, people were packing up. Annie began to stuff Spidey's toys into her bag. "Not much to tell. We share his bed and he sleeps and I don't."

"That's . . . boring."

"Isn't it?" She grimaced. "I mean, we're getting along. That's wonderful. I really like him and he says he wants to be in the baby's life. He says he wants me to stay for a while longer so we can get to know each other."

"Are you?" Katherine looked curious.

Annie sighed, wiping down a slobbered-on Kong bone

with a cloth. Spidey immediately ran to her side, thinking they were going to play, and she handed it down to him, instead. "I don't know. I like the ranch and no one has made me feel unwelcome."

"But?"

"But . . ." She licked her lips, thinking. "So when we first got together, Katherine, we kissed all the damn time. Every time we saw each other, it was instant attraction. It was like we couldn't stay apart from one another."

"Ah. And now you're fat and pregnant and he's not kissing you?"

"Ouch." Annie gave her friend a hurt look. "You go right for the jugular."

"Sorry. I mean, you're not really fat. You're Hollywood fat. That's like what, a size four?" She winked at Annie. "Besides, all of your fat is around the middle with that baby. What I should have said if I had a polite bone in my body was that you look different now and because of that, he won't touch you, right?"

"Right." Annie sighed again, gazing down at Spidey. The Boston made happy little grunts, chewing on the end of his favorite toy as if he didn't have a care in the world. "I know it's small in the scheme of things, but I wish he'd give me a kiss like he did before to show me that he still likes me. That he's not just tolerating me to get near the baby."

Katherine frowned at her then said sarcastically, "Yeah, because guys are totally more into babies than boobies. That sounds like a dude thing."

"Oh, be quiet."

"Look, I'm just saying, if you want him to kiss you like he did before, you have to remind him that pregnant women have needs, too. Maybe he doesn't want to push you into anything because you're tired all the time." She shrugged. "Guys are guys. I'm not entirely sure that they don't think pregnant women are aliens. My sister Laila? Her husband kept saying he didn't want kids. When she got pregnant, he was devastated. Turns out the dumbass thought that it meant no sex until she stopped breast-feeding." She rolled her eyes. "Men can be dumb. Tell him you need to get laid."

Annie's cheeks grew hot as she zipped up the bag, focusing on it. "I can't say that!"

"Why not? You have needs. Just because you have a baby in your uterus doesn't mean you're dead. You want your friend to send him an anonymous text message? Give me his phone number and I'll do it."

"No, it's okay. I'll talk to him tonight." It couldn't hurt, after all. They needed to get everything out in the open. If Dustin wasn't interested in her anymore, she wouldn't blame him . . . but she also wouldn't be sticking around for her heart to get broken, either.

She'd go back to LA and lick her wounds. Again.

CHAPTER SIXTEEN

Saying she was going to confront Dustin was easier than actually doing said confrontation, Annie decided.

She tried to seem calm, but her heart was fluttering a mile a minute in her breast, and she couldn't concentrate. She was distracted all through dinner, absently smiling when the cowboys teased one another or Cass tried to engage her in conversation. It wasn't their fault she was just completely out of it. They were trying to make her welcome.

She was trying to figure out the best way to broach the subject of "Do you still like me" with Dustin.

To be fair, he wasn't making things any easier. He was affectionate, sure. He'd touch her back or pull her chair out for her and make her feel doted on, but then he'd charge to his feet to get the door for Cass, or offer to take over a chore for Old Clyde and she'd wonder if he was just kind and giving to everyone and she was misreading it.

Really, the man wasn't all that easy to make out. If he'd just grab her and kiss her hard, she'd be able to blurt out all the things she was feeling. As it was, she picked at her dinner and worried.

"So . . . have you decided if you're staying?" Cass asked her as they cleared the dinner plates from the table. The men had to go out and take care of the horses before calling it a night, and Cass said they usually used this time to repair the equipment and fix saddles. In Annie's mind, it was probably a big bro-fest in the barn, but that was all right. It gave her and Cass time to chitchat while cleaning up the kitchen. Girly work, sure, but it was something she could do easily and with how pregnant she was, she didn't plan on fighting anyone over the right to oil a saddle.

"Not yet," Annie admitted. "The shoot wrapped today but . . . I don't know."

Cass made a noise that might have been agreement.

"Do you think the dogs really need training or do you think Dustin's just trying to come up with stuff to make me stay for a while longer?"

Cass smiled and looked pointedly over her shoulder. There, behind them in the kitchen, was every single one of the ranch dogs except Moose. Cass's Joy, Jim, Gable, Leigh, and Bandit were all sitting waiting for scraps, their tails wagging, eyes hopeful. Spidey was there, too—he loved being part of the pack—but Annie could have sworn the look on his face was confusion. She never gave him scraps so he didn't understand the begging. "It drives Eli crazy that I 'ruined' them," she told Annie. "We have to put everything away now or they counter-surf, and they never did before. So training them to break those habits would definitely be welcome. Is it all a ploy to get you to stay longer? I can't say that it's not. Would it be the worst thing, though?"

"No. I like it here." Annie picked up a towel and a wet plate and began to dry it. "But . . . it's complicated."

"It always is," Cass said softly. "I'll support whatever

decision you make, you know. It doesn't mean we can't be friends."

Her eyes pricked with tears. "You're going to make me cry."

"You're pregnant. That's all we do. Cry and pee and cry some more," Cass teased. "Plus, it's nice having around someone else that knows what I'm going through. Sometimes I swear Eli looks at me like I'm a space alien inhabiting his wife's body."

Annie giggled at that.

She and Cass had hot cocoas and talked babies and pregnancy while waiting for the men to return. Cass showed her the nursery and they *ooh*ed and *ahh*ed over the little onesies and swaddling blankets she'd received from distant family so far. All of her stuff was blue—she was having a boy and both her and Eli were terribly excited. It made Annie anxious for her own baby to arrive. Sometimes the waiting was the hardest part of being pregnant. Of course, then she'd have to pee for the ninetieth time that day and realized she was lying to herself.

The back door thudded, letting them know the others were returning, and Annie's anxiety hitched up a notch. They left the nursery, and Eli found his wife and immediately gave her a kiss on the lips. "You want to watch some TV with the boys? Jordy got a war movie from that new-fangled thing in town."

"Redbox?" Cass just shook her head at him. "I swear you're an eighty-year-old trapped in a hot thirty-something body. But I'll watch a movie if I get popcorn."

"One popcorn for my woman, coming right up." He kissed her again and then headed to the kitchen.

Annie could hear the others in the kitchen, too, arguing about John Wayne versus Russell Crowe. A moment later,

Dustin emerged and gave Annie a polite kiss on the fore-head. "You up for a movie with the crew or you want to call it a night?"

"I'm tired," she told him, and it wasn't entirely a lie. She was making herself completely on edge with worry, and the kiss on the forehead hadn't helped things. Sure, it was a kiss, but it was the kind of kiss you gave your granny, not your pregnant girlfriend.

But maybe she wasn't a girlfriend. The thought made her stomach clench miserably.

"All right. I'll grab a quick drink in the kitchen and then join you for some early bedtime." Dustin gave her arm an affectionate squeeze.

"You don't have to," Annie told him. "You can watch the movie—"

"I can watch a movie anytime," Dustin said, then winked at her before sauntering away. "Quality time with you is important."

Okay, that had to be a good sign, right? She hoped? More confused than ever, Annie murmured her good nights to the others and then slipped away down the hall to Dustin's room. She didn't have sexy clothes, so she went to the bath-room and gave her hair a quick combing and brushed her teeth, just in case. Then, she slowly crawled into bed and squeezed pillows around her belly, getting comfortable.

Then, she got up, because she couldn't exactly seem sexy with a pillow fort around her, could she? No wonder he didn't want to do more than hug her. Annie went to the rocking chair, instead, and adjusted her clothing, waiting.

Dustin entered the room a moment later with a bottle of water in hand. "One for you, too. I know you get thirsty."

She smiled at him. "Thank you. That's very thoughtful."

He paused at the sight of her sitting in a chair instead of in bed. "Everything all right? Your back hurting?"

"No, I'm fine." Boy, it was going to be difficult to make

him see her as sexy if he thought she was constantly hurting. This was so tricky, damn it.

Annie resisted the urge to wring her hands like a damsel. "Don't look at me like that."

"Like what?" An amused smile curved his gorgeous face.

"Like I'm going to break if you look at me sideways." She scowled at him. "I'm not that fragile."

"I know you're not. What brought this on?" He gave her a curious look, then pulled off his flannel overshirt, revealing a sweaty T-shirt underneath and the equally sweaty chest it clung to.

Her mouth went dry. "I just . . . I'm tired of being treated like a china doll. I'm pregnant. That's all. Lots of people are pregnant all the time and they don't snap like twigs."

"I know that. I've been around Cass for the last year and seen every stage she went through. If I'm hovering too much, I'm sorry." He shrugged. "It's just . . . different for you."

"Because it's your baby?"

"Because you're Annie." Dustin's beautiful mouth quirked with amusement, as if that explained everything.

It made her flush with pleasure and also left her confused. She was even more confused when he gave her a wink and then stripped off his belt, heading toward the shower as he did every night. Part of her wanted to push the bathroom door open and fling herself at him, to lick the beads of sweat off his chest like the wanton she was feeling like . . .

But what if he didn't want that?

She thought about what Kathrine had said—how men didn't know how to treat a pregnant woman. Her funny story about her sister and her sister's husband. Maybe Dustin didn't know and she did have to tell him how she felt. How she ached every day because she wanted more than just a chaste kiss or two. She wanted to lick him all over and she wanted him to lick her all over, too. Heck, she'd settle for just some quick sex. It didn't have to be earth-shattering, it just had to ease this itch in her body.

And it had to ease the worry in her head that he didn't find her attractive anymore.

If she was going to say something, it had to be tonight, she realized. The movie reshoot was over. If he told her that he really didn't like her that way anymore, then she could pack her bags and be gone in the morning. There'd be no reason to stay. But if he did like her, then everything changed.

She just needed to be brave enough to take the first step.

Sucking in a breath, Annie rose from the rocking chair and crept toward the bathroom door. The sound of running water told her that he was in the shower, and thoughts of him naked and gorgeous were enough to propel her into action. She'd open the door and join him in the shower. She'd soap his lean, tanned body up and tell him all about how she felt and he'd give her one of those passionate kisses that made everything in the world tip upside down in the best way.

Annie put her hand on the doorknob and turned.

Locked.

Well, shoot. There went that idea. Flustered, she retreated to the bed. She sat down on the edge, wiping her sweaty palms. The urge to just crawl under the covers and ignore it for another day was strong, but no. If she was going to confess her feelings, it had to be tonight.

Time for a new battle plan. She eyed the blankets and the mountain of soft pillows that were on her side of the bed. She looked down at her floral, unsexy nightie and stripped it off. The panties went, too, and so did the bra. Naked, she crawled into bed, adjusted the pillows, pulled the blankets up to her chin, and waited.

When he pulled her against him, he'd feel her naked body against his and . . . well, hopefully he'd be overcome with desire and kiss the heck out of her. Yeah, that sounded good.

So she waited.

And waited.

Gosh, the man could take a long shower. She wondered if the door was locked because he was touching himself in there, and then she wanted to cry because she wanted to be the one doing that. *Unfair, unfair, unfair.*

The door finally opened, and Annie tensed. She could smell the warm steam in the air and the scent of his soap as he moved into the room and she heard the rustle of clothing as he dressed for sleep. She wanted to tell him not to bother, to come lie next to her completely naked, but all she managed was an awkward squeak.

"Annie?"

She cleared her throat. "I'm fine. Sorry." Gosh, why was she so very shy around him? She'd known him in every sense, even the biblical one, and yet now that she was pregnant with his baby, she couldn't seem to string two words together when they were alone. It was like her brain short-circuited around him.

The bed creaked in the dark and she felt it sag under his larger weight. He reached for her, and Annie held her breath. His hand encountered bare skin, and she felt him hesitate.

"Are you too warm?" he asked, ever solicitous.

"No."

A long pause. "Uh."

"I want to have sex," Annie blurted. "Like we did before. But only if you want to." And then, to her horror, she burst into tears.

"Whoa, whoa, hey," Dustin murmured, shoving the fortress of pillows aside and pulling her against him. "What is it? Are you all right?"

Sobbing, she punched his arm lightly. "Are you deaf?" She managed to choke out. "I want to have sex. Please."

"Then why are you crying?" His voice was full of tender amusement and that just was all the more infuriating. He stroked her hair, and she was torn between cuddling against him like a greedy kitten and smacking him in the chest with her fist for being so freaking hard to read.

"I'm crying because I'm pregnant and emotional," Annie snapped at him. "And because I don't know if you like me anymore."

Dustin was quiet for a long moment. "You think I don't like you?"

"I don't know." She dug her fingernails into her palms because she was doing her best to stop crying. Crying never led to sex, she was pretty sure, especially not pregnant crying. "You don't act like it."

"Don't I?"

"No," she wailed. "You kiss my forehead when you should be giving me French kisses! You hold my hand when you should be grabbing my butt. You're nice and kind and polite but you're like that to everyone. I don't know how you feel about me because all you do is treat me like I'm your grandmother instead of your girlfriend and I don't know what I am to you."

He was silent. The only sound in the room was her sniffling.

"Say something," she hiccup-demanded after a tense moment.

"You think I treat you like my grandmother?"

"Well, you don't treat me like you did before."

"Before, when you weren't pregnant? Annie, you're carrying my baby. The last thing I want to do is hurt you or make you more uncomfortable than you already are. You spend all day rubbing your lower back and turning green at smells. You run to the bathroom every twenty minutes. Of course I'm being careful with you." He paused and then continued in a lower voice, "It'd kill me if I hurt you in any way."

"You're killing me right now with kindness," Annie whispered. "I want what we had before. If the way you feel has changed, I need you to let me know now, so I can figure out how I feel—"

Before she could finish speaking, he took her hand and placed it on his body.

Right on his cock.

His very hard, very erect, clearly aching cock. It strained against the material of his boxer briefs, and even through the fabric, she could feel pre-cum wetting the head.

"You think I don't want you?" His voice was husky with need. "You think I haven't been fighting how bad I need you every minute of every day?"

Annie sucked in a breath, utterly entranced by the feel of him in her grip. Unable to help herself, she slid her hand up and down his rigid length, caressing him through the fabric. "You never told me."

"You never indicated that you wanted me. I didn't want to push you. I was waiting for you to give me a sign." He reached up, caressed her breast and lightly thumbed the sensitive nipple. "You think we're sleeping in the same bed out of coincidence?"

"Oh." Okay, she had thought it was a little odd. "I guess I'm just as willfully blind as you are."

Dustin chuckled. "I figured I'd give you time to get settled so I could romance you proper. It's been hell trying to keep my hands off you, though. I have to practically tie them behind my back so I don't grope you while you're sleeping."

Her heart thrilled to hear that. "Even though I have the world's ugliest nightgowns? They don't exactly make tons of sexy maternity wear."

"I don't care what you wear. I find you sexy. I'd find you

sexy if you were wearing a burlap sack." His thumb lightly stroked over her nipple, and oh, she ached so badly that she could scarcely stand it. "I think you're utterly beautiful. I always have."

"But I'm fat now," she began.

"Don't say that," Dustin murmured, pulling her closer to him. "You're pregnant with my baby. You're beautiful. Saying you're fat is ridiculous." He leaned in and his nose brushed against hers. "And if you want deep tongue kisses, sweetheart, all you had to do was ask."

His mouth closed over hers and she moaned against him, her fingers curling at his nape. It felt like it had been a hundred years since he'd touched her, and the need in her was aching so fiercely that she could barely contain it. Dustin's tongue stroked lightly against her own, teasing, and her body clenched in response. Oh wow. Even kissing him felt heightened while pregnant. With a little whimper, she kissed him back, losing herself in the feel of his mouth possessing hers. Nothing had ever felt so good, so very right. She was drowning in a sea of sensation.

Dustin pulled away from her mouth and she made a little sound of protest. But he only nipped at her lower lip. "I don't know anything about pregnant ladies," he admitted in a low voice between kisses. "So if there's something you can't do or something I shouldn't touch, you should tell me."

"Touch everything. Kiss everything," Annie panted, and then blushed at how desperate she sounded. "I . . . I can't lie flat on my back, though. It's bad for the baby."

He nuzzled at her neck, and she thought she would die from the pleasure of it. Then he nipped the lobe of one ear and she nearly cried out. "So . . . standing? Hands and knees? On your side? You on top? You tell me how you want it, and I'll give it to you."

And oh, didn't that sound wonderfully filthy? Annie moaned again.

"I'll give you time to decide," he teased her, and then he was caressing her breast again. "You're so beautiful. Look at how pretty these breasts are. I thought they were perfect before, and they're perfect now. Are they sensitive?"

"Very," she breathed.

"I want to taste one," he told her, and heat pulsed between her thighs. Annie wanted to roll onto her back so she could experience this in full glory, so he could move over her, but she remained carefully on her side as he tucked a flat pillow gently under her belly and then slid forward in the bed, curled against her so he could nuzzle at her breasts. It didn't matter that she was very pregnant, she realized. He'd make this work. He'd take good care of her.

He always did.

The thought made swift tears rise in her throat again. Stupid pregnancy tears. Even when she was losing her mind with how turned on she was, she was still weepy. But then Dustin's lips closed over her nipple and desire clawed through her, fast and hard. She gasped, clutching at his head as he lapped at the peak, teasing it with his tongue and then gently sucking on it.

Oh, heaven help her, she was going to come if he kept doing that. He wouldn't even have to touch her again. She'd just spontaneously combust from his mouth on her breast. "Dustin," she panted. "I need . . ."

His tongue flicked against one hard tip.

She cried out, her sex clenching tight in response.

"Are you close?" he murmured, his hand skimming down her belly even as his lips toyed with her breast. "Let me feel how wet you are, sweetheart." His fingers brushed over the curls of her sex and then he grazed her folds lightly. "So damned wet. Look at that."

"Please, Dustin. I need you."

"Don't worry, sweetheart. I'll give you everything you need. I promise." His fingers danced along her folds and then he slipped deeper, exploring her with gentle touches. "You're so damn soft. I love this. I want to kiss you all over, touch you everywhere. Will you let me?"

For once, her voice failed her. Annie nodded helplessly.

"My beautiful Annie," he murmured, and stroked one finger gently into her.

She gasped, arching against him. It had been so long since he'd touched her that his caresses felt downright shocking. Then his mouth closed over her nipple again and he suckled as he stroked into her. His thumb brushed over her clit and that was enough—her entire body clenched in a spasm of bliss and then she was coming, her mind lost to the pleasure of it all. Gasping, crying out his name, Annie seemed to climax for forever. When she finally came down, she was panting and exhausted . . . but gosh, she felt good.

So, so good.

Dustin shifted in the bed and then he was kissing her again, his mouth hot and urgent on her own. She lost herself in his drugging kisses, letting the sweet pleasure of his embrace take her away again. His lips slanted over hers, and the kiss grew in urgency until she felt desire pooling in her belly again. She moved her hands over his chest, felt his shirt, and tugged at it. "I'm naked and you're not," she panted. "That hardly seems fair."

"You want me to get naked for you?" He kissed the tip of her nose.

"Absolutely."

Without protest, Dustin sat up in bed and ripped his shirt over his head. She could make out his outline in the darkness, enjoyed the gorgeous flex of his arms and the ripple of his muscles. Was ever a woman so lucky? He was masculine perfection and he was in bed with her. Annie couldn't help herself, she reached out and caressed one hand over his flat stomach, fascinated with touching him. She made a sound of disappointment when he got out of bed, but then realized he was stripping his boxer briefs off and slipped back under the covers a moment later.

And because she was greedy, her hands immediately went to his cock and she caressed him. Oh yes, she remembered this, how big and wonderful he was. He cupped her face in his hands and kissed her again, and she moaned against him even as she stroked his hard, hot length. His hips flexed, as if he were trying to pump into her greedy hands, and she loved the feel of him. She wanted to give him pleasure like he'd given her. "Tell me how to touch you."

"Forget touching," he told her with frantic, urgent kisses across her face and neck. "I want to be inside you. Are you too tired?"

For this? "Never."

With a low groan, he kissed her deeply again, and then she pushed him away, tugging the covers off their bodies and getting on her hands and knees. Annie felt weird and ungainly, but Dustin caressed her hips and breasts as she did, and told her how beautiful she was, and any sense of shyness or awkwardness fell quickly away. She wanted this as much as him. When she was in position on the bed, she settled a pillow under her belly and then tossed her hair back. "I'm ready if you are."

He caressed her buttock even as he rose onto his knees. "You're comfortable? You'll tell me if you hurt?" When she nodded, Dustin moved behind her on the bed, his hands on her hips.

Anticipation and arousal flared as he shifted against her, and his grip teased over her sides and thighs before moving back to her hips. His cock prodded against her core for a moment, and then he pressed against her, slowly, achingly pushing inside her.

And oh, it was so, so good.

Her entire body quaked in response, and she clenched at the blankets, crying out.

Immediately, Dustin tensed behind her. "Sweetheart? Should I stop?"

"No," she panted. "Feels good. Never stop. Ever."

"Magic words," he gritted out, and she felt his hips flex as he drove deeper into her.

He took his time, and Annie was practically itching with impatience as he inched into her. She knew he was being careful, and nothing hurt or felt uncomfortable, and so all she felt was a greedy sort of need. She wanted more of him. She wanted him pulsing into her with short, hungry bursts. She wanted him to lose control.

She needed it.

Dustin groaned deeply, rocking against her. "Still feel good?" When she nodded, he grunted a response and then began to slowly pump into her, starting a rhythm.

And oh, that was nice. So nice. Annie closed her eyes, enjoying the feel of their bodies pushing together as he thrust into her from behind. Her full breasts—so large and alien like her stomach—swayed with every motion, and her belly rubbed against the pillow, but that didn't matter. His slow, methodical thrusting felt incredible, and she gave a little sigh of pleasure as the slow curl began in her belly. He always knew just how to touch her to make her feel so good. So beautiful.

He reached forward, one hand moving to her hair, and then he twined his fingers into it, anchoring her in place even as his body began to move faster. A little moan escaped her, and she was surprised at how much that simple motion could turn her on. It was like he was holding her against him, and hot need coursed through her even as her body clenched around him.

He bit out a curse, panting. "You feel amazing, sweetheart."

"Dustin," she breathed, the pleasure in her body building with every moment. "Go faster. I need more."

"I won't hurt you?"

"Never. Please." She reached back for him, trying to touch him. "More."

He gave her more. With a groan of her name, Dustin redoubled his efforts, his thrusts harder, his thighs slapping against her own, and she was lost in his possessive takeover. Before she knew it, Annie cried out as the waves of another orgasm pulsed through her, and then Dustin's movements took on a jerky, wild rhythm. He bit out her name, tensing against her, and then slowed his movements, his breathing heavy and ragged, and she realized he'd come, too.

"Couldn't last long," he panted, caressing her hip even as he gently rocked their joined bodies. "Felt too good to be in you bare like this. My sweet Annie. My girl."

She sighed blissfully, her toes curled with pleasure. "Thank you."

He chuckled. "Well now, you're most welcome." With one last caress, he pulled away from her and then gently helped her to her feet. "Let me help you clean up, sweetheart, and then I'll get you a drink." He hesitated, then pulled her against him and pressed another hot, delicious kiss to her mouth. "I'm glad you said something. I've wanted you ever since you showed up again, Annie. Never doubt that."

"I won't," she told him shyly, but she knew it was easier to say it than believe it.

CHAPTER SEVENTEEN

Dustin woke her up at dawn for some steamy kissing, caressed her until she climaxed, and then instructed her to go back to sleep. She did, gratefully, and when she woke up some hours later, she stretched and smiled up at the ceiling, dopey with happiness.

Life was wonderful.

She tested her muscles as she crawled out of bed and headed to the shower, but everything seemed to be fine. A little tight in places here and there, but nothing she couldn't live with. The baby was flipping and tossing in her belly as if saying hello, and really, she couldn't remember a time she'd been so darn happy.

Dustin wanted her.

The sex was just as good as she'd remembered. And afterward, he'd held her so carefully and so tightly against him, naked, that she'd fallen asleep as if curled in a nest, pillows on one side and cowboy on the other. She'd never slept so well. The wake-up call had been nice, too. Annie dressed, combed her wet hair, and went to grab breakfast for herself and for Spidey, who'd been in the bathroom all night and probably needed to have a walk as soon as possible.

Cass was in the kitchen, making breakfast, her fluffy dog Joy bouncing at her heels and begging for treats. She looked over at Annie and Spidey, smiling. "Morning. Want eggs and bacon?" She gestured at Spidey. "When I woke up, Dustin was bringing him in from a walk in case you're wondering."

He did seem rather calm, her little guy. That was sweet of Dustin, to think of her pup, too. Then again, he was just wonderful in every way. Of course, that might be the hormones talking. She was sure he had flaws. She just didn't see them at the moment. "I'd love breakfast. Let me take him out for another quick walk just in case, and then I'll do the dishes."

Outside, Spidey sniffed tuft after tuft of brown autumn grass and didn't seem in a hurry to pick out a spot to do his business. That was fine with her. Hugging her oversized sweater to her body, Annie lifted a hand to her brow and scanned the horizon, looking for men on horseback, cattle, or any of the ranch dogs that inevitably followed at the horses' heels. In the very far distance, heading up a rolling hill, she saw someone on horseback riding alongside a bunch of cattle. The dogs were spotted. That would be Jordy, she suspected. Eli's dog was an enormous, snow-white Great Pyrenees, and Old Clyde had a pair, one of which was white. Moose had dark markings and he'd be at Dustin's side. She looked for her man, but the ranch was sprawling and she didn't see him anywhere by the time Spidey was done and the cold was getting to both of them. Her dog sat at her feet and waited patiently, an indication for her to pick him up. "No, buddy, not for a few more months." She rubbed her belly. "Sorry."

Once inside, she saw Cass sitting at the breakfast table,

taking bites of bacon and feeding the ends to Joy, who looked enraptured by the treats. It was clear Cass loved her dog, but it was also clear why Joy was so bad at listening. Joy had her big white paws on Cass's leg, her face practically in the woman's plate. "Ten bucks says that's your counter-surfer," Annie told her as she joined her.

Cass grimaced. "Really? But Joy's so small compared to the other ranch dogs. She's barely the size of Jim and only half the size of her mother."

"It's harder to untrain them once they've learned that people food can also be their food, but there's things we can do," Annie said, smiling at Cass. "I'm not here to lecture. I just want to help so we're not reinforcing bad behavior. One of the first things we can do, though, is to start spraying the counter at night with a substance that tastes bad so when they get up there and start licking things, it won't be very appealing. I'm not sure how effective that will be unless you leave food out, but we can always try a treat spot, instead."

"Treat spot?" Cass asked, curious. She finished her food, wiped her fingers, and then started rubbing Joy's head. It was obvious from the way the dog laid her head in Cass's (shrinking by the day) lap that she was well loved. "How do we do that?"

"We create a spot in the kitchen that we start rewarding them at. Basically, we teach that they only get treats when they're sitting in that spot. Like, if you wanted to set a mat down in the corner by the door, we train them that if they're sitting on the mat, they get treats. No mat, no treats. That way, you can still reward her and give her nibbles, but it'll stop her from jumping all over you or sticking her face in your plate to snatch a treat."

Cass brightened. "That sounds great. I know Eli isn't a big fan of spoiling the dogs but . . . I can't help it. I love them. They're like children to me." She gave Joy's ears a rub and then planted a smacking kiss on the dog's head. "She's my baby girl."

It was nice to be around people that clearly cared for their pets as much as each other.

They talked for a little longer about training, and then the talk switched—as it always did with them—to babies. Cass had gotten in a few more boxes of items she'd ordered online, and after breakfast, they fussed over the little booties and rattles and a mobile with dangling stuffed puppies that made squeezy noises when touched. "You seem happy this morning," Cass told her, folding one tiny little blue outfit after another. "Relaxed. Like the nervous edge is gone."

Annie could feel her cheeks heating. Was it that obvious they'd had sex? "I do feel good. Dustin and I had a great talk last night about . . . us. And the future." Well, future more or less. Just that they had a future together. Right now that was enough for her.

"Ah. The boat conversation?" Cass chuckled. "I swear he talked about that thing for months to anyone that would listen. So is that still on for the spring, then? I have no idea how you guys will work that with a newborn, but I know he's been looking forward to it for a really long time."

"Boat?" Annie asked, her stomach giving a little clench of fear. "What boat?"

Cass stopped, her smile fading. "I . . . oh. I just thought . . . never mind. I'm sure it's nothing."

"Please tell me about the boat," Annie said quietly, touching Cass's arm. "It's probably nothing but if it's something I should talk with Dustin about, I want to know. We're in a good place, but we're also still figuring each other out."

Hesitant, Cass bit her lip. "I feel terrible that I brought it up. I just . . ." She sighed, spreading her hands. "Eli and Dustin talk, you know? And Dustin told him a while back that he was probably going to move on in the spring. That he'd always dreamed of having a boat and sailing up the coast and going to new places. You know that man has rest-less feet."

"I know," Annie murmured, thinking about Dustin and how he'd left home because he couldn't stand to be his fa-ther. Her heart gave a painful squeeze.

"He always talked about that stupid boat." Cass shook her head. "Didn't matter that he'd never had a sailing les-son. He said he wanted to learn. You know how Dustin is—there's no mountain he thinks he can't conquer with sheer will."

Annie laughed, hoping it sounded more lighthearted than she felt. "That sounds like him, all right." And she made a mental note to ask about boats and springtime.

Just because she was changing her life to suit the baby didn't mean that she would demand it of him. He needed to be free to make his own choices, even if they conflicted with hers.

After the kitchen was clean, the two women went out and fed Cass's chickens, and then Cass showed her the stables. The chickens made her laugh, especially when Spi-dey stared at them through the wire mesh of their run, ut-terly fascinated. Even funnier were Cass's names for the chickens themselves—this one was Jerkface, that one was Creep, there was Pecker and Bossy and Meanie. Every chicken had a ridiculous name that made Annie snicker, even more so when Cass just shook her head and solemnly said the chickens were assholes.

The interior of the barn was mostly empty because the men (and the horses) were out in the field, Cass explained. Even so, there were two horses in their stalls that the women stopped by to pet and feed carrots to, and to Annie's surprise, Moose sat in the hay, watching them with a cau-tious thump of his tail. A moment later, Dustin appeared, sweaty and shirtless, a pitchfork in his hands as he mucked out one of the empty stalls. He was filthy and covered in sawdust and was up to his ankles in poopy straw and . . . she still wanted to kiss the heck out of him. Annie blushed and blushed until they went inside, her red cheeks only exacerbated by the knowing smile her man sent in her direction.

When Cass headed inside to do laundry—there were always dirty clothes with four cowboys, she explained with a grimace—Annie headed to her room to make a few calls. First to her agent, and when she got voicemail, she sent an email, instead, to let her know that Annie planned on staying in Wyoming for a while and wouldn't be looking for any jobs until further notice. She knew her agent wouldn't be thrilled, but that was all right. She'd known a call like this was coming anyhow the moment she'd realized that Annie was too pregnant to travel much.

Change was inevitable, and she wouldn't feel guilty about it.

The next call was to her mother. Kitty picked up on the second ring and without a greeting, immediately said, "How much weight have you gained?"

"Why does that matter?" Annie asked, confused.

"There's a role for 'miserable pregnant lady two' in the movie I'm shooting." As if it was her movie and she wasn't just a bit part. "The lady that had the role delivered early and so now they need someone else to fill it in. They got another lady to come in but she had preeclampsia and was on bed rest. I think she should have come in for the shoot, but whatever. I told them my daughter was pregnant but that you were really fat and not watching your figure."

"Mom."

"*Kitty*. And it's Hollywood, darling. You know how it is. They want you to be pregnant but also still gorgeously attractive. Still, the role does say 'miserable' so I thought it might suit you. If you drive back today they can shoot the scene this weekend and you can get paid. How does that sound?"

"I'm going to pass." She shook her head. "I've told you before, I really don't want to be on screen. That's why I work with animals."

"Well, I know. But I just thought it'd be money for the baby. Speaking of, how are you doing, darling? Still not sick all day I hope."

That was her mother—obsessed with appearances even as she turned affectionate to her daughter. It was a confusing sort of relationship, but then again, Kitty was a complex person. "No, I'm doing fine. The mountain air is pretty nice here. It's very cold and I think that's helping things."

"Bundle up that little rat you call a dog. You know he shivers at the slightest breeze."

Annie chuckled. "Spidey is at my feet as we speak and wearing a very obnoxious red coat. How are you doing?" She was stalling, she knew it, but sometimes it was easier to ease into the "bad" news. "How's the movie going?"

"Other than the fact that our pregnant ladies are selfishly dropping like flies? It's not bad. The director remembered my name. I'm hoping that'll mean I get a few more lines."

"Are you sure it wasn't just because you were hitting on him?" she teased. She knew how her mother worked. "Is he young and cute?"

"Please, darling. If he was even slightly hetero you know I'd be all over that. But he's a very good director. Very straightforward. I swear we've only had to reshoot half a dozen scenes. You sure you don't want to drive down here? Easy paycheck and your movie should be wrapping soon, right?"

"Actually, it wrapped yesterday," Annie confessed. "But I think I'm going to stay up here for a few more days and spend some time with Dustin."

Her mother made an unladylike sound on the other end. "That cowboy? So he's decided that now that you're knocked up with his baby he should change his ways? Did he dump the other woman for you then? You know how you get them is how you lose them, darling."

Hoo boy. Annie didn't know whether to be annoyed or amused. Her mother didn't know the truth about Dustin, though. "He didn't cheat, it turns out."

"*Mmhmm.*" Kitty didn't sound impressed.

"No, really. There was this woman in town who said that to scare me off and it wasn't true." Saying it aloud made it seem . . . flimsy, though. She trusted Dustin, she did. But she also realized she needed to talk to this Theresa person herself and settle her mind once and for all. "He's really been great, Kitty. I promise that there's nothing to worry about."

"You're my daughter. There's always something to worry about." Kitty sighed. "I just want you to be happy. I don't want you to feel as if you're making the wrong decisions because you have to. He might be a perfectly nice man, but that doesn't mean you have to stay with him, darling. I raised you all by myself and look at how wonderful you turned out."

That might have been the sweetest thing that Kitty had ever said to her. "Thanks, Mom."

"Even if you are terribly fat right now."

Annie giggled through her tears. "It's called pregnancy."

"Oh, I know. I'm just giving you a hard time. I suppose you can't help porking up. So what are the plans, then?"

"Plans?"

"Short term? Long term? Ease your mother's mind. Tell me what you two have in mind. Are you going to raise the baby here? There in that podunk town? Who's going to be your doctor? Does he have money put aside? You know babies aren't cheap, even in the wilds of Montana."

"Wyoming," Annie corrected, and for some reason, she thought of Dustin and the boat, and she felt a little niggle of worry in her belly. "And we haven't gotten that far yet. We're still figuring out where we're at in this relationship."

"Well, don't you think you should talk about it, darling? Babies come early all the time. Though hopefully not too early, because I've got a bit part on a TV show next month that needs an 'aging go-go dancer' and I need to make sure I'm available. You hold that little nugget in for as long as you can," Kitty said affectionately. "Squeeze those thighs tightly together."

Annie smiled into the phone absently. "You're crazy, Kitty. You know that?"

"It's Hollywood. It fries your brain and makes you impossible for normal people to understand. But these are serious questions."

"I know, Mom. I'll get some answers, I promise. We're just taking things carefully. One step at a time and all that."

"I suppose this is the point where I should say that if he was so careful, you wouldn't be fat and pregnant, but that might be uncharitable of me."

Annie just rolled her eyes.

"I can hear you rolling your eyes at me, darling. I'm a mother. We have a sixth sense when it comes to our children."

Despite the conversation, Annie found herself smiling. Some things changed, but Kitty Grissom never did. She'd toss a backhanded compliment at you in one breath and make you realize just how much she cared (in her own way) in the next. "I love you, Mom. I'm going to stay here for a while longer and I'll let you know what my plans are as soon as I figure them out, okay?"

"Love you too, darling. And remember, you have options. You're pregnant, not trapped in his basement. You can come home at any time."

Annie giggled again. "Thanks, Kitty."

* * *

Even though her mother was a little loopy at times, she did have a good point, Annie realized. She and Dustin might be good right now, but they needed to talk about the future and what it meant for them. It was a conversation they hadn't had yet, and with the baby on the way, they definitely needed to talk it out.

Plus, there was that worrisome conversation with Cass about boats and leaving the ranch.

Not that Annie cared if they stayed or left. She liked the ranch; she liked the dogs, the people, the animals, the scenery. It felt serene here, and safe. She'd be happy here . . . but she'd also be happy going back to Los Angeles and spending time with her mother and friends. Annie had a life there, and it didn't make sense for her to give it up if Dustin was planning on disappearing off onto a boat in the next few months.

Boats were nice, but Annie was pretty sure they were no place to raise a newborn . . . not that she'd been invited.

She was determined not to panic or stress too much, though. Just because they hadn't had the conversation yet didn't mean it would be a bad one.

Annie was determined not to make herself anxious over nothing at all. Not yet. She'd already panicked once and it had sent her back to LA an emotional mess . . . and she'd been wrong. She needed to trust him right now. He'd given her no reason not to.

So to distract herself, Annie spent the afternoon working with the dogs that were at the house still. Most of the ranch dogs headed out with the men every day, but Joy and Frannie, Eli's dog, were at the house with Cass. The dogs didn't pay much attention to Annie, though, no matter how much she tried to bribe them. They followed Cass's footsteps and watched her carefully, and Annie wondered if they knew something she didn't. "You feeling okay, Cass?"

The other woman gave Annie a smile. "Just a backache today that won't let up."

"Is it—"

"No, I don't think so. No contractions." Cass rubbed her belly. "And this is supposed to drop a few days ahead of time, right? I've been checking in the mirror every day to see if anything's shifted, but it all looks the same to me." She made a face. "So it's just another thrilling pregnancy ache."

"Why don't you let me help with your chores, instead? I can clean up and do laundry." She got to her feet and pulled a towel out of Cass's hands. "You can relax, you know."

"I can, but I'm also paid to be the housekeeper here." Cass snagged the towel back from Annie's hands, smiling. "You're just the guest. And we need more towels. I'd blame the towel situation on Jordy or Clyde but the truth is, Eli uses more dang towels than anyone I've ever met." She shook her head. "It's like if it grazes a bead of water, it goes into the laundry."

Annie chuckled. "Fine, I'll help with other stuff, then. Maybe the chickens? Or lunch?"

Cass beamed a grateful smile at her. "I love having another woman around, just so you know. It's not the chore thing. If I left every single thing in the house undone, Eli would never complain. He'd just do it all once he came in for the night. I love having you here, though. I never thought I was lonely before, but having someone else to talk babies and girl stuff with all day? It's just wonderful."

"I feel the same way," Annie admitted shyly. Her social awkwardness flared and she fidgeted. It was awkward to hear such things, but it was also nice, too. "I hope you'd let me know if I ever overstayed my welcome."

"I don't think such a thing's possible. You've met Jordy, right?" Cass arched an eyebrow at her.

Annie just giggled again.

They spent the afternoon doing laundry and then mending socks. Cass joked that she felt like a pioneer every time she sewed up holes in the socks, but every time the dogs found a stray sock, they chewed on it, and it ended up being cheaper to try and mend things than to just buy new socks all the time. Annie worked in the kitchen, making food that would be easy to reheat for dinner in case Cass wasn't feeling up to snuff, though she'd probably deny any aches and pains. Annie made muffins and banana bread, then threw a roast into the oven and chopped up some potatoes. Pot roast was one of those things that tasted better reheated anyhow.

Cass laid down for a nap shortly after lunch, and Joy and Frannie trailed after her. Annie made a mental note to mention it to Dustin when he got in, and she sat down on the couch to watch some of the news in a quiet moment.

The next thing she knew, a hand was gently shaking her awake. "Sweetheart?"

Annie jerked upright with an ungraceful snort, swiping at her mouth. "Oh no, did I fall asleep? The roast—" The house smelled wonderful, like simmering meat, and her mouth watered.

"Not burned. Definitely cooked, but not burned." Dustin hovered over her, concern in his handsome face as he tipped back his hat and studied her. "You all right?"

"Just tired." She smiled at him and extended a hand. "Help me up?"

He did, and instead of letting her go, he pulled her against him and slid his hands up and down her back. "How was your day?"

"It was great, but I didn't get much work with the dogs done." She told him how they were following Cass, and he nodded. "I might have to do most of the training of the dogs at night after they're in for the day. I don't want to pull them away from their ranch duties."

"There's no rush on any of it," Dustin told her. "Just relax and take care of yourself."

"But I want to do it," Annie insisted, doing her best to keep the stubborn note out of her voice. "I need to feel like I'm contributing more than just a womb here."

He grinned at her. "Fair enough. I'm not trying to make you all barefoot and pregnant in the kitchen. I just know you're tired and the movie was stressful. You're allowed to take a few days to rest."

Mollified, she slipped her arms around his waist and buried her face against his chest. He was warm and hard against her, his clothes smelling like sweat and the outdoors. It was a rather pleasant combination, and she wanted to snuggle up against him forever, especially when he put his hand in her hair and stroked it. "Can we talk after dinner?" she asked him eventually.

"We don't need to wait for dinner to talk," he teased.

"It's a serious conversation," Annie told him. "A private one."

She felt him stiffen. "Do I need to worry? Is something wrong?"

"Nothing's wrong. We just have stuff we need to talk about, that's all." When he hesitated, she looked up at him and smiled. "I promise I'm not doing another runner. It's just conversation, nothing more."

Dustin relaxed and then impulsively kissed her. "Good, because I don't want you leaving me behind ever again."

And really, how could a girl get mad over that?

CHAPTER EIGHTEEN

Dustin watched Annie carefully through dinner, looking for signs. Signs that she was unhappy, that something was lurking behind her eyes, that she was hiding something from him. But she smiled and chatted with Old Clyde, listening to stories about ranch dogs in the past, and how he'd first gotten started ranching after the war. His Annie was a fantastic listener and so pretty and thoughtful that it made his chest hurt. Dustin suspected that if she wasn't claimed by him, he'd have to fight Jordy and Clyde both for her affection.

She fit in so easily with everyone at the ranch that it made him feel a sense of both pride and pleasure when he would glance over and see her laughing with the others. It made the long, hard day worth it. It made coming home to her a joy.

It made him wonder how he'd ever survived the last eight months without her.

Impossible to think about, but after only a few short days, Annie had worked her way under his skin once more. He'd somehow always pictured himself as a loner, able to enjoy the company of others but never settling down in one place or with one person. Somehow, though, that was slowly changing. The thought of Annie leaving him again was like a knife in the gut; he'd do anything to prevent that from happening. Her happiness was his priority now, her smile his focus.

Being alone and without strings attached had lost its appeal overnight. Maybe he'd never met the right person until she'd come into his life. Maybe that's how these sorts of things worked.

He didn't know, and he didn't much care as long as Annie was happy.

But she wanted to have a "conversation" tonight, and that worried him. He wondered what had come up. Was it something about the baby? About Theresa? He really needed to go into town and set that woman straight if she was still harassing his Annie. Protectiveness for his woman and his baby swept over him.

He needed to make sure they were happy and safe, and if that meant giving the entire town a piece of his mind, he'd do just that. So as the others talked and laughed, Dustin pretended to listen, smiling when appropriate. In his mind, though, he planned. He needed to show Annie off to others more. He needed them to realize he was serious about her, and it'd take more than just one dinner in town to convince them of such things. It would need to be small gestures at first, so they seemed casual and normal. Tonight, for example, he could run to the mini-mart and pick her up some ice cream and pickles. That was what pregnant ladies liked, right? Gus would be behind the counter, and Dustin would make a joke about the upcoming baby and still show how proud he was of things. He'd make sure to talk about Annie and how much he cared for her. Tomorrow, he'd go see Hetty over at the souvenir shop and discuss what he needed to do to get a wedding band for his girl.

They could be engaged for as long as she felt comfortable, but if he was asking around, people would know he was serious. Dustin knew he could just head in to Casper and look for a jewelry store, but if he did it here, in Painted Barrel, it'd be all over the town in a matter of days. They'd all be talking about how Dustin Worthington, cowboy "Lothario" as Annie had called him, was ready to settle down.

Yeah, he could get this all working perfectly. And he'd stop by the pharmacy when Theresa was working and give her a piece of his mind.

There was a magazine rack at the pharmacy, too. Maybe he'd see what he could find about babies so he could read up and not be so clueless.

Annie looked over at him and smiled, her freckles lovely and bright across her cute nose, and his chest felt tight with how badly he wanted this to work out. He jumped to his feet, ready to put his plan into action. "You want ice cream, sweetheart?"

"I . . ." She looked puzzled. "Like, right now?"

Everyone was looking at him oddly. Well, except Eli. Eli just smirked as if he had an idea of what was going through Dustin's mind.

"Yeah, I need to get some gas for my truck. Figured I'd pick you up a snack."

"Okay?" She smiled faintly, as if still confused by his request. "Cookies, too?"

Cass groaned at her side, rubbing her belly. "Oh man, I didn't think I could eat anything else until you mentioned cookies. Now I want some."

"Isn't there a whole plate of baked goods in the kitchen?" Jordy asked, confused.

"Not the same thing," Dustin said quickly, and was relieved when no one contradicted him. He went to Annie's side, kissed her quickly, and then snagged his hat from the peg by the door. "Be back soon. Come on, Moose."

The big dog lumbered after him, tail wagging.

Two hours later, Dustin was headed back to the ranch, several pints of Ben & Jerry's tucked into a bag next to him, along with every kind of cookie the mini-mart had on its shelves. Gus had smirked at the sweets and joked that his wife had always wanted peanut butter when she was pregnant, and so Dustin picked up some of that, too. Gus had also asked Annie's due date, and Dustin had given a vague answer. It bothered him that he didn't know the details of that just yet, and he made a mental note to ask.

He'd stopped by the pharmacy, too, but Theresa wasn't there. A teenager—one of Rebecca Hill's daughters from the nearby Hill Top Ranch—was working the register and gave him a blank look when he asked about baby magazines, then slapped a thick book onto the counter.

What to Expect When You're Expecting. He'd bought it, a little bewildered at how thick the dang thing was. He'd always thought of himself as a pretty smart guy, but the sight of a baby book that thick threw him for a loop. How much did one have to know about having a baby?

Suddenly he felt as if he was falling down on the job of fatherhood. He needed to pay attention to these things, he realized. He needed to start preparing.

Everything was going to change the night Morgan arrived. Or Lee. Whatever Annie wanted to call him. Or her.

He went inside the ranch house, offered Cass her pint of ice cream and pick of the cookies, then headed in to his room. It occurred to him—so many things were hitting him tonight—that they didn't have a place for a baby to sleep. There was no extra room, and Cass and Eli had turned the office into a room in anticipation of their baby. All right, he'd talk with Annie about it, and see what she wanted to do. Maybe they could make something work here at the ranch. If not, maybe they could rent a place in town and he could drive out to the ranch every morning.

Unless she wanted to go back to LA. Dustin shuddered at the thought. He was a roamer, sure, but he'd never been much of one for crowded places like that. He'd gone to New York City once, on a whim, and then promptly left again. It was too busy, too packed, too dirty, too clustered. He preferred the open air of the countryside, the scenery of the mountains, and most of all, the quiet.

He wondered which one Annie would prefer.

The door to their room was shut, so he knocked politely, then stuck his head in. His woman—man, he liked saying that—was in bed, playing a candy game on her phone and she sat up at the sight of him.

"Brought you ice cream." Dustin set the now-drippy container on the nearest dresser and grimaced. "I'll go get you a spoon."

"I'm not hungry," Annie told him, and clasped her hands in her lap. "Dustin, are you avoiding me?"

"What? No. Not at all. Let me put this away, then—"

"Dustin—" she called, but he disappeared into the kitchen, sticking the ice cream in the fridge. Was he avoiding her? Hell, maybe he just didn't want to hear whatever bad news bomb she was going to lob at him. He didn't want to hear her talk about leaving him. He didn't want to hear any of that, so yeah, in a way, he guessed he was avoiding her. He headed back to the room, and then shut the door behind him. Annie looked so pretty and so concerned that he moved to her side and pulled her against him.

Maybe he could kiss that worried frown off her face. Tipping a hand under her chin, he lifted her mouth and captured her lips with his in an intimate kiss, a slow, thoughtful one that would tell her just how much he adored her.

Annie pulled away from him, breathless, her eyes confused. "Are you trying to distract me?"

Busted. He chuckled. "Maybe a little."

"I do want to talk." Her gaze slid to his mouth and her

fingers toyed with the front of his shirt. "We can kiss, but after we discuss some stuff, okay?"

"All right." Dustin braced himself, ready to hear the worst. He concentrated on memorizing the feel of her body against him, just in case this was the last time he got to hold her tight. If she wanted to go, he wouldn't keep her, no matter how much it'd kill him, but it didn't mean that it wouldn't destroy him inside.

But this wasn't about just him and what he wanted, so he waited.

Annie took a deep breath . . . and then began. "Dustin, I need to know what your plans are."

His plans? He wanted to laugh with relief. Was that what the urgent, private conversation was going to be about? He gestured at the fat book on the dresser. "Well, first I'm going to read up about pregnancies, and then I'm going to shower—"

She patted his chest over his heart, frowning. "No, I mean . . . us. As a family. Or separate. What's your plan? What do you want?"

He captured her hand in his, brought her fingertips to his mouth and lightly kissed them. "You have to ask? I want us to be a family. You, me, and Morgan. It is Morgan, right?"

She nodded, a hint of a smile coaxing from her mouth. "I think so. And . . . I just want to be sure we both want this."

"I wanted you the moment I met you. That hasn't changed one bit. If anything, it's only intensified with every breath I take." He nipped at her fingers. "The baby is just a wonderful surprise."

"And where are we six months from now?" she asked, gazing up at him.

"Together, of course. Six months into a loving, happy relationship."

"I want that." Annie shook her head slightly. "But I

mean . . . where are we together? Where is our location? Where do you envision us?"

"Ah." He held her hand over his chest. "Well, my thing is I don't rightly care where we are as long as I'm with you and the baby."

"Do you want to stay in Wyoming?"

"If my other choice is LA? Yeah, I'd rather be out here." He grinned to take the sting out of his words, stroking his thumb over the back of her hand. "If you want to go back to California, I'll pack up here and go with you, but there's not a lot of cowboy work in that area, I hear."

"No, I imagine not." Her lips twitched with amusement.

"It'd make more sense for us to stay here in Wyoming," he ventured slowly, and then squeezed her hand. "I have steady work here, and there's room enough for both of us here at the ranch. But only if that's what you want to do."

Annie bit her lip. "I like the ranch. I like the people here, but adding another person and their dog is a change for everyone. Adding a person, their dog, and a newborn baby? That's going to be rough on everyone. Are you sure it's all right with Eli and Cass and Jordy and Old Clyde? I don't want to impose on them."

"Eli won't care. Cass will be thrilled. Old Clyde likes you, so he'd be fine with it, and he's good with babies, or so I hear." He rubbed her back, tucking her against him. "And Jordy, well, much as I like Jordy, the kid has different plans."

"Oh?"

"Yep. Told Eli a few weeks ago that he's joining the navy. We thought he was going to ship out in spring after calving, but it seems that there's some sort of incentive for him to join sooner, and so he leaves in about a month. We could always use his room as the baby's room once he moves out and then decide what to do if and when we get another ranch hand. It always takes a bit of time to replace someone."

"I see." She looked thoughtful, resting her cheek against him. "No one would mind if I stayed? You're sure?"

"Of course I'm sure."

"Because I'm training the dogs?"

Because I want to marry you, he wanted to tell her, but he bit back the words. Not yet. He wanted the proposal to be a surprise—and he wanted to do it in public so everyone in Painted Barrel would know that Annie was his. "Because you're with me," Dustin said, instead. "And nothing else matters. You don't have to train the dogs if you don't want to. You can take time off. If you want to do nothing but sit around and grow a baby for the next year, I'm totally fine with that."

She patted his stomach. "Wow, you really do need that baby book if you think it takes a year more to gestate a baby."

He laughed. "I'm just joking. In all seriousness, I want you to be happy. You said you were done with movies for now. Take time and figure out what you want to do. Write a script. Train more dogs. Hell, train the cattle to do tricks. I don't care as long as we're together." Dustin squeezed her hand again. "If you're worried about money, I have some. I have a nest egg I've been saving up for a while. It's more than enough to cover anything that'll come up for a while, so relax and let me take care of you for a bit."

For some reason, the mention of money just made her look even more worried. "What about you?"

"Well," he drawled, teasing, "I was kind of hoping I was still included in all these plans I'm talking about."

Annie blushed, glancing up at him. "You know what I mean. Doesn't this go against everything you wanted? Settling in one place? Staying in one location for a long time? Starting a family?" She hesitated, then continued. "Cass told me about the boat. How you'd been talking about it for a long time. I don't want you to abandon your dreams for me and the baby."

The boat.

Huh.

Funny, he hadn't thought about the boat in days now. It always seemed like an interesting idea for the future, something to do to alleviate the boredom of settling down in one place. He didn't feel that way anymore, though. The nagging, itching boredom was gone. Instead, all he could think about was the baby and Annie and a sense of anticipation for the future. They'd be shorthanded at the ranch come spring with Jordy leaving, but he was all right with that. Annie would be here, and Morgan would be here.

Just the thought of that brought a fierce happiness to him. "Plans change, Annie sweetheart. We go with the flow." And he leaned in and gave her another kiss.

She smiled up at him, but the uncertainty was still in her eyes.

It'd disappear when he gave her a ring, he figured. Dustin made a mental note to slip away from the ranch tomorrow and have a word with Hetty in town, kill two birds with one stone.

The sooner his Annie had his ring on her finger, she'd rest easier. And him?

He'd be so damned happy. His Annie. His baby.

For once in his life, it felt like that was all he needed, and that was a great feeling.

They made love gently and sweetly that night, and Annie was exhausted when she finally curled up in her nest of pillows, Dustin's big body behind her as they drifted off to sleep.

Well, he drifted. She remained awake, her mind worrying over their conversation. He told her not to worry about the boat. That it didn't mean anything to him now. That he was focused on her and the baby. It sounded wonderful, and just what she wanted to hear . . . which was why she worried about it, of course. She remembered a conversation with Dustin months ago, where he'd told her about his father and how he'd had to settle down once he'd gotten Dustin's mother pregnant.

Dustin had hated the thought of settling down so very much that he ran away from home.

And here they were, about to repeat history.

He couldn't be happy about it. No matter what he said to her, it had to be a big change to how he viewed his future, and the thought made her ache. It might not bother him right now, but in two months? Four? A year? If he was already talking about leaving the ranch in the spring and was staying now? She worried he'd come to resent both her and the baby for holding him back.

Annie loved him, she realized. It was fast, and it was messy—like much of their relationship—but she really, truly loved him. And because she loved him, she wanted his happiness . . . even if it wasn't with her. Even if it meant that they'd have to go their separate ways. He said this was what he wanted right now, though. He told her she was being silly and worrying over nothing.

Her heart hurt. She didn't know what to do. She knew she should leave and prompt him to leave, too. That if she was back in LA, he'd follow his dream of boating and exploring the coast. He could come visit them a few times a year, she figured. The baby would have the best of both worlds. Dustin would have his dream.

And Annie? Well. She'd figure something out, eventually. She wouldn't be happy with him gone, but she also didn't want to be the reason he felt trapped.

There was no right answer. She hugged one of the pillows against her chest and tried not to worry too much just yet.

CHAPTER NINETEEN

Life settled into an easy, comfortable pace for the next week. Annie loved being at the Price Ranch. There was always more to see and do, and the ranch chores were never-ending and always interesting. One day she and Cass took one of the all-terrain vehicles and hunted down the location of a few wandering cows while the men fixed the fence. One day they worked on setting up a beautiful changing table that Cass had ordered online, and it showed up with no instructions and thirty-two different pieces. They'd ended up giggling hysterically at the monstrosity they put together, and then turned the project over to Eli to finish.

It was nice to have a friend outside of work, and it was especially nice that they were both going through pregnancy at the same time. They shared advice and discussed things that they felt comfortable only talking about with each other and not their men. Cass gave Annie clothes, and Annie worked with Joy, who now went to her mat in the corner of the kitchen, tail politely wagging as she waited to be gifted cheese—every dog's favorite treat.

The others at the ranch didn't seem to mind Dustin's announcement that Annie would be staying for a while. In fact, they didn't even look surprised, which made Annie wonder if Dustin had perhaps had that conversation with them prior to having it with her.

Kitty texted Annie all day long, demanding pictures of her "fat belly" and then cooing over them. Cass referred Annie to an obstetrician in Casper that she went to. Cass was going to have a home birth and Doc Parsons—the vet at a nearby ranch—was going to attend her. No one thought this was weird, so Annie just rolled with it (though privately she still wanted a hospital and a doctor on hand).

Spidey had settled in, too. His nervousness had disappeared and he loved having the other dogs to play with. He followed Joy around all day as if she were his big sister, and when the cowboys came home at night, Spidey curled up with Moose and they shared toys as if brothers separated at birth. Moose, patient, silent soul that he was, tolerated all of it with the occasional meaningful look toward Dustin.

And Dustin . . . gosh.

Dustin was wonderful. Every day with him was better than the last. He made Annie feel special every day, and he showered her with constant affection now that he knew it was welcome. He pulled her into his lap, ignoring her protests, and held her while the others talked around the dinner table. He made sure to spend private time with her every night, away from the others, even if it was just quietly watching TV or reading a book together in his room. On the weekend, she'd complained that his sheets were old and worn, so he'd patiently driven her all over Casper while she shopped for new bedding, and then took her out to dinner. He held her hand everywhere they went, carried her bag when her back hurt, and turned the heads of every woman they passed by. It made Annie feel good to know that everyone appreciated how sexy her cowboy was, strangely enough. She wanted others to recognize how beautiful a man he was . . . while at the same time acknowledging he was hers.

Hormones, she supposed. She was full of them right now. Most of them manifested in weird crying fits, strange food cravings . . . and sex. She wanted sex all the time, even to the point that she'd wake up Dustin in the middle of the night. He was all too happy to oblige and never needed encouragement, and he always, always made sure she came at least once before he finished.

He was thoughtful, and sweet, and funny. He was so kind it made her heart ache. He was such a ridiculous flirt that she found it adorable and ridiculous at the same time.

She was crazy in love with him.

With every day that passed, she was also worried it wouldn't last. Maybe it was because her father had never been in the picture, or that they'd "broken up" for eight months. Whatever it was, every time Dustin smiled at her, Annie's heart squeezed a little more, and she tried to memorize his face.

Just in case all she would have at some point were memories.

"You're sure he has no idea?" Annie asked as Old Clyde parked his ancient truck on Main Street. It was a crisp, clear Thursday morning and Jordy was leaving on Sunday to visit family before joining the navy. They'd decided to throw him a party and had worked out almost all the details with Wade at the bar. The celebration would be held Saturday night, and Annie needed to check with Wade to see what he needed to ensure that everything was in place, and to put down a deposit to hold their tables.

"Jordy? Know about the party? Boy's got all the intuition of a sack of rocks," Old Clyde told her, opening his door and slapping his leg. "C'mon Gable. C'mon Leigh. You too, Spidey."

Annie watched with amusement as the trio of dogs headed after the elderly cowboy. She didn't know if she should feel jealous that Spidey seemed to love everyone (and every dog) at the ranch so much that he didn't shadow her nearly as much anymore as he used to. Still, she was happy to see that he was having so much fun. Clyde loved him, too. She often found him sitting in his favorite chair at the ranch, Spidey sitting on his lap with his round head being scratched, grunting in bliss.

"Before we head to the bar, I gotta make a pit stop at the souvenir shop," Clyde told her. "Be right back."

"Okay," Annie said, bewildered. She remained bewildered when he appeared a moment later with a bundle of fresh flowers.

"Hetty gets a shipment every Thursday," was all Clyde said in explanation. "You need to run errands before we head to the bar to talk to Gus?"

"Oh." Annie hesitated at the pointed look he gave her. "I thought, uh, I'd stop by the library?" It was more like Painted Barrel's "library" was two shelves of donated books in the city hall-slash-post-office, but she thought she'd see if they had books on anything of interest, like gardening. She'd been thinking about starting one in the spring, just to see what she could grow, and Clyde had told her she'd need to run errands before he'd be ready to go to the bar. She had no idea why he was so adamant about it, but when he crossed the street, the three dogs trotting at his heels, she watched as he headed to the front desk of the Painted Barrel Hotel and offered the flowers to the elderly woman behind the counter.

Aw. Did Clyde have a girlfriend? That was sweet. Annie

made a mental note to tell Cass that they needed to make sure she was invited to the party on Saturday. How stinking adorable. She found herself smiling at the pair of them through the window, and then when Old Clyde glanced out on the street and scowled in her direction, she quickly turned away, heading for the city hall. Clyde wasn't much for "sappy stuff" as he liked to put it, and he wouldn't appreciate her knowing. That was all right; she'd tell Dustin all about it when she got home.

Home.

Funny how the ranch had become "home" so very quickly. How she'd settled in so fast. How being with Dustin could make her feel so very complete, down to her bones. Just one slow, flirty smile from him made her feel like the sexiest, most attractive woman on earth. One word from him could leave her smiling for hours, and one touch of his hand could make her feel so safe. So content.

Yeah, she had it bad.

Smiling to herself, Annie walked (well, waddled) down Main Street, a hand at her lower back. Everything seemed to be spreading a bit more lately, which meant she was less graceful each day. But the baby flipped and turned and danced in her belly, and so she figured there were worse things than being a bit ungainly. She headed slowly down Main, heading toward the city hall . . . and then paused.

There was the pharmacy.

Theresa might be inside.

Annie's stomach clenched and she stared at the little sign, wondering if she should go in.

She'd been avoiding her for days now, though, and at some point she was going to have to confront her and settle things, if only so Annie could move forward. Taking a deep breath, she pushed open the door to the pharmacy and stepped inside.

The buxom blonde was behind the counter, dressed in a

tight golden sheath dress that looked completely appropriate for fall and completely inappropriate for working a cash
register. She leaned against the counter, talking to a gray-
haired man holding a cowboy hat, smiling up at him with a
flirty look, her bright red lips in a welcoming smile. Theresa was beautiful, Annie realized again, and it made her
ache. Her figure was a perfect hourglass, her breasts perky
and prominent, and her hips were something that would
make Marilyn Monroe jealous. That should have been
enough for any one woman, but she was also gorgeous to
boot. Annie felt frumpy and bloated as she stood in the
pharmacy in her maternity pants with the gathered waist
and oversize green poncho sweater.

Both of them turned to look at Annie, and the look on
Theresa's face changed from welcoming to sour, her eyes
narrowing.

The gray-haired cowboy beamed at her, though. "Well,
well! You must be Annie. Dustin's told me so much about
you." He extended his hand in a warm welcome.

"He has?" Annie echoed, surprised and pleased.

"Of course. I ran into him chasing down a few cattle on
the border of our ranches and he told me all about his Annie and baby Morgan." He gave her stomach a happy smile.
"I'm Doc Parsons from Swinging C."

"Oh! You're going to help Cass with her baby," Annie
remembered, a smile coming to her face. "We haven't had
a chance to meet! I'm Annie." Then she blushed, realizing
he already knew that.

But Doc only winked at her. "Pleased to meet you. I'm
just up on the side of the mountain, so if you ever need
anything and that man of yours isn't around, give me a call.
Happy to help out."

"Thank you," she told him, touched by his offer. How
long had she lived in LA less than a hundred feet from her
closest neighbor and never met them? This man lived a fair

drive away—a ranch "neighbor" might be miles and miles up the road—but was offering freely to help out. "I really appreciate it."

"I was just telling Doc there must be something in the water up there at Price Ranch," Theresa said, her tone sweet but her smile catty. "So many babies."

"Two isn't exactly a baby boom," Doc said, and squeezed Annie's hand in either sympathy or support. "I'll be at the party for Jordy on Saturday. You'll be there?" When she nodded, he gave her another wink. "See you then. And call me anytime. Pleasure to meet you."

"You too," she murmured, forcing herself to keep smiling politely even though she wanted to move over to the pharmacy counter and snatch that bright blonde hair off of Theresa's gorgeous head.

Hormones, she told herself. It was hormones making her violent.

Doc left the pharmacy a moment later, and the two women stared at each other in silence. Finally, Theresa broke the tension with a tight smile. "I have to give you credit for being clever. Wish I'd thought of getting knocked up. Then maybe I'd be standing there instead of here."

"No one planned this," Annie blurted, then could have kicked herself. There was no point in explaining anything to Theresa. She wouldn't listen. "You and I need to talk."

"I have nothing to say to you." She grabbed a magazine from the counter, sat down on the stool, and crossed her legs, angrily flipping through the fashion pictures. "You can leave at any time now."

"Are you this unpleasant to everyone or am I just lucky?" My goodness, where did that come from? Hormones. Had to be hormones. She was going to blame everything on hormones for the next two months. "Because if anyone should be mad at anyone, I should be mad at you for lying to me."

Theresa gave the magazine another angry flip and

glanced up at her. "What about? I didn't lie to you. I barely talked to you, bitch. In fact, I'd prefer to keep it that way." And she pointed at the door.

This woman was like a cartoon villain. Good lord. "You told me that you were Dustin's girlfriend!"

"I am!"

Delusional, too. "No, you're not. He told me he only went out with you twice. In fact, everyone I've talked to says that you two aren't dating."

Theresa rolled her eyes. "It's called the 'long game,' honeybun. I'm letting him realize how much he needs me before I make my move. When he's ready to settle down, I'll be right here."

"You . . . do realize I'm with him, right?"

"Temporarily," Theresa acknowledged with a sniff. "Only because you're apparently fertile as hell." She shrugged. "He'll get tired of you squashing his dreams and come back to me. I can wait."

For a cartoon villain, Theresa certainly knew where to hit. Annie clenched her hands. "Squashing his dreams?"

"Oh. Did you not know?" Her smile was pretty . . . and petty. "About his boat and his dreams of sailing around the coast? Doc and I were just talking about that." She gave her head a little shake. "Poor Dustin, trapped by his good heart. He had plans to leave in the spring and travel, you know. He told me all about it. I guess dreams don't matter when you have a baby on the way, though." She shrugged one slim shoulder. "I just wonder how long you'll be enough for him, you know? I'd never make him give up his dreams." Her smile turned bitter. "I understand having something so close to your reach only to have it snatched away."

Her hand on her stomach, Annie sucked in a breath and left the pharmacy without saying another word. What an awful, bitter woman. Outside, she took deep, gusty lungfuls of air and tried not to panic. Normally she cried at the drop of a hat, but today, there were no tears. She just felt oddly numb inside.

Theresa had said everything that Annie herself was worried about. Dustin had dreams and plans before she'd come back. He'd had goals and apparently he'd told everyone in town about them.

And he was giving it all up for her and baby Morgan. Annie caressed the growing bulge of her belly and tried not to feel guilty. She'd never implied that he had to stay or that he had to give up his dreams . . . so why did she feel like she was going to ruin his life by having his baby?

Dustin drove the fence post into the ground and then paused to wipe his brow as Eli pushed his boot into the earth around it, locking it temporarily in place. He glanced up at the skies, sunny and bright blue despite the fall, and it was almost unseasonably warm. He liked it, though. "Nice day."

Eli gave him an odd look. "Same day as any other."

"Yeah, but today just seems . . . I don't know. Nice." Dustin grinned at him. "I'm turning into a lovesick fool, aren't I?"

"Just a hair," the other cowboy said drily. "But I guess I can't hold that much against you. Imagine I was the same around Cass when she first moved in."

"Only then?" Dustin joked, and then moved out of the way when Eli kicked a clod of dirt in his direction. He chuckled, picking up his post pounder and then moving along to the next one. The cattle had leaned on this end of the fence—damn things loved a good lean in the sunlight— and knocked out every post for a good stretch. They'd rounded up the runners this morning and while Clyde was driving them into the nearest pasture, Eli and Dustin fixed the fence. It was an inconvenience, sure, but ranching meant doing whatever chores came up that day, and a lot of the time, it was just fixing fence.

For some reason, it didn't bother him at all. It might have a few months ago, but now he looked at it as an opportunity to spend time in the sunlight, to get sweaty with a day's work, and of course, he had Annie to go home to.

Way he saw it, things were pretty damn perfect.

Eli straightened, wiped his brow, and glanced at the distant herd. "Gonna be a busy spring," he said, voice deceptively mild. "What with Jordy taking off and all."

"He's still a kid," Dustin agreed. "Still has wild oats to sow. He wants to see the world. It'll be good for him."

"He ain't the only one that wanted to see the world," Eli said pointedly.

"*Mmm*," was all Dustin said.

Eli grunted, shrugging his shoulders. "Well, talked to Doc Parsons the other day. They sold off a bunch of their cattle in the last roundup and haven't seen fit to replace just yet. Money flow problems, I imagine."

"Happens." Dustin waited.

"He was supposed to get a guy there in the spring to help out with calving, but won't have the work for him. Reckon we could offer him a spot here. Doc's nephew. Says he's a good guy, was a little wild when he was younger but he's settled in well. Did some ranching for a summer in Montana. Looking to settle in."

"Well, he'll need some training, most like, but they all do," Dustin said agreeably. "Another pair of hands will be useful given we've got a hundred more cattle than last spring, and that one was a doozy."

"Another set of hands would be good," Eli echoed, and then shot Dustin a look. "Curious what your plans are. Friend to friend and all."

"For the spring?"

Eli shrugged. "Spring. Fall. Winter. Everything. You

talked about moving on. Said you had restless feet. Talked about the boat until I wanted to shove your head underwater at the nearest pier in Florida." When Dustin just laughed, Eli continued. "Thought I was gonna lose two ranch hands instead of just one, but you clammed up the moment Annie showed up. I'm wondering if anything's changed with your plans or if your boat's just gonna seat three instead of one." He put his hands on his hips and studied Dustin. "I'm not telling you to go or to stay. I just need to know so I can make plans for the spring. I'm gonna have a new baby on the way, too. Won't be good for my wife if I'm out twenty-three hours a day. She'll need help with the kid."

Dustin nodded. It made sense. More than any of them, Eli felt a sense of obligation to the Price Ranch. He'd been here a long time. Not as long as Old Clyde, but as time went on, Clyde was content to let Eli run things. Dustin knew Eli was stressing over Cass and the upcoming baby, and the plans for the spring. He'd never show it, but then again, Eli never talked all that much, and he was just chatting up a storm this morning, which meant he was fishing for answers from Dustin. He needed to know where the other man stood, and Dustin understood that. If he was in Eli's spot, he'd be wondering the same thing. "You don't have to worry about me."

"I never 'worry' about you," Eli replied, voice dry. "I'm just a mite curious is all."

Dustin glanced at the distant mountains, the sky, the rolling grasses, the herd as it was carefully led off to the nearest pasture. It was quiet and peaceful right now, the weather nice and just lightly frosty with a hint of snow on the horizon. There'd be more snow in the upcoming months, so much that he'd get sick of it before it was gone. He'd thought he wouldn't stick around for another Wyoming winter . . . or if he did, it'd be his last one. Now, well . . . now he found himself looking forward to what Annie would think of the snow. The smile on her face when the dogs played in it.

The smile on her face when she welcomed him home, Morgan in her arms.

He found he was smiling, too. "It's funny," he began. "Never pictured myself as a family man, but now when I think about being happy, they're the first thing I think of. Not Florida. Not a boat." He shrugged. "Just home and my girl and my kid." He glanced over at Eli. "The restlessness is gone. It wasn't that I wanted to go to Florida or wanted to spend my time boating, really. I just wanted a new adventure."

"And now?"

"Adventure sounds good and all, but it's not the right time for it. I'm more interested in family and coming home to them every night. Putting in a good day's worth of work and then spending my evening with them." Dreams changed, he was realizing. Before, he thought there was nothing better than meeting new faces, seeing new people and places every time he opened his door. Now, when he thought about happiness, it involved the same people. The same places.

Annie's smile.

"So you're staying?" Eli asked.

"For as long as you'll have me and as long as Annie's happy," Dustin agreed.

"Good." He clapped a hand on Dustin's shoulder. "Now that we're done talking about the sappy stuff, let's finish this fence."

Sounded good to Dustin.

CHAPTER TWENTY

Dustin might have the sexiest butt in this part of Wyoming, Annie reasoned, but he was also the most disorganized man ever. She shook her head in a mix of fondness and exasperation as she cleaned out drawer after drawer in his dressers. So far she'd found photos mixed with socks, underwear mixed with sheets, pillowcases under a packet of paperwork, and she still had no idea where he kept his shirts. In the closet, probably under his boots, she thought with a snort.

This was a project she'd been wanting to tackle for a few days now, but she'd hesitated because it felt suspiciously like digging through his things and snooping. She'd asked Dustin about it last night as they'd lain in bed, snuggling, and he was fine with it. He told her she needed to make room for her own stuff, and he had no secrets from her, so she could clean and organize to her heart's content. Then, he'd kissed the heck out of her and told her to do it tomorrow.

So . . . here it was, tomorrow.

She smiled absently to herself, still feeling the press of his lips against hers, the way his teeth had expertly nipped her ear, the way his mouth . . . well. *Ahem.* Now she was getting herself all worked up and he wouldn't be home for hours. She forced herself to concentrate on the project at hand as she opened another dresser drawer and found it full of receipts. Oh dear. This man really was the worst at organizing. She threw all the papers in a box and then sat at the tiny table in the corner to go through them. She wasn't sure what he needed to keep, but she could organize them by date, at least, and then go over them later. Picking through the paperwork, she smiled happily to herself. Was this nesting? She'd heard it was something pregnant women did when they wanted to prepare for the baby. Cass was a busy bee around the ranch despite her upcoming due date, but Cass was also on the payroll as the housekeeper. It made sense for her to dig into every chore possible. Annie helped, of course, because she couldn't sit around and do nothing all day. She glanced around Dustin's masculine room and pictured it with a few small things of her own here and there, intermingled with his items. She'd have to send for her things in Los Angeles . . . and she'd probably need to invite Kitty out for the birth, even if Kitty probably wouldn't leave California. Idly she made a mental note to ask if there was room for her mother to stay at the ranch or if it would be better to have her in town.

Probably town. Kitty liked to wear heels and she wouldn't last five minutes outside in those. Annie pictured her glamorous mother in Wyoming and bit back a chuckle. She'd wither at the realization that there was no Starbucks for miles and miles. Still, it'd be good to see her. Despite her glamorous facade, Kitty liked children, but she might balk at being called "grandma." There were a few years for that yet, at least.

Annie's searching hands slid over a pamphlet, and she idly picked it up and flipped through it.

Her heart stopped in her chest.

It was the usual sales brochure, advertising a high-priced item. This one in particular was for a boat. She flipped through the pages, gazing at the pictures. She didn't know anything about watercraft or boating but this one seemed nice enough . . . and small. Very small. Room-enough-for-only-one person small. He'd kept this. But then again, he'd kept receipts for gas stations and drive-thrus so maybe he was just a receipt hoarder. It didn't mean anything.

She flipped to the back of the thick booklet and a printed piece of paper fell out even as she noticed there was scribbled writing in the back of the pamphlet. Annie recognized Dustin's handwriting, and there was a phone number and a name scrawled on the booklet—Marcus S—along with a few words and prices. She picked up the piece of paper and saw it was an email, from the same person.

Mr. Worthington,

Your option selections won't be a problem at all! I can send you the new quote, but if you won't need financing, a cash payment in person will do just fine. I've talked with the dock manager at the marina of your choice and they can reserve a slip for you when you're ready. The boat can be there to meet you the moment you step foot in Florida. Just let me know when you're ready to pull the trigger and we'll make this happen. Can't wait for you to enjoy your new Islander!

Marcus Salter
Sales Manager
Islander Dreams

The knot in her throat felt enormous. Annie fought to swallow. Dustin had mentioned that the boat wasn't serious. That it was just fine to give up that dream, but for some reason, she'd thought it was something he was talking about in the distant future. A "someday" sort of dream. A man that contacted a salesman and picked out options—who'd already discussed payment and boat slips—wasn't a man that had a distant dream. That was a man working to make the dream happen. The email was dated two months ago, and her stomach plummeted.

Two months ago, he didn't know Annie was pregnant. Two months ago, his future was completely different.

He was going to resent her for changing everything, she knew. He'd pitied his father so much that he'd left town, never to return, and here she was, about to turn him into the same man.

How could she do this to Dustin if she loved him? Annie set down the brochure and wept.

Annie couldn't stop thinking about that damn boat.
      She didn't say anything about it to Dustin, of course. He'd just reassure her that everything was fine, even if it wasn't. He'd give her a laughing smile, tease her, and then kiss her until she was distracted and that would be the end of it. So she said nothing, even though she thought about it.

And thought about it.

And thought about it.

It was on her mind all through the evening. Dustin commented that she was distracted, so she went out of her way to be attentive and loving. They watched a movie with the others in the living area, and she snuggled next to Dustin on the couch as he held her hand. She might have wept extra hard at the parting goodbye of the two characters at the end of the movie, but she blamed her sobbing on hormones. Hormones were an easy answer.

That night, she told Dustin she was too tired for sex and so he just held her close and murmured in her ear how much he loved her and how he couldn't wait to meet Morgan, and she wanted to cry all over again.

The next day, she thought about the boat even though it was a busy day, full of preparations for the going-away party. She and Cass drove out to Casper to hit up the big grocery stores there and then a party supply store for paper plates and banners and decorations. They picked up an enormous cake at a bakery and then hauled it all to the private room in Wade's bar so it would be ready for the party a few hours later. Cass seemed distracted, which was good, because then she didn't ask about the fact that Annie was rather distracted, herself. They headed back to the ranch to change clothes, wait for the men to come in and wash up, and then everyone headed into Painted Barrel for the celebration.

Everyone in town, it felt, had shown up for Jordy's going away. The bar was more crowded than Annie had ever seen it, but it made her glad that Jordy was so loved. Drink after drink was bought for the young cowboy, and he was patted on the back and hugged by everyone. The decorations were nice, the food they'd brought was being gobbled down at a record pace, and it was a good party.

She should have been happy.

Instead, all she could think about was that stupid, stupid boat and Dustin's tanned arms as he worked the ropes on the sails. How his eyes would light up as he went to each new location. How much he'd enjoy the adventure of it all.

How the cabin was built for one person only.

"Speech!" someone called out as Jordy was handed another beer, and then the entire room picked up the chorus. "Speech!" more people called. "Speech! Speech!"

Laughing, Jordy stood atop one of the round wooden

tables. He was handed another full mug of beer, and he took a long drink—to much applause—before clearing his throat. "I want to say thank you to everyone here in Painted Barrel for making a greenhorn like me feel welcome." At that, there were more cheers. "Just because I'm leaving doesn't mean that it'll be forever, or that I won't miss each and every one of you. This town really made me feel like I belonged, and I thank you all for it. Now, if you don't mind, I'll be off to serve my country." With that, he chugged the rest of his beer.

Annie smiled, Dustin's arm around her waist as she clapped. Jordy was a good guy and she'd miss seeing him around. He had the sunniest personality, as if nothing fazed him, and she wished she could be more like him. More carefree. Instead, she was wondering if she was ruining the life of the person she loved most in the world.

As if he could hear her worried thoughts, Dustin glanced down at her and gave her hip a gentle squeeze, a silent question. She smiled up at him, and he leaned down and kissed her gently, and she felt her heart break all over again.

Jordy put a hand up, still on his perch up on the table. "Wait, wait guys. Before I get down, I wanted to say that there are people here tonight that are very important to me. Their happiness is very important to me." He was so drunk he was slurring, Annie noticed with a wry smile. He turned and pointed around the room. "Eli and Cass. They've been great to me. Like my own parents."

Eli wore a smile on his hard face, but Annie noted that Cass looked distracted, her face tight. She hoped Cass wasn't feeling sick. Earlier she'd mentioned her back was hurting again. Annie made a mental note to go and talk to her once Jordy's speech was done.

Jordy turned again, pointing this time at Old Clyde. The weathered cowboy had his hat on, and his arm was around the gray-haired Constance, who ran the hotel. "This guy here," Jordy continued. "This guy's the best damn cowboy I ever met, even if he did make me stick my hand in the uterus of every cow from here to Oregon."

The room filled with titters.

"And Dustin," Jordy said. "Dustin's a great, great, great, great guy." At Annie's side, Dustin snorted. "Great, great," Jordy continued. "Unselfish and very caring. And good taste in women." He gave Annie a drunken, obvious wink. "In fact, his taste is so great, Imma let him take the floor for a moment."

Annie's smile grew a little confused. Take the floor? Were they all going to give speeches, then? Her social anxiety flared, just a little.

"First, let's get you down off that table," Dustin said, letting go of Annie and stepping forward. He helped Jordy down, gave the other man a pat on the shoulder, and when Jordy flung his arms around Dustin, ended up bear-hugging the guy. Dustin watched with amusement as Jordy bear-hugged Eli and Clyde both, and then he turned back to Annie.

The entire room was watching them now. Dustin smiled at her.

Annie felt a cold sweat break out over her body.

What was this?

Dustin extended a hand toward Annie, and when she put her fingers in his grip, he tugged her out on the floor in front of everyone. Her nervous sweating intensified, and she wanted to run and hide. It wasn't that she didn't want to be with Dustin, but did it have to be practically a performance in front of the entire town? Everywhere she looked, people were smiling at them with knowing expressions, as if there was a secret they were all in on except her.

And that made her stomach clench all over again.

"Annie," Dustin began, holding both her hands and gazing at her. "You and I met here at this very bar about eight and a half months ago. If I remember correctly, I hit on you and you were distinctly uninterested." A few chuckles rose from the group. He just grinned down at her. "That was when I knew you were the one for me." More laughter.

Oh no. No, no no. This was wonderful and a nightmare both.

"After that initial meeting, we connected right away and I fell in love with your generous spirit, your sense of self, and the way you always knew exactly what you wanted in life. I thought, now there's a woman to fall in love with. She's a keeper. And I made it my goal to win you over. I, ah, had a bit of a speedbump along the way, though, and we were apart for seven months."

More laughter rippled through the group.

Annie smiled. She smiled, but it felt painful. She knew what was coming, and she wanted it even though she knew she shouldn't. This loving, public confession could only lead up to one thing. She tried to pull her hand from his, shaking her head to signal him to stop.

Dustin ignored it. He gave her hand a squeeze, mistaking her reluctance for shyness. "Since we've been together again, I've never been happier. I can see myself with you and our child, sharing adventures and enjoying life. I can see us growing old together, and that's why I wanted to do this tonight."

He dropped to one knee.

She burst into tears.

"Annie Grissom," Dustin continued, smiling. "I love you. I want to be with you for the rest of my life. Will you marry me?"

Annie wanted to say yes. Oh, she wanted to say yes.

But she kept thinking of that traitorous boat. Of Dustin telling her about his father.

"Please, please get up," she whispered, tugging at his hand again. "Let's not do this here."

He got to his feet, a hint of a frown on his handsome face as he pulled her close to him. "Annie, I wanted to do this publicly so everyone in town would know how serious I am about you," he whispered. "I want them to know that you're it for me. That you're my woman and I love you—"

"I love you too, but we can't do this right now," she continued, panicked. "Please. Let's go home and talk."

His eyes flared with hurt as the once-laughing room got deathly quiet.

"Annie," Dustin said quietly. "Do you not want to marry me?"

His words sounded as loud as a shotgun in the stillness. She inwardly winced, and swiped at her cheeks with one hand that she managed to wrestle free from his grip. "I want to," she admitted, voice teary. "But . . . Dustin, I can't."

"Why? Why not?" The look on his face was intense. "Tell me—"

A low groan echoed in the room and all heads suddenly turned toward Cass, who sagged against her husband.

"Not to be a party pooper," Cass panted, clutching at her stomach. Her skirt was suspiciously wet down the front. "But I think my water just broke."

CHAPTER TWENTY-ONE

The nearest medical center was a good half hour away, so Cass was cleaned up, given towels to sit on, and then driven back to the ranch with Eli and Doc Parsons sandwiching her in the truck.

Dustin and Annie rode back in Dustin's truck, and it was utterly quiet between the two of them. Annie could tell Dustin was upset. She didn't blame him. She just sat and cried and stole glances over at him as he drove, his jaw clenched and his gaze locked to the roads.

"I guess I'm confused," he said finally, and she looked over at him. His hands gripped the steering wheel so tightly she could see his white knuckles. "About what this is between us. I thought you loved me, Annie."

Oh god. She hated how much raw pain was in his voice, how much betrayal. "I do, Dustin. I really do love you. But . . . I think this is all wrong. We can't get married."

"Why not? I thought that's what people did when they

loved each other?" He looked over at her. "When they have a baby on the way."

"I don't want you to marry me just for the baby—"

"I'm not and you know it."

She did. She tried again. "Dustin. You had plans and dreams before I showed up pregnant on your doorstep. Those plans and dreams did not involve starting a family right away. Those dreams did not involve staying in one town for a long time with a family to support. Those aren't your dreams, and I know it. Those are your nightmares."

He gave her a narrow-eyed look. "That's not true."

"It is true!" Annie cried. "Dustin, when we first met, you told me all about your father and how you hated the choices he'd made. You didn't see how he could give up his dreams to stay home and marry the woman he got pregnant. What do you think we're doing? You wanted to go to Florida. You wanted to buy a boat. You wanted to sail the coast and explore new places. Last time I looked, this wasn't it." She spread her hands wide. "This is the same place you've been for the last few years, you got me pregnant, and now we're settling down, and I keep thinking in my head that this is never what you wanted, and I keep waiting for the day that you start to hate me."

"Hate you?" This time the look he gave her was incredulous. "Are you insane? Annie, I love you. I'm thrilled you're pregnant. I can't wait for our life to start together. I would never hate you."

"You say that now," she continued stubbornly. "It's only been a few weeks. What about when work turns into the same old, same old and the baby needs his diaper changed at two in the morning? What about ten years from now when you're in the exact same town doing the exact same job, except you have me and the baby holding you back? Are you still going to be thrilled? Or are you going to wish you'd made other choices?"

"I won't regret you and Morgan, if that's what you're asking."

Her heart squeezed painfully to hear him say the baby's name, as if he—or she—were already part of the family. "Dustin," she said softly. "I love you. I love you with all my heart and soul. But if the timing's not right for us, it's just not right. There's nothing wrong in admitting that. It's better than trying to make this something that it shouldn't be."

"So what are you saying?" His tone was flat, dead.

Annie continued, because it needed to be said. "I'm saying that you shouldn't change all of your plans because of me. I came back here not because I wanted to demand that you take part in the baby's life, but because I felt you had a right to know. I didn't expect to fall in love with you." Her voice choked on the words. "And I think that's wonderful, but I can also admit when the timing is all wrong."

"Maybe it's not the timing that's wrong," he said, voice harsh. Dustin wouldn't look at her. He stared straight ahead at the dark road. "Maybe you're afraid of commitment."

"Maybe," she admitted. "But I can't marry you right now, Dustin. If I did, I'd be anxious for the rest of my life, worrying if this is the day that you wake up hating me for turning you into your father."

"That won't happen—"

"Really? Have you called him?"

"Huh?" He turned and stared at her, confused.

"Your father. You've had such a spiritual change of heart . . . have you called him? Told him you were wrong all those years ago? That you're okay with going down the exact same path he did?" When his jaw clenched stubbornly and he turned his gaze back to the road, she knew she was right. "I'm not saying I don't love you. I'm just saying the timing isn't right for now."

"So what do you want from me, Annie?" His voice was hoarse with emotion.

She was going to start crying. Any moment now, she'd lose it. Somehow, though, she managed to continue speaking, her voice bright. "I want you to call that guy about the boat. I know you were close to pulling the trigger on it. Call him and go buy it. Go up and down the shore for as long and as often as you want. When the baby's ready to be born, I'll call you so you can be there. And when you're ready to settle down, I'll be waiting for you in Los Angeles." Her voice dropped. "And if that never happens, that's okay, too."

It was so quiet for so long that she wondered if he'd ever speak to her again.

"What about us?" Dustin's voice was gentle.

Her eyes burned with tears. "Maybe someday there will be a time for us, but I don't think it's now."

Cass's baby boy was born somewhere around three in the morning, just after Annie finished packing her bags. She held little Travis Elijah Pickett for a few minutes, telling Cass what a beautiful baby he was and smiling at proud Eli, who was grinning for what felt like the first time since she'd met him. She admired the baby for a few minutes, then handed him back to his mother and father, saying she had to go to sleep.

Then, she harnessed Spidey and slung her bag over her shoulder and went to say goodbye to Dustin. He was in his room, sitting in the rocking chair, the baby book in his hands, unopened. His normally laughing face was full of pain and her heart clenched all over again. She wondered if she was doing the right thing . . . but if she didn't give him the opportunity to seize his dreams now, they'd both regret it for the rest of their lives. He looked up at her with his heart in his beautiful eyes.

"Don't go, sweetheart."

She swallowed back the tears that threatened and went

to his side. When he got to his feet, she took his hand and clasped it in hers. "This isn't goodbye, all right? I still want to be part of your life. I still want you to be Morgan's daddy. Nothing on that end has changed." It was just her own happiness she was sacrificing.

"It changes everything and you know it." Dustin squeezed her hand, his eyes begging her to stay. "I would never resent you, Annie. I love you."

She smiled at him. Touched his cheek.

And left, because she didn't know what else to do or how to fix this. All she knew was that if she stayed and things continued like they were, one of them would regret it. And she was pretty sure it wouldn't be her.

Dustin had to decide on his own what he wanted, and he'd never be able to do that with her right in front of him, carrying his baby. She'd forced her hand on him once by returning, and she wouldn't do so again.

The drive back to Los Angeles was a long one. Annie hated every minute of it. She might have cried all through the drive out of Wyoming and Arizona and right into California itself. She was always crying it seemed, and this time, she couldn't blame the hormones. A dozen times she thought about turning around and returning. It was late, after all. The middle of the night. She could say she would be leaving soon enough and then just . . . not go. That would be easier. Dustin would welcome her back with open arms and kiss away her tears.

And then . . .

And then she'd be right back where she started, wondering about that boat and his happiness. Everyone in town had known that he wanted to leave. They'd known his wandering nature even before she did.

She was doing the right thing.

She was.

Why did it feel so very wrong, then? Like she was making a huge mistake?

Annie drove all night. She was tired, but the thought of going to a hotel and sleeping alone filled her with despair, so she kept driving. She stopped every hour to use the restroom, or grab a snack, and to walk Spidey. She was so lost in her own thoughts that she was on the outskirts of Los Angeles before she realized it. Home already.

Except, even as she drove up to the familiar driveway of her mother's even-more-familiar house, it didn't feel like "home" anymore. Home was with Dustin. Home was a sprawling ranch house nestled in the mountains of Wyoming where a few cowboys and one cowboy's wife lived. Home was the man she loved waiting for her with a smile.

She wondered if she'd ever feel at home again.

Annie parked the car, unbuckled her dog, and then headed inside. Kitty came out of the kitchen, a martini glass in her hand, her heavily penciled brows rising at the sight of her very pregnant daughter. "Home already? I thought you were staying."

"Hi, Kitty. Bye, Kitty," Annie said, dropping her bag and heading to her bedroom. She'd talk to her mother later.

"Oh no, that's not enough of an answer," Kitty said, following her, the skewered olive making a *tink* noise in her glass. "Why are you back?"

Annie eased onto her bed—no dramatic belly flop when seven months pregnant—and hugged her pillow. "Because Dustin asked me to marry him and I said no."

"Hmm." Kitty sat down on the opposite side of the bed. "Why?"

"I don't want to talk about it, Mom."

"You know I hate it when you call me that. And if you don't want to talk about it, your mother's just going to have to guess." Kitty took a sip of her martini, thinking. "He's got a wife."

"No."

"He's up to his ears in debt."

"No. Mom, seriously, just leave me alone."

Kitty gave her a pointed look for using "mom" instead of her name. "He's got a raging venereal disease—"

"Mom!"

"Then what is it?" Kitty gave her a pointed look, and when Annie closed her eyes, Kitty poked her in the shoulder with a manicured nail. "This isn't like you, darling."

"I love him. But I don't think we can be together."

Kitty was silent, so Annie opened an eye and looked over at her mother. Sure enough, her mother was squinting at her, a line furrowing her normally immovable brow. "Why ever not? He wants to stay in that hideous Wyoming and you wanted to come home to civilization, right?"

She sighed. It was clear that Kitty was going to guess—and keep guessing incorrectly—until Annie answered her. So she told her mother the entire story—of how Dustin's parents had settled down and his father had been trapped into a marriage of convenience for the baby's sake. How Dustin had vowed that would never be him and had left home. About the damned boat and how everyone in town knew about it, so it meant something to Dustin. About her fears of becoming the thing that held him back from his dreams. When she was done speaking, Kitty was silent. She stroked Annie's hair back from her face and sipped her martini thoughtfully.

"Well?" Annie prompted, curious.

"Do you want me to sugarcoat it, darling? Or do you want me to tell you what I really think?"

"Tell me what you really think."

"I think you're being foolish, darling." She gave Annie's shoulder a little pat. "This is a stupid idea."

Annie frowned at her mother. "I think I should have asked you to sugarcoat it."

"You have a man that wants to be the father of your child. He obviously has money or he wouldn't be buying a boat. He loves you. He's handsome—I assume he's handsome, yes?" She shrugged. "I don't see the problem here."

Annie propped up on one elbow and gave her mother an odd look. "And if he resented me?"

"It's marriage, darling. It's not meant to last forever. Is Wyoming one of those states that gives you half his money if you divorce? If so then I'd say you really messed up."

She lay back down again, closing her eyes. It figured that her mother would look at it that way. "Forget I asked."

Kitty took another drink of her martini. "Don't be mad, darling."

"I thought you'd be supportive. You, of all people, the most independent woman in Hollywood who has no time for any man."

"I didn't say I didn't want a husband, Annie." Kitty's voice turned gentle. "I said he didn't want me. I told him about you and he rejected me and the baby both. That destroyed me and for years I wondered if I was doing you a disservice—if I should find some low-end producer or even a cameraman like Julia Roberts and just get married so you could have a father figure in your life. Do you think if your father had wanted me that I'd have walked away? Everyone wants to be loved, darling." She patted Annie on the shoulder. "Just don't be so quick to push him away because you're worried about being rejected."

"That's not what this is—"

"I'm your mother, darling." Kitty's expression grew wise. "You think I don't know my own daughter? You ran away from him once because you were afraid of getting hurt. Now you're doing it all over again for the same reason. At some point you're going to have to acknowledge that your problem is not entirely of his making."

Annie just stared at her mother. That sounded . . . wise. And startlingly close to home.

Kitty beamed at her. "See? And you thought all those prismatic therapy sessions were a waste. Your color right now is very, very purple. Purple is the shade of regrets, Annie dear." She paused, considering. "I think. Maybe it's blue."

The baby kicked in Annie's belly and she shook her head. What was done was done. Dustin deserved to be able to make his own choices, and she'd give him that at the very least. So she patted the bed, and when Spidey hopped up next to her, she hugged her little dog against her pregnant belly and closed her eyes. "I'm tired, Mom."

"You sleep, darling. I'm meeting the girls for happy hour. Call me if you need anything!"

Kitty exited in a flourish of tinkling jewelry and Annie was alone with her dog. She rubbed his ears and snout, thinking. Was her mother right? Was Annie running before she had the chance to have her heart broken? Was this just another excuse because she was worried Dustin would abandon her like her father had Kitty?

There were no simple answers, only more questions.

And hormonal tears. There were always more hormonal tears.

Stupid hormones.

CHAPTER TWENTY-TWO

Dustin threw himself into work for two days straight. Eli was busy tending to Cass and the new baby, so Dustin worked from sunup to sundown herding the cattle, fixing posts, baling hay, and chasing down rogue calves. It was just him and Old Clyde and the dogs, since Jordy had left. He'd offered to stay behind, but Dustin and Clyde said they could handle it.

In a way, it was good to be overwhelmed with work. Every calf that ran into a patch of nettles, every cow that needed antibiotics shots because it'd caught a cold, every busted fence meant another moment he didn't have to think about Annie leaving him. He could push down the sense of betrayal he felt, the despair at knowing she was gone. He could ignore the hollow ache in his chest.

Nights were the worst.

His bed was cold and empty, his sheets still carrying her scent. Down the hall, Cass and Eli's new baby wailed and was quickly appeased.

So he worked and he tried to forget.

After about two days of this, though, he got sick of it. He pitched hay in the barn and when Moose ran up to him and offered his paw, cocking his head, his first thought was to tell Annie about it. Then, grief and despair hit when he realized she wasn't there. He pulled out his phone, thought for a moment, and then texted her.

DUSTIN: Are we not speaking or can I say hello to you?

ANNIE: We can absolutely talk, of course. I don't hate you, Dustin. I just think it's best if we figure out what we want before we charge into anything. Please understand.

DUSTIN: I'm trying. I miss you, though.

ANNIE: I know. I don't want to say I miss you too because then this all sounds crazy.

DUSTIN: You said it, not me.

ANNIE: You always know how to make me smile. Btw, Morgan is a feisty one today.

DUSTIN: How's she doing?

ANNIE: Have we decided it's a girl now? I'm still pretty sure it's a boy.

DUSTIN: Call it cowboy intuition.

ANNIE: Sounds good to me.

ANNIE: I like this. I like talking to you. We . . . we
can be friends, right?

Even though it killed him to think of them as "just
friends," he sent her back an answer.

DUSTIN: Absolutely.

After a few more days, Eli began to leave Cass's side for
longer periods of time and returned to helping out the
others. It was a quiet period for them right now. The calves
were old enough to not need constant monitoring, the
weather wasn't too bad, and birthing season wasn't for
months yet. Things settled down.

Which was good, because Dustin needed to leave. He
talked to Eli and Clyde and told them he had to get some
stuff taken care of before he figured out what he was going
to do. Clyde just slapped him on the back, and Eli gave him
a knowing nod.

"When you come back, we'll have a spot for you," Eli
told Dustin. "If not . . . that's all right, too."

Dustin nodded, because he didn't know if he'd be back.
After a few days of being alone again, one thing was
certain—home wasn't Price Ranch, or a boat in Florida.
Home was Annie Grissom, with her freckles and her wry
smile and her big heart, and he wanted to be where she was.
Without Annie at his side, he was feeling that restless itch,
but unlike before, this time it was impossible to ignore. It
wasn't that he hated being here, he realized.

He just didn't want to be away from her. Didn't matter if
it was Painted Barrel, Wyoming, or the beach in Florida.

But because Annie needed him to be sure, he was going to
do everything he could to ensure that he knew his own mind.

So Dustin packed an overnight bag, grabbed his damned boating pamphlets, and headed to the airport. He bought a ticket to Fort Lauderdale, Florida, just like he'd planned to do so for so many years. It was time to put his money where his mouth was and experience the dream for a few days to see what he thought of it. Before he'd met Annie, a boat on the coast seemed like the ultimate adventure. He'd have no home except the one with a sail, no one to answer to, and nothing but sunshine all year round. He'd live on the beach and soak up the rays, fish to his heart's content, and then when he was tired of the faces there, he could move along to somewhere else.

He tried.

He really tried.

Fort Lauderdale was perhaps a poor choice, though. It was crowded. It was touristy. He met Marcus Salter and toured the sales yard. He eyeballed a few different boats, but the drive wasn't there. He couldn't pull the trigger on buying the boat, and it was clear that the salesman was disappointed to see his sale walk away. Marcus suggested that Dustin check out the Florida Keys, instead, so he went to Islamorada.

It was beautiful there, no doubt. Palm trees dotted the landscape, and the beaches were gorgeous, the water Caribbean blue. Even in the fall, there were beautiful women on the beach, but he found he wasn't all that interested in them. He found himself watching the young mothers escorting children on the beach, instead, smiling when a child delightedly picked up a shell.

He talked to one of Marcus's clients, a businessman who'd cashed out his nest egg and decided to live a freewheeling life in the islands. The man was about twenty years older than Dustin, and the meet-up between them went badly. The man chased after women half his age, drank too much beer, and bragged about his boat. He invited girls to sit with them, and all of them wore bikinis, giggled a ridiculous amount, and eye-flirted like there was no tomorrow. Good Time Girls, like he'd always looked for in the past. Girls that wanted no commitment, just some fun.

Dustin hated it. He hated all of it.

Was this the company he had to look forward to, then? Tourist traps and crowded beaches filled with people he didn't like?

He excused himself early and went back to his hotel, where he emailed Marcus to tell him that he'd changed his mind entirely, and then he texted Annie.

DUSTIN: How's my baby today?

ANNIE: Morgan is bouncy today. I swear she's kicked my liver a hundred times in the last hour.

DUSTIN: So you agree it might be a girl, then?

ANNIE: Just for today. Tomorrow we'll see.

DUSTIN: And how's Morgan's mom?

ANNIE: Tired. Trying to figure out my options for employment.

DUSTIN: Do you need money? I can send you some.

ANNIE: Nope, I'm good. :) Just mostly restless.

DUSTIN: I know how that feels.

He didn't tell her he was in Florida, watching his restless dream wither away before his eyes. He didn't want her to feel pressured or that he had an ulterior motive.

ANNIE: My mother thinks I should get in front of the camera for a plethora of 'pregnant woman in supermarket' type roles. Hit that window while I have it, right? And my friend Katherine knows someone that needs a dog trainer in Vancouver for the next two months. Seems their last trainer broke both his legs in a skiing accident and now can't work until he gets some mobilization again. I haven't said yes to anything, though, but the boredom is killing me.

DUSTIN: You could do dog training. Or even dog walking. Whatever it is, you'll be awesome at it. You're smart and clever and anyone would be lucky to have you.

ANNIE: :)

ANNIE: Thank you.

ANNIE: I haven't figured anything out but I do have options. I'm just . . . not sold on any of them.

DUSTIN: I hear you.

ANNIE: How about you? How are you doing? How's Moose?

Moose was back with Eli and the others, no doubt pining away that Dustin was gone. Well, not entirely. The dog had latched on to Cass recently, fascinated with the new baby. He hovered protectively near her, his herding instincts kicking in. If Dustin decided to leave the ranch, he'd go back for Moose, but for now, he was content to leave him with the others.

DUSTIN: Everything's great here.

He wanted to tell her that he missed her. That he loved her. That Moose missed her, too. That Cass hoped she was okay and was saving baby clothes for her. That he had been to see his boat and his beach dream and had been unimpressed. He had so much he wanted to tell her . . . but he wasn't sure what to say. Their "friendship" was fragile, and he didn't want to fill her phone with how he really felt. So all the *I miss you* and *I love you* and *Nothing's the same without you* messages he wanted to send remained in his head alone. Eventually, he just texted back with:

DUSTIN: Hope you're enjoying LA. Tell Morgan I miss her.

CHAPTER TWENTY-THREE

Dustin left Florida a few unsatisfying days later. The weather was nice, the scenery was great . . . but it wasn't home. Funny how he hadn't wanted a home for so long and now it was all that he wanted. That dream was pretty dead, though, and he returned to Price Ranch. He spent time with Moose, helped Clyde and Eli catch up on the backlog of chores, and then he drove out to Iowa, back to his hometown.

He hadn't been there since he was sixteen.

It felt strange to be back. Some things hadn't changed, but other things were different. The old bank had been replaced by a Burger King. The white brick school building he'd gone to looked old and yellowed, but there were still kids running laps at the track, and the old barn that he used to sneak out to in order to meet girls was still there, as crumbling and run-down as ever.

In a world of social media and instant connections, he hadn't tried to contact his parents again. He knew he should. He didn't hate them. He didn't feel anger toward them. It was just a thing that, the longer it was left undone, the harder it was to pick up the phone and try to explain himself. It became easier to avoid.

Maybe that was part of the problem that Annie wanted him to fix, so he pulled up to his parents' old house and knocked on the door, his heart hammering in his chest.

To his surprise, a stranger answered the door. It was a woman, young, with a baby on her hip, her hair mussed, and she looked distinctly frazzled and slightly irritated at being disturbed.

"Can I help you?"

"Ma'am." He tipped his hat at her, and then was at a loss. He'd grown up in this home. Why would his parents leave it behind? "I, ah, I'm looking for the Worthingtons. They lived here a while back, I think?"

She gave him an odd look, and for a moment, his heart stopped. A gamut of awful scenarios flashed through his mind. His parents weren't here because they'd died. They were in a nursing home. Cancer. Dread roared through him like an oncoming wave, and he could barely make out what she was saying.

House built. End of Pearson Road.

Right. Okay. Whew. With a distracted nod, he thanked her and got back into his truck.

Dustin's hands gripped the steering wheel, and he realized he was in a cold sweat. He hadn't thought about something happening to his parents. He'd thought they'd always be there, waiting for him when he was ready to say hello again. He didn't think that things would change for them, too. That life went on without him.

What an incredibly weird and selfish thing to realize. Maybe Annie had been right to push him away until he found himself.

That disturbing thought on his mind, Dustin drove a couple of streets over and found the house the woman had mentioned. He pulled up to it, a little surprised at the sight. It was a very new, one-floor sprawling rancher with a charming Italian villa design and slate roof. The grounds were manicured with shaped rose bushes and a decorative gate that led up the winding walkway to the front door. Perhaps he had the wrong house again.

Dustin got out of his truck anyhow and went to the door. Before he could second-guess himself, he rang the doorbell and waited, a worried knot in his gut. What if this wasn't them, either? What then?

"Coming," a woman called out, and he recognized the sound of his mother's voice. A wave of homesickness washed over him suddenly, and he felt like a sixteen-year-old boy once more.

The door opened before he was ready, and then he was staring face-to-face with the mother that he hadn't seen in over ten years, hadn't called, hadn't texted, hadn't emailed. Her hair was grayer, her face a little more lined with crow's feet at the edges, but she was still familiar and beautiful in the way that all mothers were.

"Hi, Mom," he managed hoarsely at the shocked look on her face.

"Oh, my goodness." Her gaze moved up and down over him, taking in the boots, jeans, the flannel shirt, the cowboy hat on his head. "Oh . . . you've gone and become a cowboy, Dustin."

A smile tugged at his face. "Yeah, I guess I did."

She burst into tears, and he immediately moved forward and put his arms around her.

"I'm sorry," he murmured. He didn't say what for. There were a million things he was sorry for right now—sorry for running away, for never calling, for being a shitty son.

Mostly he was sorry for making her cry, and the realization that he'd probably made her cry dozens of times wondering about him.

"It's all right, really," she managed, but she clung to him. "Adella?"

Dustin heard the sound of another familiar voice coming down the hall, and he pulled away from his mother, his throat tight as his father appeared. John Worthington looked just as Dustin remembered—a little grayer, a little older, but the same tall, proud shoulders and lean build. He didn't look sick or unwell and Dustin was so damn glad at how lucky he was that he launched himself into the older man's arms.

"Dad."

"My boy." He said warmly, hugging Dustin, and then he was home for the first time in forever.

If nothing else good came out of Annie leaving, Dustin was glad that he'd come home. His parents had missed him and kept track of him quietly from afar, using social media and the occasional private investigator to make sure he was doing well. It surprised him to hear it, but he was glad they weren't worrying over his safety. They'd done well themselves—a few years after Dustin had left home, they'd sold the dry-cleaning business to a chain and now his father dabbled in the stock market. They were doing very well for themselves, and took vacations all over Europe a few times a year. They'd had a new house built with a design his mother had fallen in love with back in Tuscany, but they'd stayed in Iowa because "it was home."

"Just because plans get delayed doesn't mean they get delayed forever," his father told him. "Your mother and I have the time to travel and the money, more so than we ever did before. Dreams don't go away. Sometimes it's okay to tell yourself that right now is the time to settle in and wait."

Wise words. Dustin grinned ruefully, because in that moment, he felt more like his father's son than he ever had.

"I met someone," he told them. "Her name's Annie and we're going to have a baby."

Nearly a week later, Dustin drove through Los Angeles traffic, trying to keep an open mind about the place.

Visiting his parents had been real nice. There was no resentment, no guilt. They understood why he'd left even if he'd hurt them by doing it. It had bothered them more that he kept out of touch, and he resolved to not do so again. They'd exchanged phone numbers and he promised to not be a stranger any longer. They offered to come visit when the baby arrived, and he told them he'd clear it with Annie first, but he didn't think she'd mind if his parents showed up.

Heck, she'd probably love it.

It was strange to be "with" Annie and be apart. His feelings hadn't changed. They texted all week long, though he hadn't found the way to mention that he was visiting his family. He felt like if he mentioned it in a text, it'd feel like he was trying to score points and he didn't want her to feel pressured.

Going home was good, though. Well, it was home and it wasn't. His parents felt comfortable and right, but the house would never be what he remembered and the town was different. It was just the place he grew up, and he wouldn't be staying there, either. If Los Angeles didn't work out, he'd be returning to Price Ranch and sticking around for a while longer, because home wasn't a place as much as it was people, and he was learning to appreciate having a "home" instead of just a bed to sleep in.

But first . . . he had to try Los Angeles, because that was where Annie was, and he wanted to be with her. She was his home, her and Morgan both, and if she wouldn't stay with him in Wyoming, maybe he'd try California.

Emphasis on "try."

Los Angeles was . . . very different. It was crowded and warm, with so much traffic that it shocked him even though he'd expected it. It was expensive. Parts of it were dirty and other parts just ostentatious and ridiculous. Los Angeles itself seemed to sprawl for an eternity before he found Annie's neighborhood, and he found himself missing the mountains of Wyoming and the wide-open spaces. There'd be a gentle snow on the ground right about now, perfect for a hot cup of coffee before starting his morning, and the mountain air would be crisp and biting. It'd be perfect . . . if Annie was curled up in his bed.

So. Los Angeles it was.

Annie's neighborhood was as crowded as the last few he'd driven through, the houses older but charming. The yards were ridiculously tiny, and when he pulled up to the house she shared with her mother, he checked the address again just to make sure it was the right one. Place didn't seem big enough for a dog, much less two people. But the address was correct, so he went to the door and gave it a shot.

A woman answered, her age indeterminate. She was older than Annie but looked much younger than his own mother. Her hair was blonde and fell in perfect waves, her skin porcelain, and she wore an absolute mega-ton of makeup and jewelry. She carried a wineglass despite the early hour and gave him a curious look. "I know who you are," she said immediately. "This is interesting."

"I came looking for Annie, though I didn't expect to find she had a sister." Dustin gave her his most winning smile.

She only cocked an eyebrow at him. "Annie told me you were a charmer. I see she was right. You can call me Kitty," she told him. "Never 'ma'am' or Ms. Grissom or anything that sounds elderly." She gave a light shudder.

"Nice to meet you, Kitty." He took off his hat and tried not to peer behind her. "Is Annie around?"

Kitty wandered away from the front door, taking tottering steps in an enormous pair of spike heels. "She's playing with dogs at the park or some such. I don't know. She didn't tell me you'd be coming by. Wine? Beer?"

"No thank you." He followed her inside. "I didn't exactly tell her that I was coming. Thought I'd check out Los Angeles for myself since Annie lives here."

"Because you're thinking about moving to the area?" she asked shrewdly, glancing over her shoulder at him. "Not a lot of ranchers in this area I'm afraid, though you might make a fair penny modeling for a while." She turned and gave him a scrutinizing look that made his ears heat, especially when it lingered on his chest . . . and lower. "Though you're going to wrinkle like a piece of old linen if you don't start putting sunblock on that pretty face of yours. Just some friendly advice."

Damn. This woman was a piece of work. "I will keep that in mind, Kitty."

She leaned against the counter, studying him. "What are your intentions toward my daughter exactly? I'm curious."

"Well." He wondered how bluntly honest he should be with her, and then decided to just speak his mind. "I love her. I want to be in her life. If she doesn't want to be with me in Wyoming, I figured I'd come here and be close to her until she's ready to accept that I'm not miserable and I'm not leaving."

Kitty winked at him. "That's a very good answer. My daughter can be a bit stubborn, you know."

"I like her stubbornness."

"She never grew up with a father so I think she expects

all men to run off at the first whiff of a baby." Kitty shook her head and downed her wine. "I suppose that's my fault. I've always tried to show her that you don't need a man to have a fulfilling life, but maybe I went too far overboard and now she thinks she has to be alone, even when she doesn't want to be."

"I've made my share of mistakes," Dustin admitted. "But I'm hoping Annie and I can meet somewhere in the middle for Morgan's sake."

"Morgan?" Kitty stared at him blankly.

"The baby?"

"Ah, she's picked out a name? I didn't know."

Was it something Annie had only shared with him, then? He liked that. "I hate to cut this short, Kitty, but I mean to tell your daughter that I love her and propose to her again. And if she won't have me, I need to find a hotel nearby. So do you think you can direct me to this dog park . . . ?"

Kitty smirked at him, pouring herself a new glass of wine. "If I must. Can I come watch?"

"I'd prefer to talk to her alone."

She just sighed dramatically.

Turned out there was a dog park "downtown"—the word meant nothing to him given that all of Los Angeles felt like "downtown" to a country boy—but with his phone app, he managed to find the place. It was just as crowded as any other place in this ridiculous city, but he spotted a pregnant woman near the entrance and parked his truck hastily, then jogged out to meet her.

To his surprise, Annie had no less than eight dogs on leashes in one hand, being dragged forward at a quick (for a pregnant woman) waddle as she headed down the street.

"Annie," he called out as she headed in the opposite direction from him, her concentration elsewhere. "Wait up!"

She paused, swayed, and the dogs jerked her forward again. Dustin raced to her side and managed to snag the leashes before she lost control, and then wrapped an arm around her hips to support her.

"Dustin," she breathed, clearly shocked. "What . . ."

The dogs jerked at his arm, two of them snapping at each other in their eagerness to run. "Where the hell'd you find so many dogs?" He asked, picking Spidey out from the bunch, his white coat obvious. "Did you adopt all these while I was gone?"

A breathless laugh tumbled from her. "What? No. I'm testing the waters to see if I want to start a dog-walking business." She leaned against him gratefully.

"What's the verdict on that?" he asked, struggling to keep control of the beasts.

"I'm thinking it's a no," Annie told him, and buried her face against his shoulder. "Dustin . . . what are you doing here?"

"Well, right now I'm holding back what feels like the hounds of hell because they want to be set loose on the streets of LA." Good lord, now another pair were fighting, and the entire cluster was tugging at his arm as if they wanted to rip it off. How had his tiny woman managed to keep them under control?

She giggled, the sound light and sweet and it tugged at his heartstrings. "I meant here, in Los Angeles, silly." Her hand moved to his chest, over his heart. "Not that I mind. I . . . I love seeing you here."

"I love seeing you, too. Now how do we get rid of these dogs so we can have a talk?"

CHAPTER TWENTY-FOUR

Dustin was here. In Los Angeles. He'd come to see her. Annie's heart wouldn't stop fluttering.

It continued to jitter nervously in her breast as they walked the mob of dogs back to their collective owners, and it struck out an entirely new samba when he linked his fingers with hers as he held Spidey's leash in his other hand. They walked to a nearby dog-friendly restaurant and sat out on the patio to have some sunshine and privacy, Spidey parking himself in a chair opposite them as if he were one of the diners. She gave him a peanut butter bone to keep him busy, but she shouldn't have bothered. He was giving Dustin so many adoring looks with his big dark eyes that she knew he wouldn't go anywhere.

He was a sucker for the cowboy as much as she was.

"You're here," Annie said again, shaking her head. "I can hardly believe it."

He slid his chair closer to hers, ignoring the looks that other diners gave them as he moved closer. "I missed you.

I got tired of being apart and so I thought I'd come here and see if you still wanted nothing to do with me."

"I never said that," she protested. Heck, seeing him here, feeling his big body against hers, she was thinking that her steadfast decision to part ways was a rather foolish one. Annie hadn't anticipated how badly she'd miss him and how much she'd wish for him to be at her side. How much it would hurt to sleep in her bed alone. How the thought of being without him every day made her feel all hollow inside. She'd been so happy when he'd texted her, and even though it was probably a bad idea to keep chatting, she couldn't help herself. She'd never get over him at this rate.

She wasn't entirely sure she wanted to.

Annie had struggled with the conflicting feelings as days had passed into a week, then two. She went to doctor's appointments and took odd jobs walking other people's pets just to keep busy. She went to lunch with her mother and her friends. She even saw Katherine, who was just about to head off to work on a Civil War television show that was filming in Vancouver.

It was nice, but . . . that's all it was. Just nice. She was still restless and feeling unsettled. Some of it was anticipation for the baby, she was sure, but most of it was that she missed Dustin, and she felt like she'd made a mistake cutting him out of her life.

So to see him here? It thrilled her down to her toes (which were currently curling with delight).

He'd come for her. He'd missed her so much that he'd braved the wilds of California to join her at her side. And judging from the slightly perplexed look on her cowboy's face, he wasn't a fan of Los Angeles, but he was trying for her sake. He picked up a menu and studied it. "What's good here?"

"Kale salad?" she offered, just to see his reaction.

He blanched. "What's good here that once had a face?" he corrected.

Annie smothered a giggle. "Chicken sandwich?"

"All right." He tossed the menu aside and slid his arm around the back of her chair, consciously scooting her closer, as if their chairs were one big sofa just for the two of them. Her heart fluttered anew. "Hi," he murmured.

"Hi," Annie whispered, unable to stop smiling.

"Is it inappropriate to kiss one's pregnant girlfriend in public here?"

"Does it matter?"

"Don't suppose it does," he agreed, and leaned in. His lips grazed hers in the sweetest, most perfect kiss ever, and she wanted to weep with the sheer joy of his nearness. She could smell his aftershave, feel his warmth, the strength of his body. She wanted to wrap herself around him and revel in all of it.

Breathless, she gazed up at him, trying to compose her thoughts. "So . . . how is the ranch?"

"I wouldn't know, seeing as how I've been traveling."

"To Los Angeles?"

"Among other things."

Annie pulled back in surprise. He hadn't told her that he was traveling to other places. "Where else?"

"I took to heart what you said. I went to Florida and checked out the boatyards. Checked out a few places in Florida, actually."

Her heart's happy, anxious flutters turned to something slow and ponderous. Her soul hurt. She'd pushed so hard for him to get that boat, to make that lifestyle choice and she should be happy for him. Instead, she just felt . . . crushed. He'd bought the boat and was going to Florida, then? She braced herself, waiting for him to gush about how amazing the beaches were. "How's your boat? Is it everything you wanted?"

Dustin gave her a slight smile, rubbing her shoulder absently. "I didn't buy one."

"No?" She shouldn't be thrilled. She really shouldn't. She'd told him to buy one. She was the one pushing him, darn it.

"No. I got to the place I'd initially picked out and hated it. Then I went to another place that was supposed to be even better, and I didn't like anything about it, either. I didn't like the people. I didn't like the boats. I didn't like the weather. I didn't like all the women in bikinis everywhere."

She snorted at that.

"Well, okay, that wasn't exactly hard on the eyes." He grinned at her. "But they were at the beach to have a good time and I didn't want them to have it with me. I wanted you and Morgan. I wanted to be sitting somewhere, rubbing your feet and getting you ice cream and pickles, because everyone says that pregnant ladies love that." He played with a lock of her hair. "I gave the dream a shot. I really did. I soaked up some Florida sunshine and walked on the beach and then I decided it wasn't for me. So then I went and visited my parents."

Annie blinked at him, not entirely sure she'd heard correctly. "You what?"

"Visited my parents. I remembered us talking about them. You kept saying you were worried I was going to turn into my father and that I'd hate you. I went to visit them because, well, I remembered my father being happy with my mother. I remembered them always smiling and laughing together and going on dates on Saturday nights. I remember them sneaking kisses in the kitchen. I didn't remember them arguing or my father resenting my mother. So I went to visit them to see if everything was as I remembered." He paused, twining her hair around his finger. "And because I was an awful son and I should have let them know how I was doing."

"How were they? What did they say?" She was frozen with excitement and fear both—she wanted to hear good news from Dustin about them, but she was terrified it would be something awful, and she'd feel responsible. He hadn't contacted them in over ten years. So many things could go wrong.

Oh no, what if she'd pushed him in that direction and they hated him? Or he hated them?

"They were good," he said softly. He watched her so closely and intensely she could feel her body prickling in response, as if his gaze was a tangible thing. "Real good. They'd sold the business and had a pretty little house they built for themselves. They'd traveled a lot. They were happier than I'd ever seen them. And they'd missed me."

"Of course they missed you!" Annie exclaimed. "You're their son."

He nodded and told her all about his visit—how it had felt to return home and see the changes. How his mom had hugged him so tightly and how his father had been just the same as he ever was. Their new home and the photo albums of their vacations in Europe covering the coffee table. How worried he'd been that he'd lost them, and how relieved he'd felt to find them whole and happy.

And how lucky he felt realizing that there was still time to be in their lives.

Tears pooled in Annie's eyes as he spoke. "It's not too late, then."

"It's never too late. Don't cry, sweetheart."

"It's just hormones—"

He chuckled. "You always say it's hormones. Could it just be that you're softhearted?"

"Or it could just be hormones," she insisted, blushing. "I'm so glad you went." She clasped his hand in hers, and she wanted to hold on to him forever. "You needed to re-connect with them."

"I guess I did. Dad pointed out something very wise to me, in fact." At her curious glance, he gave her a slow, pleased smile. "It's that plans change."

"They do? I mean, of course they do. But why is that significant?" And why was he bringing it up now? Hope sprang up in her chest, but she quickly squashed it again. She'd told him to follow his dreams; she didn't have the right to hope he'd abandoned them. She'd given up any right to claim him the moment she'd walked out.

And yet . . . it didn't mean she couldn't yearn to hear him tell her those very things.

"Yep. My father was a happy man when I was younger. I saw him again a few days ago, and he's equally happy. Following his dreams didn't have anything to do with his happiness or how he felt about my mother. They're still as in love as they ever were, and he's finally getting to see the world like he'd always wanted. He told me that just because you put off dreams for a couple of years—or even a couple of decades—doesn't mean that they die. It just means that it's life. It happens and just because the path forks doesn't mean it's a bad path to take."

He gave her a long, meaningful look that made her heart swell with love.

"That's why I'm here, Annie," he murmured, pulling their joined hands to his mouth. He kissed her knuckles lightly, then nipped at one just to watch her shiver. "I'm here because maybe this isn't where I planned on seeing myself for all these years, but that doesn't mean it's a bad thing. It just means that plans change. It doesn't mean that I don't want you or the baby. I kept thinking for so long that I wanted no ties on me, that I wanted to roam the world without a care in my head, but now that I've met you, even that would be empty. I wasn't looking for a purpose with travel. I was looking for something that would ease my boredom. And you know what I've found?"

"What?" She could scarcely breathe.

"I'm not bored when I'm with you. I'm happy. I like thinking about coming home to you every day. I like the thought of waking up with you in my arms. I like the thought of changing diapers at three in the morning and holding my son—or daughter—and watching their first steps. It doesn't matter if I'm here in Los Angeles or if we're in Wyoming, or even if we're in Florida, as long as we're together. That's all that matters to me."

She licked her lips, flustered and full of love. "Oh, Dustin."

"Being apart for these last few weeks was good, though, I admit. You were right for us to split up. Not because I think we should stay that way, but because it was a good chance to see what I didn't want. And that's a life without you."

Yep, definitely crying at this point, and Annie suspected it had very little to do with hormones. "I love you," she whispered.

"I love you too. If I propose to you again, are you going to turn me away?" His eyes gleamed with amusement and he rubbed her knuckles against his lips, smiling.

She shook her head.

"Good, because I brought the ring." And he got down on one knee, right on the patio, in front of two dozen other diners.

Spidey immediately climbed out of his chair and sat next to Dustin on the patio, then offered his paw, and she burst into laughter. (And tears, sure.) When she could finally speak, she said yes.

She said yes a thousand times.

They had a quick lunch.

Theoretically. Annie didn't remember much of it, but at some point their plates were cleared and the check was paid and they walked several blocks back to her mother's little bungalow. Not that she paid much attention. Her senses were filled with Dustin, his nearness, his pleasure at holding her hand.

Her joy felt overwhelming.

Once they returned to the house, her mother was gone. That meant they had privacy. Annie flung herself on Dustin, her arms around his neck, her belly pushing against him and making kissing awkward. It didn't matter. Within moments, they were stripping each other naked with hungry, quick motions, and then he carried her to her room and laid her gently on the bed, on her side. They made love curled up against each other, with Dustin's big body spooning hers and her cowboy holding her so tightly against him as he kissed her ear and whispered words of love.

Afterward, he cupped her breast and kissed her neck, and they remained tangled in bed together, content.

"So," he murmured between nips at her shoulder. "We moving to LA?"

"God, no. You met my mother, didn't you?"

"I did. She's a real nice lady."

"Kitty? Kitty Grissom?"

Dustin chuckled, caressing her skin. His hand slid down to her full belly, rubbing over the mound of it. "She's not like anyone I ever met before, but she's real nice."

"She likes kids but she's not keen on the idea of being a grandma. Besides, LA is expensive. And wouldn't you miss Wyoming?"

She felt his big body tense against her, and he hesitated. "I want to be where you want to be, Annie."

"I want to be with you. And I liked Painted Barrel." She pulled his hand from her belly and kissed his palm. She could kiss him for days and days on end. "Do you like being a cowboy?"

"I do."

"Well, there's a lot more of that sort of work in Wyoming than there is in Los Angeles."

He laughed, his breath sweet against her hair. "Fair enough. But I don't want you to feel as if you're giving anything up."

"I'm not. I didn't enjoy the last movie I worked on." She played with his fingers, admiring the engagement ring he'd given her. It had a woven band that looked like a vine, and in the center of a delicate flower was a tiny diamond. It wasn't big and ostentatious like the rings that were in all the shops in Beverly Hills, but it was unique and pretty and she loved it with all her heart. "I still like dogs, but the movie part wasn't fun. I've never wanted to be on camera or live the Hollywood lifestyle. My mother loves it. I'm not much like her."

Dustin made a thoughtful sound. "No, you're not. So what do you want to do?"

"I'll figure something out. There has to be a need for pet services in Painted Barrel, I would imagine. If they can't come to me, maybe I can go to them. A roving pup truck of some kind."

"I like that."

"I do, too." Actually she liked it the more she thought about it. She could visit clients and groom, trim nails, give shots (provided she got the right certifications), and work on training a bit. She could pet sit. She could do all kinds of things, really, and it didn't have to involve horrible directors or traveling all over the world to teach a dog how to sit patiently while some idiot tried to start a wildfire around him. "What about you? Will you be content at Price Ranch?"

"Yeah. Eli and Clyde need the help and I like it there. It's a good place to raise a kid. Maybe five or ten years from now we can get a vacation house on the shore, and then you and me and Morgan can figure out what kind of adventures we want to have, together."

Together. That sounded amazing. "That's fine with me. I just want to be with you."

"And my baby," Dustin agreed, kissing her shoulder as he touched her belly.

"That's right," Annie whispered. "My cowboy and my baby."

EPILOGUE

"Happy Mother's Day," Dustin told Annie, waking her with a kiss. "You get breakfast in bed this morning."

"I do?" She yawned, her breasts feeling heavy. That meant the baby would need to be fed. "What about Morgan?" She rubbed her eyes, sitting up, and then smiled blearily at the sight of her cowboy with their daughter perched on his hip, a breakfast tray in his other hand. Morgan, bless her fat little cheeks, had her father's hat in her hands and was busy chewing on the brim. It was her favorite thing to do, and Dustin's favorite cowboy hat was looking a little misshapen lately, but the man loved his daughter so much that he didn't care. He wore the hat, bite marks and all, as if it were a badge of honor.

And if that wasn't the cutest thing Annie had ever seen, she didn't know what was.

She sat up in bed and propped up against the pillows, smiling at Dustin. "How long have you been up?"

"Long enough to change a diaper, make coffee, change

a diaper again, walk the dogs, and then make Mommy oatmeal." He grimaced, setting the tray down with a movement that required a lot of balance. "I wanted it to be bacon and eggs but Morgan's a handful this morning."

She put her arms out, and Dustin settled their chubby daughter in her mother's embrace. Annie tugged down the neckline of her nightgown and the baby immediately latched on to her breast, hungry. "This is so sweet of you, Dustin." She smiled up at him, her hand brushing lightly over Morgan's red-gold floss of hair. "You're the best daddy. Two diapers, huh?"

"Two explosive diapers," he agreed. "You're welcome."

She chuckled. "Welcome to my world, cowboy."

"Kind of makes me happy that all I have to do is hunt down cattle and pry babies out of their hindquarters when they get stuck."

"You make it sound like you do that all day long."

"Some days it does feel like I do that all day long." He winked at her, then settled at the edge of the bed, watching her feed the baby. "You get enough sleep, sweetheart?" When she nodded, he smiled. "Good, because I have a surprise for you."

Annie glanced up from watching Morgan's fat cheeks as she nursed. Her daughter was beautiful—the fattest, happiest baby she'd ever seen. But she was probably biased. "Uh-oh. Good surprise or bad surprise?"

"Well . . . it depends." He was all mischief, this man. She could practically see the impish humor bubbling out of him, and it made her smile, too. "I figured since it was your first Mother's Day, we might make it special."

"It's already pretty special," she told him, and glanced down at her daughter again.

"I know." There was a husky note in Dustin's normally laughing voice, and it warmed her heart to hear it. If Annie was obsessed with her daughter, Dustin was even more so. The man would move mountains for one gurgling Morgan laugh. He was a great dad, always trying to help her out with the baby and taking her for entire afternoons so she could work on launching her Pupmobile "Training and Grooming to Go" business. There was nothing cuter than seeing Dustin come home with groceries, baby carrier strapped to his front, Morgan's fat little legs jouncing, both Moose and Spidey at his heels.

"And since it's your first Mother's Day," Dustin continued, "I wanted you to have everyone you loved around you."

She looked up at him, her eyes wide.

"Your mother's flying in at one, and my parents will be driving in sometime this afternoon. Morgan's going to spend her first Mother's Day with all the mothers in her life."

Annie's lip trembled. "Oh, Dustin—"

"No tears," he warned, picking the coffee up from the tray and offering it to her. "I thought we were done with hormones."

"Temporary flare-up," she told him, and sipped the coffee. He'd made it just the way she liked; the man was the most thoughtful human alive. How on earth did she get so lucky? "How did you manage this?"

"To invite everyone here without telling you? Or do you mean how did I manage to get Kitty to hop on a plane knowing that she was going to be called 'grandma' at some point today?"

Annie giggled. "Yes to both."

"She was drawn to the siren call of baby Morgan. No one can resist her." With a wink, he leaned in and gave Annie a quick kiss on the forehead. "I'm told that we'll have our choice of babysitters tonight, which means Mommy and Daddy are free to have some alone time."

"This is quite the Happy Mother's Day, then," she

murmured, anticipating that even more. Moments of alone time were normally stolen and didn't happen often enough. "I'm a lucky woman."

He gazed down at her, his hand curving along her cheek, and a smile lit his tanned face. "Don't make me fight you for the title of 'luckiest one' in this relationship."

"Pillow fight for the title," she teased him, switching her daughter to her other breast.

Dustin watched her, eyes gleaming. "You're on."

Mother's Day was going to be her favorite holiday, she could already tell.

Keep reading for the next Cowboy
romance from Jessica Clare

A COWBOY UNDER
THE MISTLETOE

Coming soon from Jove

It was the middle of December, and Jason was sweating.

He walked along the snowy sidewalk in Painted Barrel, focusing on the quaint buildings that lined the main street of town.

It had been six years since Afghanistan. He could have sworn he was getting better. But because it was a blustery winter and the town was small, it was quiet out.

Too quiet.

No one came out of the souvenir shop across the street or went into the hotel. The gas station at the far end of the street—the only one in town—was empty. The lights were on, and he could see the clerk reading a magazine behind the counter. Painted Barrel boasted a bar that doubled as the town's only restaurant, but it was closed because it was midday. No one was around. Despite the festive wreaths that hung on the doors, it was like the entire town was deserted.

His sweating grew more intense. Jason could feel his heart speeding up, and adrenaline rushing over his body. The sky overhead was bright blue, despite the fresh layer of snow on the ground, and it felt . . . open. Too open.

Open was bad.

It reminded him of the day that everything happened. He was visiting a village just outside of Kabul when a gunman opened fire, killing his buddy, and shooting Jason three times, nearly taking his life.

Ever since then, quiet, wide-open spaces bothered him.

Kinda dumb for you to take a job as a cowboy, then. He could hear Kirk's voice in his head, even though Kirk had been dead for the last six years. And heck, maybe it was dumb, but Jason really thought he was better. Even after his PTSD service dog, Truck, passed away in the spring, he hadn't had many breakdowns. He thought he was past that.

Guess not.

His sweating increased and his self-preservation instincts kicked in. He needed to find someplace to hide. Anywhere, really. He just needed to get out of the open, and fast. Panting, Jason raced down the sidewalk and tried the first door he came to. Locked. With a low growl of frustration, he sprang to the second one, and flung himself inside when it opened.

A wall of heat hit him and he skidded on the tile floor, his wet boots unable to find traction. Jason slammed into the wall and stayed there for a moment, trying to calm down. He sunk down low, the urge to crouch and hide overwhelming.

To take cover.

Someone cleared their throat. "Hi, can I help you?"

Jason closed his eyes. He didn't know where he was at the moment, but he was pretty sure he'd just made a spectacle of himself. And since Painted Barrel was a small town—population about two handfuls—it was sure to be on everyone's lips in less than a day. That was bad. The last thing Jason needed was his new employer finding out that he suffered from PTSD.

Great. Just great.

"Are you . . . here to return a library book?" The voice was kind, quiet. Soft.

He cracked an eye open, willing his racing pulse to slow down. "I need a moment."

"Take all the time you need," the woman said. "Let me know if I can get you anything."

Huh. That wasn't the normal reaction he got when he lost it. People panicked when he did, assuming that because a nearly seven-foot-tall man was freaking out there was something to freak out about. Because of his height, Jason wasn't real good at blending in with the crowd, and when he lost control, everyone noticed.

He was rather thankful that the woman left him alone. He leaned back against the wall and tried to focus, to ground himself in reality. No one was shooting at him. There were no snipers in nearby windows. It was quiet, not because people were waiting to attack, but because it was just quiet.

So he focused on coping mechanisms, wishing again that Truck's warm, comforting presence was at his side. He forced himself to pay attention to his surroundings. He noticed Christmas music playing somewhere nearby—Bing Crosby. Wood paneling on the walls. Serviceable metal-armed chairs—two of them—across from him. The room itself was small, and off to one side there was a shelf of books that all looked as if they were twenty-years-old and hard-used. There was a computer in a corner with an uncomfortable looking chair parked in front of it, and a solitary counter. Behind the counter were rows of what looked like metal mailbox cubbies, and there was a woman.

A woman in a very ugly Christmas sweater and a headband with stuffed reindeer horns.

She smiled at him, noticing his attention. "No rush. You're not the first person to come in here sweating at the thought of paying your bills." Then she winked, as if that wasn't the most ridiculous thing to say.

He laughed, the sound nervous. "I didn't come in to pay a bill."

"Library fine, then?" She arched a brow at him.

Jason found himself laughing again. He took off his baseball cap—cold with damp sweat—and ran a hand through his military-short hair. "Is that where I am? The library?"

"You are in the municipal building of Painted Barrel, Wyoming," she told him in a voice that was somewhat proud, somewhat wry. "We handle the water bills. And the mail. And the library." She gestured at the sad shelf of books. "And animal control, but I have to warn you that if you've got anything bigger than a stray dog, I'm going to need help bringing him in."

He stared at the woman in surprise, noticing her appearance—well, beyond the ugly sweater and antlers—for the first time. She was about his age, maybe a few years younger. Pretty, golden-brown hair that hung like a curtain past her shoulders. Round face. Dimples. Gorgeous eyes, gorgeous smile, and a welcoming expression.

He liked her immediately, more so because she hadn't acted like he was crazy for storming in and collapsing. "Are you the mayor?"

"I am a municipal clerk," she admitted, moving to one side and picking up a coffeepot. She poured some coffee into a ceramic mug and then came from behind the counter and approached him, holding the coffee out. As she came closer, he noticed that while her sweater was ugly and boxy, her legs were thick but shapely and she had a great, round bottom. She didn't look like a model like the kind of girls he normally dated, but for some reason, he liked that she was different. She didn't look like someone who wanted to go out to the club and drink the night away. She looked like someone who'd be happy curling up on the couch.

And he liked that most of all.

"What's your name, municipal clerk?"

"Sage, like the herb," she announced, crouching next to him and offering the coffee. "If you don't like caffeine I can make a pot of decaf."

He took the mug and gulped half of it down before he could think about it. He was feeling more normal with every moment that passed, and Sage-like-the-herb was a great distraction. She was pretty, she was sweet, and she apparently had a sense of humor. "You offer everyone coffee when they come in to pay the bills?"

"In the winter I have to spike it with something once people hear just how bad their heating bill is." She winked at him and then got to her feet. "Kidding. I don't offer coffee to everyone, no. We've only got a few mugs and I won't keep foam cups here because it's bad for the environment. You just looked like you needed something to drink." She tilted her head, studying him. "And you must be . . . Jason Clements, right? Jordy's cousin?"

Jason stiffened, all the pleasure rushing out of him. "Why, because I came in here with my head all messed up?" His tone was abrasive, accusing. "Is that the rumor around town?"

Her big brown eyes widened. "No," she said softly. "Because you didn't know who I was. Painted Barrel's kind of small. We don't get a lot of newcomers that wander in." Her smile returned, but it was hesitant, tight around the edges.

He felt like an ass. "Sorry. I'm a little distracted today."

"It's okay."

"And a jerk."

One of the dimples returned. "You said it, not me."

He found himself smiling again. "I, ah . . . have a bit of

a phobia about being outdoors when it's real quiet." Jason hated to admit it, but he didn't want her looking at him strangely. He wanted to keep her smiling. "Sometimes it sneaks up on me."

To his surprise, she nodded and went back to standing behind the counter. "I had an uncle who was agoraphobic. I recognized the look."

She did? She wasn't judging? He ran a hand over his mouth, and then drank the rest of the coffee. Most times when people heard he had PTSD from the war, they either acted like he was utterly crazy and about to snap, or they gave him pathetic, pitying looks and treated him like a drooling idiot. He hated both reactions.

Jason found himself getting to his feet and returning the coffee cup to the counter. "I appreciate the understanding. I haven't told many people about that."

The woman—Sage—flashed him another dimpled smile and picked up a stack of mail, sorting Christmas catalogs into piles. "This is a no-judgment zone. Well—" she amended, tilting her head and making the reindeer antlers cock. "Unless you came here to use the library computer to look up porn like the high school kids do. Then I'm going to judge you."

He snorted. "No, ma'am."

"Miss," she clarified, and to his surprise, she turned bright red in the cheeks. "It's miss. I'm not married."

"Ah." He didn't know what to say. She looked distinctly uncomfortable, her face as red as the reindeer nose on her sweater. She was pretty, and charmingly sweet, but it was clear his head was still a damned mess. Asking her out would be a bad idea. He doubted he'd be in Painted Barrel for long and didn't need commitments. Besides, she probably had a boyfriend in a town as small as this, especially with how utterly adorable she was. He cleared his throat.

"I'd appreciate it if the whole PTSD thing stayed between you and me."

She made a locking motion over her mouth and pretended to throw away the key.

Cute. Everything about her was cute, and that was bad news for his heart. He forced himself to look at his surroundings. "I guess it's a good thing I'm here at the library."

"Oh?" She tucked a strand of long, silky hair behind her ear, and he tried not to look at how cute—or small—that delicate ear was. "You need a book?"

"Yeah. On ranching. Something like *Ranching for Dummies* would be great."

Her pretty brown brows furrowed and her mouth pursed. He noticed that she had full, pink lips that would be perfect for kissing, and then he got mad at himself for noticing that. For a man not interested in dating, he sure was liking everything he saw about Sage. "I'm sorry, did you say a book on ranching?"

"I did."

"I . . . thought you were a cowboy? Working out at Price Ranch?"

He managed a rueful smile. "Hence my dilemma. I need to know a lot, and real quick before anyone finds out I don't know what I'm doing."

ABOUT THE AUTHOR

New York Times and *USA Today* bestselling author **Jessica Clare** writes under three pen names. As Jessica Clare, she writes contemporary romance. As Jessica Sims, she writes fun, sexy shifter paranormals. Finally, as Jill Myles, she writes a little bit of everything, from sexy, comedic urban fantasy to zombie fairy tales. She lives in Texas with her husband, cats, and too many dust bunnies.

CONNECT ONLINE

jessica-clare.com
facebook.com/AuthorJessicaClare
twitter.com/_JessicaClare

Ready to find
your next great read?

Let us help.

Visit prh.com/nextread

Penguin
Random
House